Dear Reader,

I hope you're enjoying your visit to Marble Cove. I sure have fun getting better acquainted with Diane, Margaret, Beverly, and Shelley. They're all so different in regard to interests, backgrounds and age. And yet they mesh together so sweetly—almost like family. But have you noticed one common denominator in their lives? They all seem to have reached a stage of reinventing themselves.

Oh, Margaret is further along with her painting, but she did used to be an accountant. Shelley is trying to launch her baking business, and even Beverly is turning her career in a new direction. I can probably relate to Diane most, since she, too, is a writer. I had numerous and rather varied careers before I discovered my true "calling." I taught preschool when my children were small. Later on, I worked briefly in interior design and then in international adoption. I also worked in publishing for a few years before I became a full-time writer.

Although it makes for a strange résumé, I'm thankful for these diverse occupations (and I didn't even list everything!). I think all of the different experiences add layers and texture to my writing. (At least I hope they do!) I'm sometimes asked why I waited so long to write seriously. My only answer is that I was on a journey, and it took some twists and turns to get here. I see the same thing happening with the Marble Cove characters. Again, it's a case of life imitating art...imitating life. And it's just one more reason that I love what I do!

Blessings!
Melody Carlson

MIRACLES *of* MARBLE COVE

STILL WATERS

MELODY CARLSON

New York

Published by Guideposts Books & Inspirational Media
110 William Street
New York, New York 10038
Guideposts.org

Acknowledgments

Every attempt has been made to credit the sources of copyrighted material used in this book. If any such acknowledgment has been inadvertently omitted or miscredited, receipt of such information would be appreciated.

"From the Guideposts Archive" originally appeared as "Cave In!" by Chris Merkel in Guideposts magazine. Copyright © 1993 by Guideposts. All rights reserved.

Cover and interior design by Müllerhaus
Cover illustration by Jeremy Charles Photography
Typeset by Aptara, Inc.

Printed and bound in the United States of America
10 9 8 7 6 5

CHAPTER ONE

Shelley looked at the handsome man standing in the doorway of the lighthouse. Who was he? And how had he gotten in?

She and her three friends—Beverly, Diane, and Margaret—had heard that the mysterious man who'd been asking about the lighthouse was in town and might be at the lighthouse itself. Then, as they'd headed this way, the lighthouse beam had come on. After generations of darkness, it was on! And now they stood here confronting the stranger.

But he had eyes only for Beverly.

"Anna?" The man's dark eyes grew wide as he stared directly at Beverly. "Is that really you?"

"Look, mister," Diane said, "no one here is named Anna."

"You must be thinking of someone else," Margaret said.

The man bowed his head to get a better look at Beverly. "Anna, it *is* you. I can't believe it."

The five of them stood there in shocked silence. Shelley thought Beverly looked more embarrassed than shocked, though.

"Excuse me," Diane said, "but this is *Beverly.*" Then Diane proceeded to introduce all the women to the handsome stranger. Shelley thought it seemed slightly absurd, as if they'd casually gathered at the lighthouse for a Tupperware party. They shouldn't be sharing any details with this stranger, even if he did look a bit like a younger George Clooney.

"Nice to meet you all," the man said, finally tearing his eyes from Beverly. "My name is Jeff Mackenzie, and I'm doing research on the lighthouse."

"But at night?" Margaret asked.

"I just wanted to try something when it was dark," he told them. "Kind of an experiment."

"So you were the one making the light work?" Diane asked.

He chuckled. "Yes. I hope it didn't bother you."

"We figured there was a logical explanation," Margaret said.

It was funny now, as if everyone was relaxed and enjoying the moment. Except for Beverly. She still seemed upset. Shelley wasn't sure why, but something was definitely wrong.

"You girls go on and head home without me," Beverly suddenly told them. Her expression was hard to read. "Mr. Mackenzie is an old acquaintance of mine, and I really need to speak to him privately." And with no further explanation, Beverly stepped away from her friends, then followed this strikingly handsome stranger around to the other side of the lighthouse. Just like that, she left Diane, Margaret, and Shelley standing together outside the heavy door.

"What is going on?" Shelley demanded. "Why did she go over there with him?"

"It seems that Beverly already knows Mr. Mackenzie." Margaret sounded irritatingly nonchalant, as if it was of no concern that Beverly had gone off with him.

"Apparently they want to be alone," Diane said wryly.

Margaret chuckled. "Can't blame her for wanting to get reacquainted. He's an awfully good-looking man."

"But I don't get it," Shelley said. "At first she seemed so scared. Then she goes off with him. And why did he call her 'Anna'?"

"I'm sure we'll find out soon enough," Diane said. "In the meantime, I'm tired. And I left Rocky home alone."

Margaret hooked her arm in Shelley's. "Remember what curiosity did to the cat, Shelley. Better get you home." She turned her flashlight beam back toward the beach, and the three of them slowly headed back toward town.

Naturally Shelley continued to ponder the strange occurrence, trying to get her friends to speculate with her. But the fact was that no one really knew what was going on. As mysterious as this Jeff Mackenzie had seemed initially, Beverly's reaction seemed even more mysterious. Perhaps they didn't know her as well as they supposed.

CHAPTER TWO

The following morning, Diane called out to Shelley as they both stepped outside to pick up their newspapers from their front porches.

Diane crossed the street and came to stand on the edge of the Bauer front yard. "Beverly agreed to meet me for coffee."

Shelley smiled nervously. Embarrassed to be caught outside in her bathrobe and slippers like this, she quickly reminded herself it was only Diane, and it wouldn't be the first time she'd seen Shelley looking less than her best.

"And Margaret plans to come," Diane told her. "Anyway, can you possibly make it too?"

"I'd love to! I'm dying to hear Beverly's story."

Diane nodded. "See you at nine."

Shelley dashed back into the house, eagerly searching for her husband. "I've got to go meet the girls for coffee," she told Dan. "Can you stay with the kids for an hour?" Fortunately—or not, depending on how one looked at it—Dan wasn't working today, so he really had no good reason to say no. "I just have to get to the bottom of this," she said as she kicked off her slippers.

"You mean the lighthouse's mystery man?" He chuckled. "Well, as long as you come back and tell me what's up with her and that strange guy, I guess I don't mind too much."

Though she scrambled to get dressed and put everything together for Dan and the kids, Shelley knew she was running late. As she hurried to get a bottle of milk for Emma, she glanced at the clock on the stove, but that clock, just like two of the stove's burners, was not working. "Dan," she called as she capped the baby bottle, giving the formula one last quick shake, "don't forget to call your mom, okay?"

"Oh, sure," he said jokingly. "Right in between feeding and changing Emma and stopping Aiden from terrorizing the dog, I'll be sure and call Mom, and we'll have a nice long chat." He leaned down to prevent Aiden from grabbing Prize by the tail. "Stop that, Aiden!"

"Welcome to my world." Shelley grinned as she pecked her frazzled husband on the cheek. "But thanks for sticking around."

He rewarded her with a crooked smile. "And you'll be back in an hour, right?"

"Sure." She shook her finger at Aiden now. "Listen to your dad, and stop picking on Prize. I thought you liked your puppy."

"I *do* like her." Aiden struck a superhero pose with fists raised and biceps flexed. "But I am Spider-Man! Prize is the bad guy and I'm taking her to jail." Then he took off chasing Prize, sliding down the hallway in his footed pajamas.

"It's time for Spider-Man to get dressed," Shelley called after him. Then she exchanged glances with Dan. "I think Aiden is overdue for a playdate."

He nodded as he took the baby bottle from her and jiggled Emma in his arms. "Have fun with the girls," he called in a slightly helpless voice.

Shelley made a quick exit. She closed the front door, took a deep breath of the fresh sea air, and hurried down the walk.

She jogged toward town, knowing she was at least ten minutes late. But it wasn't easy for her to drop everything. Not like it was for them. She tried not to envy their freedom as she hurried on her way. She hoped they hadn't gotten too far without her. Maybe they were caught in the Cove's morning caffeine rush, still ordering their coffees and pastries. Surely they would wait for her to arrive before questioning Beverly.

"Hey, Shelley." Brenna jerked her thumb over her shoulder. "Your gang's all back there. Want your regulah?"

"Thanks, Brenna." Shelley nodded, then hurried back to where Beverly, Diane, and Margaret were already nestled into a cozy corner table casually sipping their coffees.

"Sorry I'm late." She sat down and peeled off her polar fleece jacket. "Did I miss anything good?"

"Not particularly." Margaret poured a sugar packet into her cup. "I was just telling the ladies about how Adelaide wants to dye her hair...*purple*, of all things." Margaret's brows drew together.

Shelley laughed. "Yes, Adelaide told me about that a few days ago. She saw someone on TV with purple hair, and she thought it was pretty."

"Well, I'd appreciate it if you tried to convince her that it's a silly idea," Margaret said. "She might respect your opinion, Shelley, since you're closer to her age."

Shelley sometimes forgot that Adelaide was in her midtwenties; her condition made her seem so much younger. "Maybe we can talk her into hair extensions," Shelley suggested. "They come in all different colors, and you just pin them into your hair."

"Marvelous idea." Margaret nodded.

Shelley looked directly at Beverly now. "Okay, excuse me for cutting to the chase here, but I am dying to know more about last night's mystery man. And why did you stay inside there with him like that? And why did he call you Anna?"

Suddenly the focus of the table turned to Beverly, and she stiffened as she folded the paper napkin into a triangle and creased it tightly.

"That was a lot of questions," Diane said to Shelley. Her eyes twinkled. "Perhaps you should just start with one."

"Sorry." Shelley grimaced. "I guess I was in such a hurry to get here that I was still racing. So…" She took in a slow breath, smiled apologetically at Beverly, and wondered where to begin. "Okay…we know his name is Jeff Mackenzie, and we know he's extremely good-looking, and you obviously seem to know him since you sent us all home without you." She gave Beverly a sly grin. "But I'm dying to know exactly *how* you know him."

Beverly took a slow sip of her cappuccino, then cleared her throat as she set the mug down. "Jeff and I are simply old business acquaintances, from back in Augusta. I actually hadn't seen him in years. And, certainly, I never expected to see him here in Marble Cove, let alone in the lighthouse at night. Naturally, I was quite surprised." She gave them a stiff smile.

"So what is he doing here?" Diane asked curiously. "He mentioned he was working on a research project for the lighthouse. But what sort of project is it?"

"He didn't go into that." Beverly said this crisply, as if to suggest she didn't care to continue this conversation. "Don't any of the rest of you have news?"

"Not right now, we don't," Margaret said with a wink. "What I want to know is, how did he get a key to the lighthouse? We've been trying for months."

"I'm not really sure." Beverly looked down at the newspaper sitting on the table near her. "Oh, look, they're going to open a craft and antique mall in the old cannery building. Won't that be nice?"

"That's a great idea," Diane said as she glanced at the headline. "It's about time someone put that old building to some good use. When does it open? Does it say?"

"It sounds like they're aiming to open before Christmas." Beverly read a bit of the article aloud to them.

Shelley wanted to pound her fist on the table and insist that they get back to the hot topic of the day. Like what was really going on between Beverly and Jeff Mackenzie. "So, Beverly," Shelley began carefully, "I'm curious. Why did Jeff call you 'Anna'?"

Beverly just laughed, but something about the laugh didn't sound genuine. "Oh, *that*. Well, I think he just got me confused with someone else for a moment. Because, really, we didn't know each other that well."

"Someone else?" Shelley raised her eyebrows. "But he looked at you like you were some long-lost friend. And you obviously knew him. I mean, you seemed so shocked to see him."

"Is that how it seemed to you?" Beverly seemed to study Shelley now. "I honestly can't remember what happened last night. I was so startled to see someone open that door like that, well, I nearly fell over from sheer fright." She smiled. "I was so impressed with how brave you were, Shelley."

Shelley shrugged. "I suppose that living with little kids underfoot all the time sort of prepares you to expect the unexpected." She laughed.

"So how did Jeff make the light work last night?" Margaret asked. "Did you get a chance to ask him about that?"

"Yes." Beverly nodded eagerly. "He'd brought a high-powered beam with him and he shot it out over the ocean just as we were walking toward the lighthouse. I guess he just wanted to see what it would look like if the light worked."

"But *why?*" Shelley asked.

"Just for fun, I think." Beverly looked down at her coffee.

"And you're sure he wasn't up to something?" Margaret wondered. "I don't like to sound suspicious, but it does seem odd that he'd go out there by himself at night and send a signal like that."

"Yeah," Shelley said. "How do we know he wasn't signaling someone out on the water?" Suddenly she remembered how everyone had suspected Dan had been up to no good not so very long ago. What if this Jeff person was into something like drug smuggling?

"Oh, I don't think he was signaling anyone." But Beverly frowned now, almost as if she was unsure.

"So, for clarity's sake, Jeff is the same guy that Augie told us about?" Diane asked. "The one who's been sleuthing around town asking about the lighthouse, correct?"

"He is one and the same," Beverly said.

"But he didn't tell you exactly why he's so interested in the lighthouse?" Diane asked.

Beverly's brow creased as she took another sip of coffee. "No, he didn't."

"So you're in the dark as much as we are?" Shelley felt disappointed. She had expected more than this.

"Unfortunately, I am."

"But why did you need to speak to him privately?" Shelley knew she was veering dangerously into nosy territory now, but she just couldn't help herself. Inquiring minds wanted to know!

Beverly gave her a patient smile. Or perhaps she was trying to look mysterious, or maybe she was trying to send Shelley a polite message to back off. "Jeff and I had some old—private—matters to discuss."

"Well, now." Margaret checked her watch. "I hate to break up the party, but it's about time for me to open up the gallery." She chuckled as she stood. "Not that I expect much business now that the season is ending. But at least I'll have time to catch up on my painting now that things have slowed down."

"And I should get back to my writing." Diane took a final sip of her latte, then reached for her purse. "I'm actually starting to feel inspired about starting the second novel. An interesting character has been running around in my head and it's about time I got her down on paper." She smiled. "Or at least into a computer document."

"And I have an appointment," Beverly announced as she stood. "But it was nice seeing everyone." Then before anyone else could leave, Beverly exited the Cove.

"Something is going on," Shelley said quietly.

"What do you mean?" Diane peered curiously at her.

"I mean with Beverly and that Jeff dude. Something is up."

Margaret laughed. "Oh, Shelley, don't let your youth and your imagination run away with you."

"But didn't you see her face?" Shelley asked as they all stood. "She was hiding something."

"And what if she is keeping something to herself?" Margaret countered. "Isn't that her right?"

Shelley sighed. "I guess so."

"Maybe she's attracted to Jeff," Diane suggested with a coyly lifted brow.

"He's certainly attractive enough," Margaret chuckled as they walked toward the door.

Shelley nodded eagerly. That actually made the most sense. Jeff was handsome, and it was possible that Beverly's head had been turned by his good looks. "Yes…maybe that's it. Maybe she's hoping for some sort of romance and just doesn't want anyone to know about it. You know, in case it falls apart."

"And so, as her good friends, we'll respect her privacy," Margaret declared as they stood by the door of the coffeehouse, "and we won't press her for details until she's ready to speak. *Right?*"

They all agreed this was the best plan for the time being. Give Beverly her space.

However, as Shelley walked home, much more slowly this time, she was still curious. It would take some serious self-control not to keep pressing Beverly for more information about her relationship with the handsome mystery man.

CHAPTER THREE

Rocky greeted Diane with a happily wagging tail as she opened the door to her little cottage. "Always a warm welcome, eh?" She leaned over and patted his golden head, causing his tail to whip back and forth even faster. "And you've already had your morning walk, so you'll just have to be patient while I settle in to do some serious writing."

Diane hung her bag on a hook by the door, then went to the kitchen to put on the teakettle. Some Earl Grey tea was just what she needed to get her creative juices flowing. She puttered in her kitchen, putting her breakfast dishes in the dishwasher and washing down the soapstone countertops, until she heard the cheerful whistle of the kettle. She opened her tea tin and smiled to see some packets of the hibiscus tea that Jessie had brought during her visit a few weeks ago.

Having both Justin and Jessica here at the same time had been such a treat. She wondered how long it would be before that happened again. With Justin getting ready for officer training, it wouldn't likely be anytime before Christmas.

She poured the steaming water over the tea bag. Waiting for it to steep, she looked outside the kitchen window and into the backyard. More signs of fall were showing up each day.

Her sugar maple was vibrant with shades of orange, gold, and green. And the ash tree in Margaret's yard, backlit by the morning sun, resembled a fall-toned stained glass window.

She loved this time of year. Unfortunately, it always passed too quickly. And the older she got, the faster it seemed to go. And then winter would be upon them. As she removed her tea bag, she wondered how a winter, here by the sea, would compare to an inland winter. Would fierce winds and harsh seaboard weather make her feel more housebound than she had in Boston? Or would she relish the coziness of her little cottage with a fire burning? Would she put her downtime to good use by writing her next novel?

With her hot tea mug in hand, she went into her little office, tilted the blinds up, put on some music, sat down in her office chair, and turned on her computer. Out of habit, she checked her e-mail first. Mostly it was junk mail, although Justin had forwarded her a funny post about bears. But then, just as she was about to sign off, a new message popped into her inbox—and it was from her agent!

As usual, Diane's radar went up when she saw Frieda Watley's name in the sender column. Frieda's New York agency was the kind of business that made people in the publishing world sit up and pay attention. Diane was no different.

Hello, Diane. More news for you. Do not be alarmed, but your publisher has decided not to go with the series idea. I realize you put a lot of work into these proposals, but now it seems that the publisher has determined that series are not selling.

Diane stopped reading and, closing her eyes, took a deep, steadying breath. *How could this be?* After the editor at the publishing company had come back and practically begged Diane to write two more fully fleshed-out book proposals to go with her first novel, making it into a trilogy—now they were saying *no*? How could they be so fickle? So cruel? To get her hopes up by sending her a contract, and then to dash them just like that? It seemed unconscionable.

She took another deep breath, telling herself that it was no matter, that she could face this disappointment. After all, her life, her times...all were in God's hands. Opening her eyes, she braced herself and continued to read the disheartening message.

But, dear Diane, as I said, do not be alarmed. Do not despair. The good news is that the publisher still wants three books from you. And the novels can be linked in some way. Perhaps simply the location, which you've charmingly re-created to resemble your own little coastal town. But they do not want the novels to be part of a continuing series. According to your editor, Jane Veers, your books must stand alone so that they can be read in any order. That way, the buyer and the bookstore don't get distracted or confused by which volume comes next.

I hope this makes sense to you and that it is not too disturbing. Jane agrees that your original proposal won't need too many changes. Your storylines may still work. You simply need to make the books stand alone.

I would call you with this news, but I'm in flight to Phoenix just now. After that, I'll be meeting with an author in Montreal, and then I'm heading over to the Frankfurt Book Fair. Feel free to e-mail me with any questions. Otherwise, you can respond directly to Jane Veers.

Naturally, the advance for your three-book contract will hinge upon these revised book proposals, so I suggest you get right to it—before they change their mind again. LOL. Welcome to the wonderful but ever-changing world of book publishing!

Best, Frieda

Diane leaned back in her chair and let out a long sigh. She had to rewrite the two proposals. It seemed she had barely written and sent them, and now it was time to do it again. But what if she rewrote books two and three and the publisher changed its mind again? What if the publishing committee suddenly decided that a continuing series was the best way to go? She felt like a Ping-Pong ball that was being batted back and forth between her publisher and her agent.

Still, she realized that many writers would love to have such a problem. "Count your blessings," she said as she opened up the file that contained her series proposal. "And back to the drawing board." She chuckled as she copied and pasted the second novel proposal into a new document. Perhaps this was God's way of keeping her from getting a big head. Whatever the case, she could do it. She *would* do it.

And, like Frieda insinuated, the sooner the better. But she would keep all the old versions of the proposal, just in case the publisher changed its mind again.

Fortunately, once she dug into the project, she discovered that Jane and Frieda were absolutely right: it wasn't that difficult to turn the proposals into stand-alone books. In fact, once she finished her revisions, by late afternoon, she decided that it might even make the whole project simpler for her. She wouldn't need to keep such careful track of all the details now, making sure that they carried over into the next books. Making each story its own entity freed her to bring in more characters and have more fun.

"Oh, Rocky," she said as she stretched her hands over her head and worked the sore muscles in her neck. "You and I are overdue for a good long walk on the beach." She considered calling one of her friends to join her, but it was close to the dinner hour, and she knew that could be tricky. Besides that, the weather had turned iffy with dark clouds gathered on the horizon. She and Rocky would have to hurry if they wanted to get out and back before it started to rain.

The wind whipped her shoulder-length hair about and she wished she'd thought to grab a ball cap as she leashed up Rocky and headed across the well-worn path that cut through their neighborhood and went straight to the beach. It was hard to believe that just a few weeks ago, this path had been constantly crowded with tourists, or that the beach—nearly deserted now—had been filled with kids and dogs and people of all ages. Marble Cove turned into a completely different sort of place after Labor Day. But Diane was thankful to be part of it.

As she and Rocky wandered down the windswept beach, she remembered how many times she and Eric and the kids had loaded everything into their car and headed back to the city on Labor Day. How many times had she cast one last wistful look as they rolled out of town along with all the other tourists, wondering what it would be like to be a full-timer? And now she was.

She pulled a tennis ball out of her pocket and gave it a good throw for Rocky. Having heard a sad story of a tourist's dog that was injured when it tripped on the beach with a stick in its mouth, Diane had decided to switch Rocky from chasing sticks to chasing balls. And since she could toss the ball farther than the stick anyway, Rocky wasn't complaining either.

Still, she reminded herself as she picked up the soggy, sandy ball, she needed to look into one of those throwing implements she'd noticed some tourists using with their dogs. It looked like the tennis ball fit into a sticklike thing that was used to lob the ball even farther than she could throw. Maybe she would ask Lee Waters at the Pet Place if he knew about them.

As they got closer to the lighthouse, that familiar feeling of peace washed over Diane. To her, the lighthouse was like a symbol of God—protective, unchanging, stability, strength... the giver of second chances. Seeing the lighthouse, tall and white and stately, always filled her with a sense of hope.

She watched it carefully, hoping to see a flash of light. But, as usual, nothing changed. The few times she and her friends had seen those inexplicable lights coming from the lighthouse had been random and limited. She could probably count them on one hand. And the light they'd seen last night, she now knew, had been produced by Jeff Mackenzie. Although what he had been doing there, and what he'd been researching, was still a mystery to her. And what about the other lights they'd all seen?

Despite her attempt to appear mature and nonchalant at the Cove this morning, mostly to keep Shelley from creating an uncomfortable scene, Diane was extremely curious about Jeff and about Beverly's relationship with him. The way Beverly had acted last night, the way she had insisted on staying behind with Jeff...none of it made any sense. However, Diane knew Beverly well enough to know that if Beverly clammed up about something, there was no point in prodding her. That would only drive her away. With Beverly, patience seemed to pay off. Diane would have to wait.

Fat raindrops started to fall now, splatting down on her head and face, and Diane knew it was time to turn back. "Come on, Rocky," she called as she started to jog back down the boardwalk. "Let's get home!"

By the time they got to her front porch, Diane was soaked to the skin and Rocky was dripping. She peeled off her soggy jacket, hung it on the banister, and slipped into the house to get a towel for Rocky. Before long, she had changed into dry warm-ups and both she and Rocky were considerably dryer.

She got a fire crackling in the fireplace and started thinking about dinner.

But as she heated soup and sliced an apple, she felt a little lonely. This was never how she'd planned to spend her "golden" years...living with a dog as a companion. It was times like tonight when she really missed Eric. In all her dreams, Eric had been here with her. And yet here she was, alone.

Rocky came over and pressed his slightly damp body against her leg, letting out a little whine, almost as if he knew she was feeling blue. She looked down into his amber eyes. "What is it?"

His tail wagged eagerly as he looked at his empty food dish, then back to her with an expectant look.

"Oh, I get it. You're hungry." She laughed. "And here I thought I was having dinner alone tonight."

CHAPTER FOUR

Margaret was in her bliss, quietly painting a moody seascape that included the art gallery's namesake—a shearwater bird perched on a rock slightly above the pounding surf. Her inspiration was a photo she'd snagged a couple of weeks ago. And although she was barely past the sketching stage and just starting to apply paint, she was very pleased with the results. Nestled in the cozy back room of the gallery, music quietly playing, and a cup of cinnamon stick tea by her side, all was right with the world.

And then the phone rang. But, as usual, she let it go to the answering machine. This was a luxury she afforded herself during the slower season. Often it was simply someone wanting to hear the gallery's hours, and the caller usually hung up without leaving a message. But this time she heard Allan's voice speaking. She paused with her paintbrush in midair to listen.

"I don't want to disturb you, dear, but I'm having a… well, a little challenge with Adelaide this morning." He lowered his voice. "She can't hear me right now, but she is a bit out of sorts. For some reason we can't find the right things for her to wear. I really don't know what to make of it, but I think she is in need of a woman's—"

"Allan," Margaret said into the receiver. "What is going on?"

"Oh, it's probably just a tempest in a teapot, but Adelaide is on the verge of getting upset, and I felt I could use some advice."

"On what?" Margaret set her brush down, wiping her fingers on her smock.

"Usually, she has no problem with getting dressed to go to the community center."

"But not today?"

"Right. For some reason, she is very frustrated. She put on one outfit, then looked at herself in the mirror by the front door and said it was all wrong."

"All wrong?" Margaret tried to imagine this. Usually Adelaide had no concerns about her appearance. One of the blessings of raising a Down syndrome child.

"Yes. So she went and changed her shirt and put on a sweater. But then that was all wrong too."

"Oh dear." Now Margaret remembered Adelaide's request to dye her hair purple. "Do you think this is some kind of adolescence? I remember reading about something like this once, but I thought we had escaped it."

"I'm not sure what it is, but I'm afraid she's not going to be ready when the bus arrives in the next ten minutes." He sighed. "I suppose I can drive her over there. It's just that I was in the midst of gluing some wood veneer, and I hate to stop midway."

"Don't stop what you're doing," she told him. "I'll pop on home and see what's troubling her."

"I didn't want to interrupt you," he said apologetically. "I just thought you might have some advice or know some female trick that I might employ with her."

"I think Adelaide just needs some one-on-one time with me," Margaret said. "I'm afraid I've neglected her a bit lately. I'll just put up the 'I'll be back' sign and come home for a bit."

He thanked her, and she removed her smock and hung the sign, then hurried home to see what she could do to help her daughter. Just as she got home, the activities bus pulled up. Margaret apologized to the driver, explaining that she'd be driving Adelaide today, then she went into the house.

"She's in her room," Allan said with a worried expression. "Sorry. I'm just not good at this."

Margaret waved her hand. "Go ahead and get back to your project. I'll see what I can do." But the truth was that Margaret wasn't so sure she'd be good at this either.

"Hey, Adelaide," she said gently as she went in her room. "What's wrong?"

"What's wrong is that I am *not* pretty." Adelaide folded her arms across her chest and sat down on the edge of her bed, making a *humph* sound.

"Yes, you *are* pretty." Margaret sat next to her, running her fingers through Adelaide's sleek, shoulder-length hair. "You've got the silkiest hair ever, and it's exactly the same color as honey. Plus you have those beautiful brown eyes, the same color as mine. You are very pretty, darling. And you're not just pretty on the outside. You are very pretty inside too. You're helpful and kind and gentle and sweet."

"This shirt." Adelaide looked down at her pink sweatshirt. It had the image of three kittens on it. It used to be her favorite. She shook her head. "It's ugly."

"No, it's not ugly." Margaret studied her daughter's grim expression, trying to figure this out. "Did someone tell you it's ugly?"

Adelaide nodded sadly.

"Who said that?" Margaret felt the mother-bear syndrome rising up inside her. How dare anyone pick on her child!

"Lisa did."

"Lisa?" Margaret frowned. "Who's Lisa?"

"A girl." Adelaide's brow creased as she tugged at the cuff of her sweatshirt, twisting it with her fingers.

"A girl at the community center?" Margaret tried to remember a Lisa.

"Yes." Adelaide stuck out her lower lip. "She's mean."

"Oh."

"She says she's prettier than me."

"Well, that's not a very nice thing to say." Margaret pondered a moment. "I know you would never say anything like that to anyone. Would you?"

Adelaide shook her head firmly. "No. It's mean to say that."

Margaret thought hard about the people at the community center. Chances were that Lisa had some challenges of her own. "I wonder if Lisa feels unhappy inside. That might be the reason she wants to make you feel bad."

Adelaide's brow creased as if she was trying to grasp this concept.

"I've found that sometimes people are mean because they have bad feelings trapped inside of them." Margaret tapped her own chest to make her point, then tried to think of an incident to further illustrate it. "Remember when I got grumpy because of the roof problems at the gallery? I was kind of short-tempered with you about something, and then I felt bad afterward."

Adelaide nodded.

"But I wasn't really mad at you—it wasn't even your fault. I just acted grumpy because of that silly old roof. And then I had to apologize to you. Remember?"

"Yeah. But you said you were sorry, Mom."

"I did."

"But Lisa never said sorry," she said glumly.

"Maybe Lisa just needs someone to be nicer to her," Margaret suggested. "So that she will feel better inside."

"And not be so mean to me?"

"Yes. Maybe she needs you to be her friend, Adelaide. You are such a good friend to people. You know how to share and help. Maybe Lisa just needs to get to know you as a friend."

Adelaide looked hopeful. "Okay."

"Would you like me to go to the community center with you this morning? Maybe I could talk to Lisa?" Margaret didn't want to intrude on Adelaide's territory. But she also didn't want to let someone hurt her daughter.

"Okay." Adelaide smiled like she was relieved.

Margaret looked at the pink sweatshirt now. The image of the kittens was a little cracked and faded. Maybe it was almost ready for the rag bag. "So is that what you want to wear today?"

Adelaide looked uncertain.

Now Margaret went over to Adelaide's closet, which was messier than usual. Probably because Adelaide had tried on several things in her search for something "pretty." Margaret pulled out a light blue pullover that she'd gotten Adelaide last Christmas. It was almost like new. "I think this sweater looks very pretty on you, sweetheart. It's the color of the ocean on a clear, sunny day."

Adelaide brightened.

"And you could wear that blue hair band that matches it. I think that would look very pretty."

Soon they had Adelaide outfitted and happy, and Margaret was driving her to the center. Her plan was to meet Lisa, have a pleasant conversation, and then put a bug in the ear of whoever was supervising today. She knew it wasn't an easy job balancing the diverse needs of the people at the center. Some had physical challenges, while some like Adelaide had mental ones. But usually they managed to get along smoothly. She hoped this Lisa wasn't truly a mean person.

Adelaide held Margaret's hand as they walked up to the low brick building.

The community center was one of the things that had originally attracted her and Allan to the small town of Marble Cove. Thanks to an endowment fund from a wealthy family, as well as some government grants and the annual fund-raiser, the community center met the needs of a number of local families, and Margaret never ceased to be grateful for it.

She pushed open the glass doors and entered the spacious lobby, waving to the receptionist at the front desk, then continued on into the big activities room. With two walls of floor-to-ceiling windows, the room was washed in sunlight. Very cheerful. And today a fire was crackling in the big stone fireplace. Cozy.

"Adelaide." Penny Tyler came over to hug her. "I'm so glad you're here. We're getting ready to do a nature walk and collect autumn leaves to make into collages."

"Oh, that sounds fun," Margaret said.

"You're welcome to join us, Mrs. Hoskins."

"I would...except that I need to man the gallery."

Penny smiled. "Well, I'm sure Adelaide will surprise you with a lovely collage."

"I can't wait." Margaret looked around the large room. "Is Lisa here today?"

Penny nodded, pointing over to a table where several people were looking at something. "She's over there."

"I'd like to meet her." Margaret smiled at Adelaide. "You want to introduce us?"

Now Adelaide looked like she was feeling shy. So Penny offered to help, and they all walked over and Margaret watched Lisa as Penny went through the introductions. It was clear that Lisa had some mental challenges too. Not Down's syndrome...but something.

"It's lovely to meet you," Margaret said to Lisa. "Adelaide told me about you. And it's so nice that you girls can be friends."

Lisa smiled brightly. "Yeah. We are friends."

At that, Adelaide looked happier.

Margaret made some small talk about the book that they were looking at on the table. Then she went back to find Penny, explaining what Adelaide had told her.

"Oh, I'm surprised. Usually Lisa is very sweet." She chuckled. "But you never know. Maybe she'd had a bad day."

"That's probably it."

"Anyway, thanks for the heads-up. I'll keep an eye out for any problems."

Margaret thanked her.

"By the way," Penny said, "I was wondering if you'll have time to do any art classes this year. Everyone really enjoys it when you do that. But I realize you're a lot busier with the gallery and all."

"I'll do everything I can to teach some classes," Margaret promised. "Allan helps to watch the gallery sometimes, so I'm sure we can work something out."

"Thank you," Penny told her. "And I promise to help mediate should any troubles arise between Lisa and Adelaide."

Margaret left the community center feeling greatly relieved. Really, compared to the kinds of problems some parents had with their children—including grown children—parenting Adelaide was a piece of cake. She hoped it would continue to be.

CHAPTER FIVE

To Beverly's relief, Jeff had assured her he was going back to Augusta on Sunday night. She had made it clear that she had no intention of seeing him ever again. And he had promised not to bother her. The past was the past, and she had no interest in going back there.

However, on Thursday afternoon, less than a week since their "chance" encounter at the lighthouse, he called her cell phone. How he'd gotten her number was a complete mystery. But she had no intention of answering. She had enough on her plate right now.

"Go ahead and take that call if you need to," Mrs. Peabody told her as she slid a casserole into the oven. "I can finish seeing to dinner." Despite the fact that Beverly was living full-time with her father, Mrs. Peabody still didn't want to give up her role as housekeeper and cook. And, really, Beverly didn't mind. Besides, she knew the old woman could use the income.

It freed up more of Beverly's time to work from home. She had imagined telecommuting for her job at the State House would be much easier than it was. However, she soon discovered that with the distractions that came with the territory, the work hours of the day sometimes slipped by too quickly. "That's okay," she told Mrs. Peabody, tucking the phone into her jacket pocket. "It's not important."

"I just scratch my head over those little phones." Mrs. Peabody reached up and literally scratched her curly white hair. "How you young people figure out how to use all those fancy devices is a wonder to me."

"Sometimes they're handy," Beverly admitted as she put the coleslaw salad Mrs. Peabody had made into the fridge. "But sometimes I'd like to just toss them altogether."

"How is the mister doing?" Mrs. Peabody asked in a hushed tone.

"He's resting." Beverly glanced down the hallway toward her father's bedroom.

"I know you took him to the doctor this morning." Mrs. Peabody looked worried. "Did you learn anything?"

Beverly sighed and just shook her head. The truth was, she was disappointed in her father's doctor. But she hated to admit this to Mrs. Peabody. She knew the old woman liked to talk, and Beverly didn't want to be the one responsible for starting negative rumors about his medical practice.

"Well, I know he loves my chicken and broccoli casserole," Mrs. Peabody said with confidence. "Maybe some good food will put him back to rights."

Beverly smiled and nodded. "I'm sure it will help." She walked Mrs. Peabody to the door, confirming that she'd return in the morning so that Beverly could meet Diane for coffee as planned. She waved as Mrs. Peabody went down the steps.

Why was it that some elderly people, like Mrs. Peabody, fared so well with aging, whereas others, like her father, did not? Her father was actually a bit younger than Mrs. Peabody. And he'd always taken fairly good care of his health. Or at least her mother had.

Standing there on the porch, she found herself replaying the conversation she'd had with the doctor while her father had redressed. "It's a normal part of aging," he'd told her. "At least with some unfortunate souls."

"What do you mean 'it's normal'?" she had persisted. "My father's memory seems to get worse each day."

"Call it Alzheimer's or dementia or short-term memory loss, it happens to some people. It's fortunate you've moved back home to care for him."

"Yes, I'm happy to be back with him. But I didn't expect that he'd need this much help," Beverly admitted.

"Do you think he's a danger to himself?"

"Oh no...not really."

He handed her a booklet. "Here are some helpful tips for patients with Alzheimer's. Some of the usual stuff like unplugging the stove and storing items he needs in full sight. But you might also want to attend a support group."

"So that's it?" she asked. "It really is Alzheimer's?"

He pressed his lips together and gave a slight shrug. "Like I said, we can call it a number of things. Mostly we have to learn to live with it."

Beverly felt like yelling now. *To live with it?* Wasn't there anything to be done to help?

He must've sensed her frustration because he reached out and patted her shoulder. "I know it's hard seeing someone you love aging like this. And it's possible that you'll need to look into some alternative care situations."

By that time, her father had emerged. He'd looked slightly disheveled, with his tie crooked and his shirt buttoned wrong. But his smile was sweet and genuine when he saw her. "You're still here?"

"Of course," she'd told him. "Now let's go home."

★   ★   ★

The next morning, her father still very much on her mind, Beverly sat down with Diane at the Cove coffee shop. "Sorry I'm late," she said as she set her orange scone and cappuccino in front of her.

"No problem." Diane smiled. "So how's your week going?"

Beverly stirred her drink and sighed. "To be honest…not so well."

"I'm sorry." Diane broke her muffin in half. "What's troubling you?"

"My father." Beverly shook her head. "I just don't understand it. He's gone downhill so quickly. Just last spring he seemed so much better than he is now. I had no idea a person could deteriorate so fast. It's as if he's aged a decade or more in the past couple of months."

"I know what you mean. I spoke to him just yesterday. I was passing by when he came out to get the mail. So I said hello and started telling him a little about the book I'm working on...because he used to be so interested in the writing process and all. Remember how he read some of my work for me, offering some very helpful critiques? That was only last May."

Beverly nodded sadly. "Yes, it's hard to believe now."

"But yesterday he seemed so confused and disoriented. It felt almost as if he didn't know me. Then I chattered away at him. You know how I can be. And it seemed like we got past that, or he pretended to. But then it was as if he didn't even remember that I was a writer. And I could tell he was frustrated."

"I suppose this is how it's going to be from now on, a steady decline." Beverly took a sip of her coffee. "Alzheimer's is such a nasty disease...the way it steals the memory from people. I just hate it."

"Are you sure it's Alzheimer's?"

"Well, that's what Father's doctor called it just yesterday. He also said it could be dementia. Anyway, it's pretty much the same thing...deteriorating short-term memory. Nothing we can do. Just be patient." She grimaced to remember how he'd brushed it off.

"But I was just reading this article in a health magazine." Diane's eyes brightened, almost as if a light had just gone on inside her. "And I know your father has diabetes. But I'm curious, has his doctor ever given him an MRI or CT scan?"

"Why would he do that?"

"Because this article said that people who suffer from diabetes are also very prone to strokes."

"Yes. I know about that. But that's not the problem, Diane. I know that Father hasn't had a stroke. He hasn't exhibited any paralysis."

"But it's possible he's experienced *mini*strokes."

Beverly leaned forward. "Ministrokes?"

"Yes. It's a temporary blockage that doesn't look like a real stroke in that there's no paralysis or the usual symptoms that we associate with strokes. These little strokes can come and go, and the person might not even know they're having them."

"So what does a ministroke do?"

Diane got a thoughtful look, as if processing something. "The interesting thing in this article was how these ministrokes, particularly in older patients, are sometimes confused with Alzheimer's or dementia because the blood flow blockage results in symptoms like temporary memory loss. As a result they are misdiagnosed, and they go untreated."

Beverly sat up straighter. "Do you think that could be Father's problem?"

"I think it's worth looking into."

"You know Father's doctor is a nice guy, but he's pretty old, and I get the feeling he's sort of old-school too. Father jokingly calls him a horse doctor."

"Maybe you need a second opinion," Diane suggested. "Or at the very least an MRI or CT scan."

"Oh, Diane, what if this is something that can be fixed?" Beverly felt a rush of hope. "What if Father isn't really suffering from Alzheimer's at all?" She pulled her phone back out. "I feel like I should call someone. But who?"

"Margaret recommended her doctor to me awhile back," Diane told her. "I've only been once, just for a checkup. But I was impressed with her. Not only was she very nice, she was intelligent too. Plus she spoke to me like we were on equal ground. I like that in a physician."

"A woman doctor?"

"Your dad wouldn't like that?"

"I don't know for sure. But I think it's worth a try."

Diane pulled out her cell phone and gave Beverly the doctor's number. "Go ahead and call right now if you want. I don't mind."

So with Diane waiting, Beverly called and quickly explained the situation, briefly giving her father's history. "I don't want to malign another doctor," she said, "but I am worried that something important might've been overlooked. Plus I know that my father's doctor is close to retirement. Is there any chance that Dr. Emerson is taking new patients?"

"Would you like to speak to the doctor?"

"Yes, please," Beverly said eagerly.

Before long Dr. Emerson was on the line, and Beverly quickly explained her concerns regarding her father's diabetes and possible ministrokes.

"I don't want to worry you unnecessarily," Dr. Emerson said, "but this could be quite serious. And, considering what you've told me, you have good reason to suspect that your father is experiencing TIAs."

"TIAs?"

"Transient ischemic attack. Otherwise known as a ministroke," she explained. "If left untreated, your father could be at serious risk." The doctor asked her to hold for a few minutes, and Beverly filled Diane in on what she'd just learned.

Eventually, a nurse returned to the phone. "Ms. Wheeland, another patient had been scheduled for an MRI, but she had to cancel this morning. I just checked with the hospital, and the appointment is still open. Is there any chance your father can make it over to Bramford by three o'clock today?"

"Today?" Beverly pressed her lips together. What would her father say if she were suddenly forcing him to go to the hospital to be scanned?

"Dr. Emerson said that she highly recommends this procedure for your father. The sooner the better."

"But what about Father's other doctor? Dr. Vernon?"

"If you decide to take the MRI appointment, Dr. Emerson will be in communication with Dr. Vernon for you. They've worked together on similar cases, and Dr. Vernon sometimes refers patients to Dr. Emerson."

"All right." Beverly decided. "I'll get him there."

"Great. But Dr. Emerson would also need to see your father here in our office first. Just to do a quick checkup and go over some things. She could probably squeeze him in at one thirty, and that would give you plenty of time to make it over to Bramford afterward."

Beverly agreed, and the nurse took some insurance information, promising to request medical records from the other doctor. Beverly asked a few more questions, jotted down some things, thanked the nurse, and closed her phone.

"Diane," she said urgently, "I need to get Father to the hospital."

Diane's brows shot up. "What's wrong?"

"No, it's not like that. They were able to set up an MRI appointment for three o'clock." Beverly put her notepad back in her purse. "But Dr. Emerson wants to see him in her office first."

"Wow, that was fast."

"I'll have just enough time to fix Father some lunch and help him to get ready to go to see Dr. Emerson. After that, we'll go directly to the hospital in Bramford." Beverly looked at her watch. "This is all happening so fast. It feels like my head is spinning. Can you believe they had a cancellation for the MRI?"

"I think it's a blessing." Diane looked relieved. "If your father's having ministrokes, you don't want to let it go undetected a day longer."

"I agree." Beverly grimaced. "And I know Dr. Vernon means well, but it's upsetting to think he might've missed something this serious."

"Doctors are only human."

"Well, I've got a lot to get done now. Sorry to cut our visit short." Beverly stood.

"I'm just glad you called Dr. Emerson."

Beverly frowned. "I hope Father doesn't give me any resistance."

"Could you use a hand?"

"Oh…" Beverly wasn't sure. She was so used to handling everything on her own. It was still strange for her to think that someone would want to help her like this. "Would you really have the time…or even want to?"

"What are friends for?" Diane put a hand on Beverly's shoulder.

"Well, I know Father likes and respects you." Beverly set a tip on the table. "At least he used to…back when his mind was working better."

"Well, let's just do this together. I need to run home and let Rocky out, and then I'm ready whenever you are."

"Can you come by the house around one?"

Diane agreed, and Beverly felt hopeful. It really seemed providential that all this was coming together. For all she knew, this could be lifesaving for her father. But by the time she got home, she felt even more worried about Father's condition. How many ministrokes might he have experienced in the past several months?

And what if she handled things poorly today? She knew he might be resistant to this sudden development. What if he decided to get stubborn about going? Or worse yet, what if she pushed him too hard or stressed him so that he had a major stroke?

Deciding she didn't want her father to sense her concerns, she knew she had to put him at ease. And so, as she fixed him some lunch, she calmly explained the initial conversation she'd had with Diane at the Cove. "We're both concerned for you," she said.

"Why are you concerned?" he asked.

"Well, you just don't seem like yourself lately."

His brow creased with that confused look that she was getting so used to seeing. "You know...I don't really feel like myself."

She patted his hand. "I know. So we think Diane's doctor might be able to help."

"Who is that?"

"Dr. Emerson."

"Dr. Emerson?" Father nervously drummed his fingers on the kitchen table, repeating the name several times as if trying to place it.

"Yes. That's the doctor who thinks you should have an MRI."

"MRI? What's that?" His frown lines grew deeper.

"It's a magnetic scan that helps the doctors to see what's going on inside your head." She set a bowl of chicken and rice soup in front of him. "Your sandwich is almost ready."

"To see if my brain still works?" He gave her a lopsided smile as he picked up his spoon.

"Something like that. The thing is, Father, it might be that your memory problems can be fixed."

His face lit up slightly. "Fixed? So I'll remember things better?"

"Maybe so." She flipped over the grilled cheese sandwich. "Wouldn't that be great?"

"Yes. I'd like that."

On that hopeful note, he became more cooperative about getting ready. He didn't even complain when she urged him to put on a clean shirt. "Diane is going with us too," she said as the doorbell rang.

"Diane?" He looked slightly confused again.

"Remember our neighbor Diane?" she said. "The one who writes books?"

"Books." He nodded and smiled. "Yes, I like my books."

It was just a little past one by the time Beverly had her father seated in the passenger's seat and Diane in the back. To Beverly's relief, Diane kept up a sort of one-sided conversation going as she told them about the latest developments in her novel. And Father actually responded positively to Diane's chatter about her book's characters, nodding as if he understood, when it was obvious that these fictional people had nothing whatsoever to do with his life.

Perhaps that was how his life felt these days. With his loss of memory, it was possible that everyone in his world felt unreal to him. How frustrating would it be to be surrounded by characters that came and went as they pleased, constantly changing and never quite what he expected? Poor Father.

The appointment with Dr. Emerson went smoothly, and Father even seemed to like the no-nonsense physician. He didn't question that she was a woman—and a relatively young woman at that. But perhaps her strawberry blonde hair and ocean green eyes helped. In fact, unless Beverly was imagining things, her father was actually flirting with the pretty doctor.

"Dr. Vernon's office faxed over your medical records," she told them both, taking care to look directly at Father. "And everything is in order for your appointment over in Bramford." She handed Beverly a piece of paper for the MRI, explaining that there could be no metal in the room during the scan. "And you can be in with your father during his MRI," she told Beverly. "It should take about thirty minutes to complete the scan, and then the preliminary report should be sent to me within the hour. If our suspicion about TIAs is correct, I'll call in a prescription for you." She patted his hand and smiled. "And then I'd like to see you again next week to go over everything."

Father just nodded, but his expression seemed to be changing from pleasure to a mixture of confusion and fear. He probably had no idea what to expect.

Beverly prayed silently as she drove to Bramford. She prayed that the MRI would deliver real answers and that Dr. Emerson would be able to help her father recover. It wasn't that she was unwilling to care for Father if his condition continued to deteriorate into real dementia or Alzheimer's. It was simply that she felt that he didn't deserve this. A man whose mind had been sharp and clear for so many years, who had been sharp and clear just a few months ago, shouldn't be living in this foggy, confused world now. It didn't seem right. And she was willing to do whatever it took to figure it out.

Chapter Six

Diane could tell that Mr. Wheeland was feeling nervous as Beverly pulled into the hospital. He kept glancing from side to side with a worried expression.

"Do you want to drop us at the entrance?" Diane suggested to Beverly. "That way, your dad and I can go inside and wait for you to park."

Beverly agreed that was a good idea. Diane waited for him to undo his safety belt, then, hooking her arm in his, she chattered pleasantly about the weather and autumn leaves as they slowly made their way inside. "I've never been here before," she said as she guided him over to some chairs arranged by a rock fireplace. "It seems like a very nice place."

He continued glancing from side to side, almost as if he expected to be accosted.

"Why don't we wait here for Beverly?" Diane set her laptop case down on the coffee table.

"Yes." He nodded nervously. "We'll sit."

Diane picked up a worn issue of a gardening magazine and pointed to a photo of a fruit stand. "I heard there's a good produce stand over on Larkspur Road. I've been meaning to get over there to pick up some fresh fruit. This is such a wonderful time of year for apples. I love making apple pies. Do you like apple pies?"

His brow creased as he considered this, but then he slowly nodded.

And so she continued to jabber on about apple varieties and making pies and how her grandmother had taught her to bake when she was a child. She knew that her ramblings were just filler, but it did seem to put him at ease. Eventually Beverly came, and they went off in search of Radiology, where Beverly filled out some paperwork and Diane chattered to Mr. Wheeland about newspaper writing.

Eric used to call her a magpie sometimes. Usually it was when she was nervous or attempting to put others at ease. And he never said it in a mean way. In fact, she knew that he had often appreciated what he called her "gift of gab."

"Okay." Beverly came back to join them. "Now we'll go get ready for the MRI, Father." She explained to Diane that she planned to sit with him. "That means I have to change into hospital scrubs too."

"It's nice that you can keep him company," Diane smiled at them. "Have a good MRI!" As she watched them walking down the hallway, she knew that had been a silly thing to say, but at the moment, it was all she had. Well, that and prayer. So for a few minutes, Diane leaned back in her chair, closed her eyes, and proceeded to pray for Mr. Wheeland's MRI, for the technician's wisdom, and that Dr. Emerson would get to the bottom of his memory-loss issues.

Then, satisfied that this was all in God's capable hands, she pulled out her laptop and returned to her current work in progress. She was nearly finished with the third chapter now, but she still wasn't comfortable with the revisions she'd made to the first two chapters. She'd followed the publisher's direction by going back and changing some of the characters and several other things in order to make this book separate from her first novel, but the more she thought about it, the more she wanted to simply scrap the first chapters and just start over fresh. Still, it was hard to throw her work away.

But then, as she looked at chapter three, she realized that it made a good first chapter. And so that was what she would do—she would chop the first two and begin with three. Imagining herself as some sort of word surgeon, she amputated the first two chapters. Although she did copy and paste them to a new document, just in case she changed her mind later. Then she bravely typed "Chapter One" atop what had previously been her third chapter.

Feeling strangely invigorated by her literary surgery, she got a cup of tea and made herself even more comfortable in the Radiology waiting area, proceeding with an entirely different beginning for her novel. Before long, she was fully immersed, typing as fast as her fingers could fly—which, after years of newspaper writing, was relatively fast—when she heard her cell phone ringing from inside her bag.

She hated to stop her work, but knew she needed to at least see who was calling in case it was one of her kids. Old "mom" habits died hard. However, the number didn't look even vaguely familiar. But then, realizing she was already distracted as well as curious, she decided to answer it. To her surprise, it was a blast from the past, an acquaintance from her college days.

"This is Barbara Craig," an enthusiastic voice announced. "Remember me?"

"Yes," Diane said with some hesitation, "I do."

"Gail Myers gave me your phone number," Barbara cheerfully told her. "She'd mentioned how you'd moved to Marble Cove a while back. And since I'm coming out your way, I thought I'd give you a call."

"You're coming to Marble Cove?"

"Yes. I'm staying at a friend's beach house for a few days, and I was hoping we could get together and catch up."

"That would be great." Diane winced. *Great* was definitely an overstatement, especially since she and Barbara had never been particularly close. But what else could she say?

"Fantastic. I'll give you a call after I get settled in tomorrow. Perhaps we can do dinner."

Diane agreed to this, then hung up and shook her head. Barbara Craig. Why on earth was Barbara Craig calling Diane, of all people? Barbara had been in Diane's sorority, but the two had never really been friends. In fact, there was a time when Diane would've considered Barbara more of an enemy than a friend. Not only was there the time when Barbara told Diane's roommate that Diane had cheated on an exam, but it was even worse when Barbara had tried to come between

Diane and Eric. That hadn't worked out for Barbara, but it had definitely driven a wedge between the sorority sisters.

Of course, Diane knew this was all water under the bridge now. But even so, she didn't feel a bit eager to reacquaint herself with the likes of Barbara Craig. Maybe she was being immature or ungracious, but suddenly Diane was hoping that Barbara would either lose her phone number or else find other things to amuse herself with during her visit.

Diane had barely gotten back into her book when Beverly and her father reappeared. Both were dressed in their street clothes and looked relatively relaxed. "How did it go?" Diane asked.

"Pretty well," Beverly said. "Father did great."

"I didn't move," he told her.

"I think you actually fell asleep." Beverly jabbed him gently with her elbow.

"I only closed my eyes."

"Anyway, we're done. So we might as well go home and wait for Dr. Emerson to call. I hope she'll have a prescription for me to pick up." She smiled gratefully at Diane. "I'm so thankful you told me about that article you read, Diane. What perfect timing!"

"And almost miraculous that you were able to get that canceled appointment too." Diane slipped her laptop into her bag. "I can't help but think God had a hand in that."

"I sure hope so."

The ride home was much more subdued, and Diane suspected by the tilt of Mr. Wheeland's head that he was snoozing again. And so she decided to use this quiet time to continue in her prayer for him to get well.

"Thanks so much for your help today," Beverly said as they got out of the car.

"You're very welcome." Diane looped the handle of her bag over her shoulder. "Let me know what you find out."

"I will," Beverly promised.

Diane considered inviting Beverly to join her for a beach walk but figured she'd probably want to be around to help her father, fix some dinner, and wait for the doctor to call. So she simply waved and headed for home. Rocky would be more than willing to walk with her.

"Hello, neighbor," Margaret called as Diane passed by her house. She was just coming out her front door and wearing her parka and a knit hat. She appeared to be dressed for a walk.

"Allan's night to cook?" Diane asked.

Margaret nodded as she looped a bright scarf around her neck. "Just heading for the beach."

"Want company?"

"I'd love it." Margaret came over to join Diane on the sidewalk.

"Just let me drop off my bag and get Rocky, and we'll be on our way."

They were soon on the beach with Rocky bolting eagerly after the tennis ball. "How do you like my new ball thrower?" Diane showed the long plastic device to Margaret.

"Very nifty."

"It's a wonderful invention," Diane said as Rocky bounded toward her with the ball in his mouth. "It keeps my hands clean, and I can throw a lot farther." She paused to pick up the ball with the stick, then launched it down the beach. "Lots easier on my arm too."

As they walked, she filled Margaret in on her surprising afternoon with Beverly and her father.

"Wouldn't it be marvelous if Dr. Emerson could help him?" Margaret pulled her hat down over her ears. "It's made me so sad to see him deteriorate like that. You know, he's really only a few years older than my Allan. I can't imagine what I'd do if Allan began to lose his memory like that. I can't even bear to think about it."

"Getting old does come with its challenges, doesn't it?" Diane gave the ball another hard throw.

"Yes, but like they say, it beats the alternative." Margaret grinned wryly.

"So how is your painting coming this week?" Diane asked. "Making progress?"

"Slowly but surely. Sometimes painting feels like two steps forward and one step back."

"How's that?"

"Well, today, for instance. I thought I'd really made some progress on my new seascape, but when I stepped back and took a good hard look, I realized it was all wrong."

"*All* wrong?" Diane had a hard time imagining one of Margaret's paintings being anything less than great.

"Yes. I don't even know why, except that I must've gotten distracted. The perspective was way off, and I actually had to paint out a portion of the seascape in order to start over."

"I know how you feel," Diane said. "Just today I threw away two chapters from my new book."

Margaret's brows shot up. "Do you think it was something in the autumnal air? Perhaps a creative thinning of sorts, like when the leaves fall off the trees and prepare for new life."

Diane laughed. "Maybe so. Whatever it was, I think it was good for my book. It needed some pruning."

"I've been grateful that foot traffic has slowed down at the gallery. It really gives me more time to paint. I feel a bit guilty though." Margaret pursed her lips. "Because I realize we need customers for the business to stay afloat. It's a crazy sort of balancing act."

"How about my idea for the giclée prints?" Diane gave the ball a good chuck down the beach.

"We're still working on it. We're looking at companies that own their own machines and do work to order. I hope to get some prints ordered soon." Margaret bent down to pick up a shell. "So for right now, I'm afraid Dan's framing for the canvases is off to a slow start." She shook her head. "But Allan's furniture orders have picked up, so he's helping Allan with that for now. It should help a little."

Diane felt a wave of concern for Dan and Shelley. She knew that the Bauers were already stretched thin financially. Shelley's baking business was barely launched, and Dan's hours at work were less than half-time now. They'd really been clinging to the idea of Dan working for the gallery. Shelley had even called it their lifesaver.

Diane looked toward Orlean Point Light now. Barely perceivable through a milky layer of thick fog, it resembled a tall white ghost. It was times like these, especially now that the days were growing shorter, that Diane wished it was a working lighthouse. How she longed to see a golden beam of light slicing through the mist like a beacon of hope.

Chapter Seven

Shelley remembered a time in her life when working on a Friday night would've felt like sheer drudgery. Like back in high school, which wasn't much more than ten years ago. However, as she walked down the dimly lit street to the Cove, she felt a guilty sense of relief to know that she'd gotten out of getting the kids ready for bed tonight.

It was ironic to think of how much time Shelley spent at the coffeehouse these days. What a change from how her life used to be—back when her average 24-7 consisted of lost binkies, dirty diapers, sticky fingers, piles of laundry, and dog messes. Now she still had all those things *plus* the responsibility of running her baking business.

Not that she regretted the evenings she spent at the Cove. What a treat it was to have the whole coffeehouse to herself! As queen of the Cove's kitchen, she was able to bake muffins, cookies, and other delectables to sell in her fledgling business as well as to fill the Cove's pastry case. Other than being away from Dan and the kids, which came with its own little guilt trip, it was a pretty handy arrangement. The coffeehouse was starting to feel like her home away from home.

To her relief, Dan was becoming fairly comfortable with her being gone too. Like tonight, instead of complaining about the fact that she hadn't had time to put away the clean laundry, he'd taken the initiative to dig through the basket in search of Aiden's Superman pajamas. Naturally, Aiden would've preferred Spider-Man, but those were still in the dirty clothes hamper.

As Shelley slipped her key in the front door, she was surprised to see that the lights were still on in the coffee-house. She was even more surprised to see that Brenna was still behind the counter.

"What're you doing here?" Brenna asked.

"Baking." Shelley unzipped her jacket.

"But we're open tonight."

Shelley frowned. "Open?"

"Yeah. It's Friday. Remember how we wanted to try staying open on a Friday night? Just to see if we get any business? If it doesn't work, we'll shut 'er down."

"Oh...I guess I forgot." Shelley glanced around to spot only one couple, sipping coffees and their reading newspapers. "Looks pretty slow."

"Yeah. Gotta expect that at first. Next week, we'll have live music and see how that goes."

"So...I can't bake tonight?"

Brenna's mouth twisted to one side. "Well, we do seem to be running low on our baked goods." She picked up the phone. "Let me call the boss and see if it's okay."

Shelley stood there waiting as Brenna explained the situation, including the barren state of the pastry case. She hung up and nodded. "You can bake tonight, Shelley. But sounds like it's just this once if we keep staying open on Friday nights."

Shelley wanted to ask why it would even matter, especially since there wasn't much business anyway. However, she knew that some rules just never really made sense anyway. At least she could bake tonight.

As she went to work, she tried not to think about her family's financial state. Yes, they were in bad shape...bad that was steadily leaning to worse, despite her friends' efforts to find ways to help. But it wouldn't make her pastries taste any sweeter to obsess over it now. In fact, she knew from experience that pessimistic thoughts could ruin a recipe faster than a wrong ingredient.

Brenna poked her head into the kitchen before eight. "I'm closing now," she told Shelley as she pulled on her coat. "Happy baking."

Shelley wiped her hands on her apron. "Maybe you guys will want to rethink staying open on Fridays now."

Brenna just shrugged. "Can't give up before we give it a good try. Live music might help."

Shelley nodded, returning her attention to rolling out the buttery croissant dough, handling it gently with her ice-chilled hands, layering it, thinking light and happy thoughts. Really, there was a sort of magic to baking...something she had difficulty explaining to a novice.

Shelley felt contentedly exhausted as she loaded the last of the baking dishes into the dishwasher. She still needed to wipe down the counters and stow her ingredients into the cabinet that the coffeehouse was allowing her to use. Already she was running out of flour and sugar and vanilla again. Tomorrow, she'd have to make a list...and hope that she could afford to fill it.

Her feet felt heavy as she walked home. It was only a short walk, but Dan didn't like it when she walked. "It helps to clear my head," she'd told him. "And it saves on gas." Still, it felt like a long tonight.

It was past midnight by the time she'd checked on the kids, cleaned up the mess Dan had left for her in the kitchen, and finally fell into bed. Dan emitted a sleepy groan, and she tried not to count how few hours were left until Emma would wake up. Would there ever be a time when Shelley didn't feel this tired?

As expected, morning came early. Emma's cries woke Shelley out of a dead sleep at 5:57. Since it was Saturday, Dan had nowhere to be and, as usual, he slept soundly. What was it about Dan that he could sleep through the cries of their children while she could not?

Emma's cries evaporated when she saw Shelley in the doorway. Instead she simply held out her hands and, with a quivering chin, rewarded her mother with a brave smile. "Hello, princess." Shelley swooped her up. "How's my good girl?" She took a sniff and winced. "A little smelly, eh?"

Emma cooed and smiled as Shelley cleaned her up until she smelled fresh and sweet and finally dressed her in a cozy set of pink warm-ups. "All better?" Shelley leaned down and kissed both Emma's cheeks. Really, being a mom might have its challenges, but who could complain about this?

Shelley was by nature an optimist and, despite being tired and wishing her daughter liked sleeping in more, she enjoyed seeing the sunrise. With Emma nestled clean and content in her arms and happily sucking on a bottle of warm milk, Shelley watched as the eastern sky filled with golden light.

This was Shelley's time to quiet her heart and pray. She usually started with a prayer of gratitude—expressing her thanks for God's protection and provision for her family. Then she would pray for what she felt they needed. And finally she would ask God's blessings on her extended family, friends, and neighbors. It was a good way to start the day.

Shelley had just gotten Emma situated with some toys on a blanket when Aiden came bounding down the hallway with Prize at his heels. "I'm hungry, Mommy." His voice was still gruff with sleep. "I want cookies for breakfast."

She ruffled his hair. "No, darling boy, you can't have cookies, but—"

"I *want* cookies," he insisted. "Daddy said you were making me cookies and I—"

"How about pancakes?" she suggested. "With blueberries."

He didn't look convinced.

"And you can help me make them," she offered. "With Mickey Mouse ears."

His eyes lit up. "Oh-*kay!*"

"First, you need to let Prize outside."

With the morning pace quickly picking up, Shelley started to pull out what they'd need for pancakes. Before long, Aiden was cracking eggs and asking her why they had "yellow balls inside" and if they could get a chicken for a pet. Shelley tried not to think about the pieces of shell he might allow in.

By the time Dan came out to join them, showered and shaved and looking a lot more energetic than Shelley felt, she and Aiden had managed to put together a lopsided stack of strangely shaped blueberry pancakes as well as an impressive mess all around the stove.

"Oh, for a self-cleaning kitchen," she muttered as she placed the plates and forks on the table.

"I made these pancakes," Aiden told his dad as he slid into his booster seat. *"Myself."*

Dan wiped a fragment of blueberry from Aiden's cheek and grinned. "Nice work, man."

"Mama helped a little," Aiden admitted as Shelley put Emma in the high chair, sitting a minisized pancake in front of her.

Dan flopped several pancakes onto his plate. "Do they taste as good as they look, buddy?"

"Mm-hmm." Aiden smacked his lips. "I already had some."

"Let's say a blessing before you have any more." Shelley bowed her head as Dan said a quick thank-you prayer.

"Did Aiden tell you he has a playdate today?" Dan asked as he poured syrup onto his pancakes.

"A *play*date?" Shelley tried not to sound as ecstatic as she felt, but the idea of having only one child to care for was hugely appealing just now. Maybe she could catch a nap herself when she put Emma down.

"Yeah." Dan nodded. "Maddie called right after you left last night, and she said—"

"Maddie Bancroft?" Shelley's glee was quickly doused with a cold bucket of reality.

Dan frowned. "Is something wrong with that?"

"No..." She shot him a warning look, like this was a grown-up conversation, and she'd fill him in later.

But now he looked offended. "You recently told me that Aiden *needed* a playdate, Shelley. Maddie called and asked if today worked, and I said yes."

"Without even asking me?"

"Since when do I need to ask you about a playdate for Aiden?" Dan lifted his hands in a helpless gesture. "Seriously, if you want to micromanage me, maybe you better find yourself a new babysitter."

Now that just made her mad. "You're their father, Dan, *not* their babysitter."

"I wanna go to Benjamin's house," Aiden whined. "Do I get to go?"

"We'll see." Shelley tried to keep her voice calm. To be fair, it wasn't really about Maddie. They had put that behind them. Even so, it just wasn't something she wanted to deal with today. Why couldn't Dan be more understanding?

Dan slid back his chair, making a loud screeching sound that probably left its mark on the worn vinyl flooring. He'd barely touched his pancakes, but it was clear he was done.

"Do I get to go to Benjamin's?" Aiden pleaded again.

"Your mom will decide about that." With a stony look, Dan pecked Aiden on top of the head. "She's in charge of you kids." Dan leaned over and kissed Emma too. "See ya 'round." And then he left the house.

Shelley tried to hide her angst as she picked up his plate of barely touched food, along with hers, and began scraping both of them into the sink. But as the pancakes slipped down the drain, she remembered their garbage disposal was on the blink again. Trying to hold back frustrated tears, she stuck her hand in and dug out the mucky mess.

Why did Dan have to go and act like that? *Why?* Maybe she had overreacted about Maddie. After all, she and Maddie were actually on friendly terms. Even if Maddie's success still made Shelley feel like a failure at times, it wasn't Maddie's fault. But for Dan to storm off like that—well, it was just wrong.

Shelley picked up a washrag and started to scrub hardened droplets of pancake batter from the stove top. The stove top that barely worked. Really, what difference did it make if she cleaned this kitchen or not? This whole space was slowly falling apart anyway. Even so, she scrubbed hard and then harder, taking out her frustrations. She continued to clean and scour everything until the small dysfunctional kitchen was actually gleaming. Appearances really could be deceiving.

"Can I go to Benjamin's house?" Aiden gave a persistent tug on her sweatpants. "Can I, Mommy? *Please?*"

Of course, Emma was fussing to get out of her high chair now. Arching her back and extending her arms like she was about to let out a screech and slip into a full-blown tantrum.

"I'm coming," Shelley told her. As she freed Emma from the chair, she wondered what had happened to her earlier sense of peace and calm. How quickly it had unraveled.

"Mommy," Aiden demanded, "I'm *talking* to you!"

Shelley blinked at her little son. Still wearing his Superman jammies, he shook a child-sized fist in the air with a furrowed brow. He reminded her of a little old man.

Stifling giggles over his indignant posture, she sat Emma on the blanket with her toys again and then, still kneeling, looked into Aiden's eyes. "What is it?"

"You *never* listen to me." Now he placed his curled fists onto his hips, probably imitating her own habitual pose. "I'm *talking* to you."

"I'm sorry, Aiden. I was busy. What were you saying?" She used the rag still in her hand to wipe the sticky syrup from his chin, listening patiently as he explained how badly he *needed* to go to Benjamin's house, almost as if he'd be enduring a lifelong prison sentence if he was forced to stay at home with her today.

"Yes, I suppose you can go to Benjamin's today," she said with reluctance. "Maybe Daddy will take you over there when he gets back." But even as she said this, she knew it was unlikely. Judging by her husband's wounded expression as he departed, she suspected that he planned to be gone for a while. And maybe that was a good thing—for everyone.

Not for the first time, she wondered why it was that daddies were allowed to storm off like that...and why it was that mommies usually got stuck at home with the kids. It had certainly been true in her life. Growing up with parents who constantly fought and a dad who eventually walked out on them had been rough—on both her and her mom. More than anything, Shelley did not want that to become the norm with her and Dan. And, even if it wasn't easy, she would do all she could to keep that from happening to her children.

CHAPTER EIGHT

After breakfast, Shelley took the kids outside to get some sunshine and play with the dog. But mostly she wanted to stall Aiden for a while in the hopes that Dan would come home and offer to taxi him over to the Bancrofts for her. That way she could work on her Web site and bakery orders. She'd underestimated how so much of this business wasn't just about baking but about management and finances and marketing too.

Still, Shelley knew that her primary job was that of being a mommy. And it was a job she'd always wanted. It's just that she didn't want to have to taxi Aiden over to Maddie's house. Not because she disliked Maddie, but because Shelley's life felt so chaotic just now, it would be painful stepping into Maddie's picture-perfect world.

Despite knowing that Maddie had her own challenges, Shelley wasn't sure she could handle driving up to Maddie's beautiful home, seeing the landscaped grounds and the immaculately decorated house. She knew there was an art to contentment, and most of the time, she felt like she got it. But still tired from working late last night combined with her silly little spat with Dan, she just wasn't in top form.

"Hello there, neighbors!" Diane waved from across the street. "Lovely morning, isn't it?"

"Looks like you and Rocky have been to the beach already," Shelley called back.

Diane nodded as she tied Rocky's leash to the porch, then crossed the street to join Shelley in her yard. "Rocky insisted on swimming. Now he'll have to dry off in the sun for a while."

"I wanna go swimming," Aiden said. "Me and Prize. Can we, Mommy?"

"It's a little cold for that today."

He peered up at that sky. "The sun's out."

"Yes, but there's a nip in the air."

"What's a nip?"

Diane laughed and tussled his hair. "Sometimes it's what a dog does to your heels."

Aiden looked confused, and Shelley just shook her head, then waved over to where Beverly was coming down the street with a newspaper in hand. "How's it going?" Shelley called out to her.

"I'm hopeful." Beverly tucked the paper beneath an arm. "Did Diane tell you the news about my father?"

"I was just about to," Diane said. Then both she and Beverly told Shelley about how they'd taken Mr. Wheeland to the hospital for an MRI the day before to be tested for ministrokes.

"The doctor was supposed to call with the results," Beverly said, "but she hasn't yet."

Shelley felt concerned now. "Beverly, if your dad gets well—and you know I hope he does—would that mean you'd move back to Augusta?"

Beverly just laughed. "Not at all. I am here to stay."

Shelley managed an uneasy smile as she shifted Emma in her arms. "I just hope that Dan and I are here to stay too."

"Isn't Dan working on Margaret's giclée print frames?" Beverly asked.

"A little." Shelley reminded them of how the Hoskinses were still waiting to get the giclée print process under way. "The plan is kind of on hold for the time being, and I'm not sure how much work there will be at first."

"But I noticed Dan going into the Hoskins house this morning," Beverly said. "I figured he was going to work."

"You saw Dan over there?" Shelley felt confused.

"Mom...?" Aiden grabbed her free hand, squeezing it in both of his. "When do I get to go to Benjamin's house?"

"Be patient," she told him. "Why don't you go see what Prize is up to? I think she's lonely."

Aiden took off toward the backyard now.

"So if Dan's not working for the gallery, what's he going to do for work?" Beverly asked.

Shelley glanced over to Margaret's house again. Was Dan really there now? And, if so, why? "Dan's still trying to figure it all out," she said slowly. Then to change the subject from Dan's job situation, she explained how she'd had a late night at the Cove. "So I guess I'm still a little worn out." She frowned down at her grubby-looking warm-ups and slippers, wishing she'd taken the time to put on "real" clothes. "As much as I appreciate using the kitchen there, it's hard maintaining a night shift and then getting up with my kids. Emma woke up before the sun this morning."

"Can't Dan help with that?" Beverly asked.

Shelley laughed, but felt no genuine humor.

"Some men don't automatically understand how to be domestic," Diane said quietly.

"You've got that right." Shelley nodded. "He tries, but—"

"Come to think of it, my father's never been terribly domestic either," Beverly admitted. "With him, I think it's his generation. Which reminds me that I was about to fix him some breakfast. He slept late this morning. I can't wait to hear from the doc and maybe get some medication to help him."

"I should probably go feed Rocky too," Diane said.

Shelley had barely told them good-bye when Aiden began to plead with her again, begging to go to Benjamin's. She glanced across the street. Was it possible that Dan was over there working on frames for giclée prints after all? She could only hope so.

"Let me get dressed first," Shelley told Aiden, and she headed inside.

"You are dressed, Mama."

"I mean dressed nice," she told him.

"Like for church?" He looked confused.

"Sort of." She looked at his mismatched outfit, mentally comparing it to the immaculate way Maddie's children were usually dressed. "And you can go put on a fresh shirt too," she said firmly. "And some clean socks while you're at it, young man."

He started to protest.

"Aiden," she said, "you have a choice. You can refuse to clean up and stay home, or you can do what I asked you and go. It's up to you."

It was close to ten by the time she had cleaned herself up and had both kids loaded in the car. It wasn't until she pulled up into the Bancrofts' circular driveway that she realized she'd never even asked Dan what time the playdate had been scheduled for. She was about to keep going past the house when she noticed someone waving to her from the side yard.

She let down her window to give a weak smile to Maddie's husband, quickly explaining about the playdate. "But Aiden was so eager to come, and Dan forgot to tell me what time, and I realized I might be early or—"

"Don't worry about it," he said. "Maddie and the kids are all here. She's probably expecting you."

"Okay then..." She nodded nervously. Then, while parking, she thought it might be somewhat amusing to catch the perfect Maddie Bancroft off guard. What if Shelley walked into some total chaotic mess? Really, it wouldn't be merely entertaining, it would be highly encouraging. However, when Maddie answered the door, she looked tidy and stylish. Despite Shelley's attempts to clean up her act, she knew she looked dowdy next to Maddie.

"Come in," Maddie said graciously.

"I've got Emma in the car," Shelley explained.

"Bring her in too!"

"Well, I—"

"Where's Benjamin?" Aiden demanded.

"Manners," Shelley said sternly.

Maddie laughed. "Benjamin's down in the family room. We just made a big batch of purple play dough."

"You *made* play dough?" Aiden's eyes grew wide.

"Yes sir. Purple. And we're just about to start on some green."

Shelley heard Emma's cries wafting out the open car window now. "I think it might be nap time," she told Maddie.

"So soon?"

"Well, she's been up for more than four hours."

"Isn't she on a schedule?"

Shelley winced inwardly. "Not really."

"Oh." Maddie just nodded, a knowing look in her eyes.

"So I really should go." She started to turn. "What time should I pick up Aiden?"

"I thought around one-ish. That way, he can have lunch here. Benjamin wanted to pack a lunch and take it outside so they can pretend like they're camping." She jerked her thumb over her shoulder. "The kids insisted on putting up a tent a few days ago. Trying to enjoy the weather while it lasts."

"That sounds like fun." Shelley smiled. "See you around one."

"Bye, now."

As she hurried to the car, where Emma's wails were increasing in volume, she knew that Aiden had landed in kiddy paradise...again. She knew he would talk about how great Benjamin's house was, how there was so much to do, so many toys, tents in the backyard, purple and green play dough. Homemade play dough! Why hadn't Shelley ever thought about making play dough? Well, at least they'd made blueberry pancakes together this morning. And they'd almost had a nice family breakfast too. Almost.

"Mommy's here," she said to Emma, fumbling around in the diaper bag for the pacifier. "We'll be home soon, little girl. Then we'll both take a nice long nap."

However, after she got Emma fed and put down, Shelley did not feel the least bit sleepy. Instead, she felt agitated and antsy. And so, in complete un-Shelley-like fashion, she decided to clean her house.

It wasn't that Shelley enjoyed a disorderly home. It was simply that most of the time, she didn't even notice the messes. Between two small children, a dog, and a partially unemployed husband, their house could get rather cluttered. And when she did notice the bedlam, she usually felt overwhelmed.

Shelley shook her head as she cleared the floor by pitching toys into a basket. She had no idea how people like Maddie managed to do it all. Oh, she knew that Maddie had her faults and challenges, and that she tried to make things look easier than they were, but really, Shelley decided as she pulled out the vacuum cleaner, she could try harder. And maybe if Dan came home to a freshly cleaned house...maybe, just maybe, they could have a fresh start too.

CHAPTER NINE

The weather turned during the church service on Sunday morning. It had been blue skies and sunshine when Diane went into the church but was dark and blustery when she came out. As a result she got a good soaking as she made the dash to her parked car. But at least her spirits were light. It had been an uplifting sermon, and, as she shook out her damp hair and started her car, she felt certain that despite the stormy weather, this was going to be a good day.

Besides, she liked a good storm. It was the perfect excuse to hole up and build a rip-roaring fire. Maybe she'd make some black bean soup, and perhaps she'd even dig out her breadmaker and attempt to bake some bread. Then she'd work on her book. She was still putting the finishing touches on her outlines and was looking forward to enjoying the freedom of writing her second book without the restraints of having it part of the series. In fact, what had been frustrating at the time turned out to be a blessing in disguise now.

With visions of a cozy writing day, imagining the comforting smell of fresh bread baking, Diane pulled up to her house and was surprised to see a vehicle in her driveway. Not just any vehicle either. A white Cadillac SUV. She waited to see if the SUV was going to back out so she could pull in, but there didn't seem to be anyone in it.

She peered through the sheets of rain to see that someone, it looked like a woman, was standing on Diane's front porch. Since she was already wet, Diane just parked on the street and raced through the pelting rain on up to her porch.

"Diane!" exclaimed the woman. "I was just going to leave you a note."

"Barbara?" Diane blinked. "Is that you?"

"Of course it's me." The surprisingly youthful-looking woman smiled brightly at her. "Are you going to invite me in or not?"

"Yes, yes." Diane opened her door to the sounds of Rocky barking. "By all means, come in."

"You don't even lock your door?" Barbara sounded appalled as they stepped inside.

"Rocky here is my security system." Diane reached down to pat his head. "Besides, I have very good neighbors." She helped Barbara to remove her trench coat, then peeled off her own soggy jacket, hanging them both on the coat rack by the door. "Come, make yourself comfortable, and I'll get a fire started."

"What a charming little cabin." Barbara walked around the compact living room, studying every detail, it seemed.

Feeling slightly unsettled, Diane knelt down and crumpled an old newspaper. Piling some kindling and a couple of pinecones on it, she lit the mound and waited for it to catch. "My fire-making skills have improved greatly since I moved here." Now she told Barbara about how she forgot to open the flue once. "Smoke everywhere." The kindling began to crackle and snap in the flames, and she carefully stacked on some larger pieces of wood.

"I heard about Eric," Barbara said gently. "I'm so sorry for your loss, Diane. He was a good man."

"Thank you. And yes, he was a very good man." Diane stood and brushed off her hands. "Now how about if I go put on the teakettle? That is, if you'd like some tea."

"Yes, tea sounds lovely." Barbara followed her into the kitchen. "My, this is a sweet little kitchen too."

As Diane got the tea things ready she told Barbara about the renovations she'd gotten done when she'd first moved here last spring. Mostly she was simply trying to fill the air, all the while wondering why on earth Barbara was here. She also wondered how Barbara, who was in her midfifties, managed to look more like thirty-something. And furthermore, why?

Diane turned from the stove with a forced smile as she handed Barbara a steaming mug of green tea. "By the way, you look fantastic," Diane told her. "I didn't even recognize you out there on the porch. You must be taking very good care of yourself."

Barbara laughed as they returned to the living room, settling in by the fire. "The truth is I pay other people to take good care of me."

"Oh?" Diane asked as she sipped her tea.

"And, believe me, it's not cheap."

"No...I wouldn't think so."

"But I do think it's worth it." Barbara tilted her chin up slightly, almost as if posing for a photo. "Don't you?"

Diane wasn't sure how to respond. "Well, uh, yes, I suppose so... I mean, if that's important to you."

Barbara's dark eyes seemed to suggest skepticism to Diane's comment, but her perfectly smooth brow didn't even flinch. Was that the effect of Botox? Diane wasn't sure she wanted to know. "Are you saying that your appearance is unimportant to you?" Barbara studied Diane carefully. "You don't want to grow old gracefully too?" She chuckled like this was witty.

Diane gave her a tolerant smile. "Actually, I do want to grow old gracefully. I suppose I just put more emphasis on the *growing old* part."

Barbara sighed. "Yes...I suppose I would have your attitude too if my life had gone along as happily as yours did. You always seemed to get just what you wanted, Diane."

"Really?" Diane set down her tea mug.

Barbara laughed. "Yes. Did you know that I was very jealous of you in college?"

"Not exactly." Diane got up to put another log on the fire.

"Oh yes. Everything seemed to come so easily to you."

"Is that really what you thought?" Diane considered this as she sat down again.

"Wasn't it true?" Barbara smoothed her sleek black hair. It was one of those styles cut shorter in back and longer on the sides, but it framed her face nicely.

Diane thoughtfully sipped her tea. "I always felt like I worked pretty hard. I took journalism seriously. I put in a lot of hours working on the college newspaper."

Barbara waved her hand in a dismissive way. "Yes, yes, I'm sure you did. And to be honest, I didn't really mean to go there right now. I mean, I did...and I didn't."

Diane felt thoroughly confused. Just why was Barbara here? And what had happened to Diane's plans for a peaceful, holed-up day?

"I'm sorry," Barbara said suddenly. "I honestly didn't mean for that to come out this way."

"All right," Diane said slowly. She was trying to remember the details of this morning's sermon. The theme had been mercy, but suddenly it seemed foggy to her. Maybe she needed to be exercising some mercy right now. However, it felt like the last thing she wanted to do.

"I'm sure you're wondering why I came here today." Barbara nervously fiddled with the mug in her hands.

"I suppose I am a bit curious." Diane looked intently at her. "As I recall, we weren't very close friends in college."

Barbara cleared her throat. "Yes, that's probably true. And it's true that I was jealous of you back then."

Diane simply waited.

"But you see, I've been doing some real soul-searching these past couple of years. It's a long story, Diane, but I realized that I hurt some people during certain times in my life, and I am trying to make amends."

Diane just stared. "Seriously?"

Barbara nodded. "So I hope that you'll forgive me for all the silly, selfish stunts I pulled in college. I took out my meanness on you."

Diane tried not to show how stunned she felt. "Of course I forgive you, Barbara. Goodness knows that was a long time ago. I'm sure we all did things we're not proud of." She gave Barbara a genuine smile now. "And I appreciate your apology."

Barbara looked relieved.

Diane glanced at the clock on the mantle. "Would you like to join me for lunch? I had planned to make some homemade black bean soup."

"*Homemade* soup?" Barbara's eyes lit up. "That sounds marvelous."

So they headed back to the kitchen where Barbara tried to make herself helpful, but Diane quickly realized that Barbara's kitchen skills, even in something as simple as using a can opener, were lacking. "Why don't you just sit here and keep me company?" Diane finally told her as she pointed to a kitchen stool.

Barbara laughed. "My last husband banned me from the kitchen."

"Banned you?"

Barbara explained how her third husband, Leland, was quite wealthy and how they had household staff to take care of practically everything. "I still miss Estella," she said wistfully. "She made the most delicious quiche."

"So is Leland... Well, did he pass away too?"

"Heavens, no. Leland is alive and well, and, thanks to California laws, he's faithfully paying his alimony too." She chuckled.

"Oh." Diane poured the minced onions into the hot olive oil and stirred a bit, then turned down the heat. "Do you have any children?"

"No. To be honest, I never really wanted kids."

"Uh-huh." Diane scraped the other chopped vegetables into the pan, listening as Barbara talked about all the exotic locations she'd lived in and how children just never fit into her plans.

Barbara didn't ask about Diane's children, but Diane felt a tiny bit relieved at this. She wasn't sure she wanted to discuss Justin and Jessica with Barbara. She was still trying to be merciful...but she was feeling a bit irritated too. The ungracious truth was she wished she hadn't invited Barbara to lunch. But what was done was done, and Diane was determined to play the congenial hostess.

"Here we go," Diane said finally. With the kitchen table set, complete with good china and cloth napkins, the two women sat opposite each other. "Do you mind if I say a blessing?"

Barbara looked a little surprised. "Not at all."

Diane asked a blessing on the food and on her "old friend," then took in a deep breath as she picked up her spoon.

"*Mmm*, this is delicious, Diane."

Diane smiled. "It's my neighbor's recipe." Diane told Barbara about Margaret and Shearwater Gallery.

"Oh, *that* Margaret." Barbara nodded with interest. "I visited her gallery and met her yesterday. I simply love her art. In fact, I told her that if I find a house I like here in Marble Cove, I might buy some of her pieces."

"Really?" Diane felt her brows raised high.

"Oh yes. I'm a great collector of original art."

"No, I meant that part about moving here. Are you seriously considering relocating?"

"I'm actually between houses right now. I came to Marble Cove to see if I'd like to live here."

"Interesting." Diane tried not to sound too negative as she picked up a piece of cheese and carefully laid it on a cracker.

"Yes. My parents used to come here when I was a child."

Diane looked up. "So did mine."

They talked about things they remembered from childhood about Marble Cove, everything from ice cream cones to sand castle–building contests.

"But do you know what I love most about this place?" Barbara asked in a dreamy tone.

"What?"

"The lighthouse." Barbara sighed. "I just adore Orlean Point Light."

Diane nodded with surprisingly conflicted feelings. "Yes, so do I."

"Isn't that amazing! Who would've guessed that, after all these years, you and I would have so much in common?"

"Who would've guessed?"

Barbara gushed on and on about how much she loved the lighthouse and how she'd always dreamed of purchasing it and changing it into a bed-and-breakfast.

Diane frowned. "Seriously?"

"Don't you think it would be delightful? Can't you imagine what it would feel like to spend the night there? To wake up to the sound of the surf and that view?" She laughed. "Of course, I'd have to hire a good cook."

"Of course." Diane couldn't believe how resistant she felt to Barbara's idea of turning Orlean Point Light into a bed-and-breakfast. But it just went against everything inside of her. Surely the powers that be would never allow such a thing. Would they?

"I have a perfectly wonderful idea," Barbara said as she was getting ready to leave. "You will have to come out and visit me at the beach house where I'm staying. I can't offer to fix you a meal like this—not homemade anyway. But I will order up something in town. And you will come out for dinner this week and—"

"I, uh, I'm not sure I—"

"You cannot turn me down, Diane." Barbara's overly full lips made a pouty expression. "After all we've been through, all we have in common, and after finally letting bygones be bygones today." She put on a hopeful smile. "Surely you'll come join me for dinner. Especially if I promise *not* to cook. And you can pick the night. *Please.*"

It seemed useless, not to mention unkind, to say no. "Sure," Diane said, wondering how far out she could push this day. "How about...uh, Friday?"

"Friday it is." Barbara smiled triumphantly.

"Perhaps I can bring something." Now Diane pointed across the street to the Bauers', explaining about Shelley and her new baking business. "I could bring dessert."

Barbara agreed to this as she glanced up and down the street. "You certainly have some interesting neighbors, Diane. Although it's not a terribly impressive neighborhood, is it? But I suppose one would get used to it over time."

Diane just smiled. With any luck, Barbara would never be forced to get "used to it."

"See you on Friday night," Barbara called cheerfully.

"Looking forward to it." Diane felt a tinge of guilt for that line. She hadn't really meant to tell a fib. But perhaps she'd have an attitude change by then and by the grace of God she truly would be looking forward to it.

CHAPTER TEN

I'm just not sure how to handle this," Margaret confessed to Diane on Monday morning. The two had met for coffee and, Margaret hoped, some mother-to-mother advice. "I know you've been through the raising of a teenage girl and, although Adelaide is different, well, I have a feeling that we're going through some slightly adolescent-like things right now."

Margaret explained how Adelaide hadn't really experienced too many of these challenges during adolescence. "I was told that it wasn't necessarily due to her special needs, but simply that she was delayed." Margaret shook her head. "But it feels like she's making up for that now."

"So she still wants to dye her hair purple?" Diane asked.

"Oh, I think we're beyond that. But she's still much more concerned with her appearance than ever before. I thought it was due to a girl named Lisa who had possibly been picking on her."

"That's not good."

"But after some further investigation, it turns out that Lisa and Adelaide are competing for a boy."

"A boy?" Diane blinked.

"Well, actually a young man. Hank is in his early twenties. Just a couple years younger than Adelaide. He spends time at the community center too."

"Ooh, a love triangle!" Diane said, her eyes sparkling. "Does Hank have Down syndrome too?"

"No. A head injury as a child. He has a part-time job too. Works in the high school cafeteria."

"And Adelaide and Lisa both like him?"

Margaret nodded.

"Well, I think that's kind of sweet." Diane smiled. "Oh, not the love triangle part, that's always difficult. Except in fiction. But I think it's sweet that Adelaide has those kinds of feelings for her young man."

"Why on earth would you think that was sweet?"

"Oh, you know the adage, better to have loved and lost than to never have loved at all."

"I don't know."

"At least you're in on it."

"But what do I do?" Margaret held her hands up. "I have no idea how to handle this."

"Maybe you just let it run its course."

"But what if Adelaide gets hurt?"

"Has she ever been hurt before?"

"Yes, of course. Many times." Margaret didn't like to think of how many times Adelaide had been hurt.

"And how did you handle those times?"

"It depended on the situation." Margaret took a sip of coffee. "But usually things blew over fairly quickly. Come to think of it, Adelaide is rather resilient."

"So what is the upside of this new development?"

Margaret chuckled. "I should've known you'd take this route. You are a regular Pollyanna, Diane."

Diane laughed. "So indulge me. What is the upside? You mentioned Adelaide is concerned about her appearance now. So why not have fun with it? Take her to get her hair done. Go clothes shopping. Get a manicure. What would be the harm in that?"

It felt like a light had just gone on. "You're absolutely right!"

"Really?" Diane looked surprised.

"Yes. The truth is I used to feel a bit sad for missing out on all those girly things with Adelaide. She just never cared about fashion or hair. On one hand, I felt slightly relieved because I've never been that good at that sort of thing." She chuckled. "Well, look at me. I'm about as low maintenance as they come."

"You're just a very practical woman."

"As a result, I'm not even sure where to begin with Adelaide. I like her appearance as it is."

"I know you do." Diane's brow creased. "Why not just do something small…something that might feel fun and special, but something that doesn't really change her?"

"Like purple hair?"

"No, definitely nix the purple hair. But what about a fancy manicure? I've seen girls with interesting colored polishes or little flowers on their nails. And you could both get one together. Wouldn't that be fun?"

"Yes. That's a good idea."

"Then maybe buy a special item of clothing. Something that makes her feel feminine and pretty. Or how about shoes—something in a fun color, maybe some pretty kitten heels or ballerinas with beads or embroidery?"

"Yes," Margaret said eagerly. "These are all good ideas."

"And it sounds like it could be fun."

"I knew you'd be better at this sort of thing than I am." Margaret added a bit more cream to her coffee. "I can't even remember the last time I bought myself a new pair of shoes." She looked down at her sturdy loafers. "But that's because I buy things to last."

"It's funny because I don't think of myself as a very girly girl either." Diane shook her head with a hard-to-read expression.

"Something wrong?"

"I was just thinking about this old college friend." Diane gave an ironic-sounding laugh. "Well, she wasn't exactly a friend. But we've buried that hatchet."

"What?" Margaret felt lost.

"Sorry." Diane explained about how a woman named Barbara was in town. "And it's not that I don't like her. It's just that I don't really care to be her good friend." She sighed. "And that makes me feel guilty."

"Well, you can't be friends with everyone."

"I know." Diane grinned. "I suppose the reason I thought of Barbara was because she'd be just the kind of person to take Adelaide out girly-girl shopping." Now Diane told Margaret about how this Barbara person had transformed herself to look much younger than her real age. "At first I was rather put off by it. I thought only a very shallow person would waste that much money, not to mention time and energy, on looking younger. But then—and it's embarrassing to admit this—I found myself examining my own face last night, imagining how much younger I might look with a little assistance."

Margaret laughed loudly.

"I know, I know." Diane just shook her head. "It's embarrassing to admit to this kind of superficiality. I hope you still respect me."

Margaret was still chuckling. "I'm sorry for laughing so hard. But the truth is I can relate to it just a little. I think that no matter who you are, as a woman you reach a certain age when you realize you're growing older...and you can't stop the clock. And, well, it's not easy for any of us. Believe it or not, I had similar thoughts about ten years ago. I blamed it on my artistic nature." Margaret gently tapped one of her sagging jowls. "I like things that are pretty."

"That's just it, though," Diane said quickly. "I honestly do believe that aging women, wrinkles, gray hair, all of that... are actually very attractive."

"Really?" Margaret tipped her head.

"I know, it sounds like I'm contradicting myself. But I remember my grandmother with her silver hair and pale wrinkled skin and the way her diamond ring hung sort of loose on her finger, and I used to think she was beautiful in a queenly sort of way."

Margaret waited expectantly. She could tell there was more to this.

"But I just wasn't quite ready to go there myself."

Margaret laughed again. "Yes. Well, welcome to the club. Except that I have moved on now."

"And Beverly and Shelley are too far on the other side to relate to me."

Margaret reached over and patted Diane's hand. "Well, if you have any questions about growing older, feel free to ask."

"I appreciate that. And the same to you in regard to parenting a daughter. Not that I'm such an expert. Jessica was relatively easy too. But if there's anything I can do to help..."

"Maybe you'd like to come with us," Margaret said tentatively.

"For your girly-girl shopping?"

"I know it's probably not exactly your cup of tea. I would ask Shelley, but she is so busy these days. I worry she's getting overwhelmed."

"But Dan's around to help, isn't he?"

"Actually, Dan's been giving Allan a hand with his furniture making again, and Allan's started to help him learn to make the frames for giclée prints. When the prints finally arrive, Dan will be ready to go to town on them."

"That's wonderful!"

"Speaking of giclée printers, we just got back some more prints of my originals from the third-party printing houses we're looking at. Allan decided to do some experimenting to compare the quality of printing. Some of them are quite good. So I'm feeling encouraged. Between Dan helping with furniture as well as framing giclée prints, we should have a nicely stocked gallery in time for tourist season next spring."

"Shelley must be so relieved that Dan's working."

"Yes." Margaret nodded. "Except that it makes her busier than ever. Trying to keep up with the kids and her baking, not to mention the business end of things...well, it's demanding. So I doubt she'll be able to drop everything and go shopping with Adelaide and me."

"Well, I would love to join you. Maybe Beverly would too."

"Wouldn't that be fun!" Margaret felt hopeful. "I'll talk to Adelaide about your ideas and see which one appeals to her. How about if I give you a call when she wants to go?"

"I'll plan on it."

Margaret looked at her watch. "And now I need to scurry. Believe it or not, I'm off to a chamber of commerce meeting." She made a puckered face. "And this is after I swore to Allan that I would never ever get involved in local politics."

"The chamber isn't exactly politics, is it?"

"It's not supposed to be. But I've heard stories."

They both stood, and Diane wished her luck.

But as Margaret made her way to her meeting, she wondered if she really wanted to get involved. However, she'd already accepted the invitation and there wasn't really time to excuse herself from it now. She hoped she could simply sit in and make some polite comments, then explain that her demands as an artist as well as a businesswoman made it difficult to join the chamber. Yes, she decided as she headed up the stairs to the meeting room, that's exactly what she would do.

Chapter Eleven

Beverly wondered who felt more nervous on Monday morning: her or Father? They were waiting for their appointment with Dr. Emerson. Father was pretending to read a hunting magazine. She knew he was pretending because his eyes hadn't moved at all.

"Mr. Wheeland?" the receptionist announced. "Dr. Emerson will see you now. In her office, second door on the left."

Father looked at Beverly with a puzzled expression, but he set down the magazine.

"I'll come in with you," Beverly told him as she reached for her handbag.

"Do I take my shirt off?" he asked quietly as they walked down the corridor.

"No, I don't think so. Not this time. I think Dr. Emerson simply wants to explain the results of last week's test." She glanced at him. "Remember the MRI?"

"MRI?"

But now they were in the office, and Dr. Emerson was coming in with a file in her hand. "Good morning," she said cheerfully. "Have a seat."

After a quick exchange of small talk, Dr. Emerson opened the file. "It turns out we were right to suspect you were experiencing TIAs, Harold."

"That's what it is?" Beverly asked. "You're sure?"

"T...I what?" Father looked more confused than ever.

"TIA stands for transient ischemic attack, Harold," Dr. Emerson explained. "It's also called a ministroke."

Father nodded as if taking this in.

"As I explained to your daughter on the phone, it's a blood-clotting problem," she told him. "Probably related to plaque and blood-sugar levels." She was writing something down. "It's serious but treatable. Besides your daily aspirin treatment, I'm prescribing clopidogrel bisulfate."

"What is that?"

"Also known as Plavix." She explained how the medication worked and what to watch for, then she looked at Beverly. "We also need to focus on keeping his blood-sugar levels in the normal range."

Beverly nodded. "We're working on that."

"And I think your father would benefit from some therapy." Dr. Emerson wrote some more things down and handed Beverly these as well as a pamphlet. "I think you're going to be feeling better soon, Harold. And your memory should improve greatly over time. Especially if you faithfully do the exercises your therapist gives you." She tapped the side of her head. "We need to get that sharp mind of yours working as well as it used to work."

He smiled hopefully. "Yes. That's what I want. More than anything."

After leaving the doctor's office, they were soon on their way back home. To her relief, the atmosphere in the car was much more cheerful than it had been earlier. Father seemed truly hopeful as he read over the material Dr. Emerson had given him. And as soon as they got home, he was eager to take his medication. Even if the meds didn't work—though she had no reason to expect that—his new positive attitude was like a tonic in itself.

★   ★   ★

Beverly had allowed her obsession over her father's health to distract her from responding, or even reacting, to the ghost from her past. Jeff Mackenzie. She realized it was a convenient excuse, but as a result, at least for the most part, she could push anxiety over Jeff into the far corner of her mind. And that was exactly where she planned to keep him. Now if only he would stop calling her cell phone. It had been more than two weeks since their disturbing reunion, and he had called her at least ten times. Naturally, she was ignoring his calls.

"Beverly?" Father's voice echoed down the hallway. It sounded like he was in the kitchen, although she'd just left him in his library.

"Yes?" she asked.

"Where is the jam?"

"Jam?" She frowned at him. It had been less than an hour since breakfast. Had he forgotten that? Certainly he wasn't hungry again.

"*Blackberry* jam," he said in a slightly irritated tone.

Why did he need blackberry jam right now? And just when she'd been encouraged to think that his memory had been improving a bit. At breakfast he'd told her all about something he'd read in the newspaper just yesterday, going into a lot of detail. And now he wanted jam? For what? But instead of questioning him, she patiently told him that the jam, as usual, was in the fridge. "Right where it always is."

"No, it's not," he insisted.

So she opened the fridge to show him, but was surprised to see that he was actually right. "Oh, I guess it's not there." Now she peered curiously at him. "Just why do you need the jam anyway?"

Now he smiled sheepishly. "It's for Diane."

"Diane?" She tried not to look too skeptical. "Why would Diane want your favorite sugar-free blackberry jam, Father?"

"She's making thumbprint cookies."

Beverly tried to grasp this. "Diane is making thumbprint cookies?"

"Yes." He looked slightly embarrassed now. "Diane and I were chatting this morning, and I mentioned how much I like thumbprint cookies, and it seems that she likes them too. So now she is baking some, but she didn't have any sugar-free jam, and I offered her ours. But now I can't seem to find it. And I know for a fact that I had some on my toast this morning."

"That's right, you did."

He smiled. "You see, I can remember that. I just cannot seem to remember where the jam is."

"Well, I cleaned up after breakfast." Beverly went over to the cupboard by the toaster and opened it. And there, right next to the honey, was the jam. "I don't know why I put it up here," she said as she handed it to her father. "I always put it in the fridge."

Father grinned as he took the jar. "Maybe my bad memory has rubbed off on you."

Beverly couldn't help but laugh. "I think your new medicine is really working. Before long your memory will be better than mine."

"I'm going to take this over to Diane's house," he said as he reached for his sweater. "She promised me cookies in exchange for jam."

"Sounds like a good deal." Beverly smiled and returned to where she'd been sorting laundry. Here she'd been ready for something weird, like her Father was going to use jam in place of his shaving cream, and the poor man was simply doing something normal. Perfectly normal. Well, it gave her real hope.

She had just turned on the washing machine when she heard the phone in the kitchen jangling. The sound of the landline ringing always took her by surprise since her father received so few calls. But maybe this was his doctor. She had run some more blood tests for him. Perhaps she'd gotten the lab reports back by now. Beverly hurried to the kitchen, picking up the shiny black receiver of the old-fashioned phone. "Hello?"

"Beverly?" It was a man's voice. "I finally connected with you!"

"Who is this?" she asked in a flat tone, although she knew who it was. At least he hadn't called her *Anna* this time.

"It's Jeff Mackenzie. I've been trying to reach you for days, and wh—"

"How did you get this number?"

"Your father gave it to me."

"My father?"

"He answered your cell phone yesterday. You were on a walk. Anyway, he gave me the house phone number."

"He did?" She twisted the curly black cord tightly between her fingers.

"I just need to talk to you. I th—"

"I do not want to talk to you." The words sounded brittle, icy. "I thought I made that clear at the lighthouse."

"I know, but I want to tell you—"

"How can I make you understand that I have no need to speak to you? Have you not noticed that I've ignored your calls? I deleted your messages. I do not call you back. I even considered changing my cell phone number. How much more plain can I be?"

"I get that, but I need to—"

"I do not want you in my life, Jeff. Can't you understand that?"

"I'm not asking you to have me in your life, Anna. I'm o—"

"*Beverly,*" she said, seething.

"Yes, yes…Beverly. I'm sorry."

"Don't bother being sorry, Jeff. Just leave me alone."

"I can't. We need to talk. You need to hear my side of—"

"I don't want to talk. I just want you out of my life. Please." She choked back a sob now. "Just leave me alone. I'm begging you."

"I can't leave you alone. There's too much that's been left unsaid. It's not healthy. Not for you or me. Can't you understand that?"

"I've tried to make my feelings clear, Jeff. I told you in the lighthouse that I never wanted to see you again. Why can't you respect that?"

"Because I don't believe you."

She felt like screaming now. Instead, she bit into her lip and considered just hanging up. Except Jeff could simply call back. And what if he called when only Father was home? What if he told Father everything? She couldn't afford to take that chance.

"What will it take to make you leave me alone?" she asked quietly.

"Just talk to me, Anna, just—"

"*Beverly!*"

"Yes, sorry. Beverly. Just meet me, and listen to what I need to tell you. All I want you to do is to just listen. Hear my side. Okay?"

"I don't know." She heard the front door opening and knew it was her father.

"Please."

"Here's what I'll do." She used her business voice now. "I will give your offer my full consideration."

"Meaning what?" he sounded frustrated.

"Meaning, I will get back to you on this. Is that acceptable?"

"Do I have a choice?"

"No. And I have your number," she said crisply as she watched Father going into the den. "So, when I have figured this out, I will get back to you. Don't call me. I'll call you."

"When?"

"As soon as possible." Now she politely thanked him for his time, and, with shaking hands, she hung up. She had no idea what she was going to do to hold him at bay or how long it would be until he started to call again, but at least she had bought herself some time. Not that it would do much good. Really, what was there she could do about any of this?

Although she had other work to do, she decided to distract herself by ironing one of her father's shirts. Normally, she never touched an iron, and really this was something that Mrs. Peabody or her granddaughter usually did. But something about being in the laundry room, sprinkling the shirts just like her mother used to do, as well as the smell of hot cotton, well, it was just extremely comforting. She hoped Mrs. Peabody wouldn't take it personally.

"Hello?" Diane stuck her head in the laundry room. "Your dad said you were in here. What are you doing?"

"Oh?" Beverly smiled. "I know it's silly, but I just got the urge to iron something. You know…to get the wrinkles out." She laughed nervously. "I really should be working."

"Well, I brought treats," Diane held out a dish of thumbprint cookies. "They are almost sugar-free. And your father is making a pot of tea. Care to join us?"

Beverly sniffed the aromatic cookies and nodded. "Those smell yummy." She turned off the iron.

"I never took you for a woman who ironed shirts," Diane said as they went into the kitchen.

"I'm usually not. But it felt therapeutic today."

"Therapeutic?" Father frowned at her.

"Just soothing," she told him. "I was thinking about Mom. Remember how she loved to iron?"

He nodded with a wistful look.

"And she liked making thumbprint cookies too," Beverly said as Diane set the plate on the kitchen table. "So maybe this is a day to remember Mom."

As they drank black pekoe tea and munched on cookies, Beverly and her father told Diane a little bit about the woman who used to run this house. And, to Beverly's surprise, that really was good therapy.

"So much was going on in my life when Mom passed away," she said finally. "Sometimes I think I didn't even take time to properly grieve…and remember."

"I know what you mean," Diane told her. "Sometimes I feel like that about Eric. It all happened so fast. There was no warning whatsoever. Then there was so much to attend to for the funeral and memorial. And I was trying to be strong for the kids and other family members. It took almost a year before I allowed myself to really cry."

Beverly understood this. More than she cared to say. So many feelings had been trapped inside of her for so long. Sometimes she wondered if they would ever be allowed to the surface. And if they did surface…how would she survive them?

"Anyway, the reason for my visit here is twofold," Diane said as they were finishing their impromptu tea party. "I wanted to invite you to join Margaret and Adelaide and me for a girls' afternoon out today."

Beverly chuckled. "A girls' afternoon out?"

Diane explained how Margaret was trying to boost Adelaide's self-confidence with a day at the beauty shop and some retail therapy. Naturally, Father took this as his cue to excuse himself back to his library.

Diane laughed as they rinsed the teacups together. "I didn't mean to scare him off like that."

"It's okay." Beverly wiped off the table. "Actually, that sounds like fun. And I think Father will be just fine on his own for a couple of hours."

"He seems so much better."

Beverly told her about the confusion over the missing jam. "It was such a relief that he actually knew what he was talking about. In fact, I'm worried he might be more together than I am lately." She hung up the tea towel and shook her head.

"Are you feeling stressed about something?" Diane asked with concern.

Beverly felt a surge of fear now. Had she let her guard down again? Was Diane guessing that all was not well in her life? Beverly gave her old "I'm okay" smile. "I suppose I'm still getting over being so worried about Father. I just need to remember that he's getting better each day."

"Then a girls' afternoon out might be just the medicine for you. And Margaret wants us to leave at one. We'll have a little lunch, then we'll do some shopping, mostly for Adelaide. She wants to be more stylish." Diane smiled. "We'll break for a trip to the beauty shop. Then we'll shop some more. Sound good?"

Beverly's smile was genuine now. "Sounds absolutely perfect." And, really, the idea of helping Adelaide, shopping with her girlfriends, and having a little lunch seemed like a good plan. If only Jeff didn't call the house while she was out. But she felt fairly certain that she'd gotten through to him. Now all she needed to figure out was how to cut him loose for good.

However, she was determined not to think about that as she and Diane walked down to Margaret's house. And, she reminded herself, it was perfectly acceptable to take time off from her workday like this since she'd spent so much time working in the evenings lately. Father usually went to bed so early that working at night had become a routine. Just one more reason to enjoy the freedom of working from home.

"We are going to have fun!" Adelaide exclaimed as she answered the door.

"Absolutely!" Beverly said.

"We'll shop till we drop," Diane said.

"Yes!" Adelaide laughed, then repeated it. "Shop till we drop!"

"But first we will have lunch," Margaret announced as she came out. "I made us reservations at the Primrose," she told them as they got in the car. "For high tea."

"Oh, is that the tea house in Willow's Corner?" Beverly asked. "I've always wanted to go there."

"What is high tea?" Adelaide asked.

"It's like a very nice lunch with lots of lovely little sandwiches and cakes and, of course, tea," Margaret explained. "It's all very pretty and proper. So we all have to mind our manners."

Adelaide giggled.

A short time later they were seated at a round table, complete with white linen and delicately arranged flowers. Beverly realized this was just the sort of place her mother would've loved. "I wonder if this was here when my mother was still alive," she said quietly.

"Oh yes," Margaret said.

"I'll bet she came here," Beverly said as she looked around.

"Oh, I'm sure she did," Margaret said.

Beverly wished she'd taken more time to come visit in Marble Cove and its surrounding areas back before her mother died. It would've been wonderful to have enjoyed tea with her here. Even so, Beverly felt her mother would be pleased to think that Beverly was here today. And with friends too. In fact, it was something her mother used to worry about. "You need more friends," she'd often told Beverly. "There's more to life than just work." Beverly smiled to herself as she reached for a cucumber sandwich. Perhaps her mother would think this made up for some of that now.

Beverly felt a little out of her element after they left the tearoom. She wasn't accustomed to shopping with "the girls." For starters, she'd never been much of a shopper. She usually purchased her clothes online through her favorite catalog stores. And being a person who liked a more classic look, she didn't go for the funky little accessory stores that Adelaide was determined to browse through. However, she found it rather interesting.

At three o'clock they went to Pinkie's beauty salon, where Margaret had called ahead for manicure and hair appointments. "I really don't want a manicure," Margaret told Beverly. "Why don't you take mine?"

Beverly tried to refuse this offer, but Margaret said her nails would only get ruined with her painting anyway.

"Well, I suppose I could give it a try," Beverly told her. "I'm not usually into nail polish."

"Come on," Diane said. "Just have fun with it."

"I want those!" With bright eyes, Adelaide pointed up to where some colorful hair extensions were displayed.

Beverly tried not to blink at the bright neon colors. Did Adelaide—or anyone—really think that lime green hair was pretty? As Beverly was settling in with the manicurist, the woman named Mimi helped Adelaide try on various colors.

Eventually she settled on a bright pink color, then got a manicure that matched, along with little flowers on each nail.

In the meantime, Beverly settled for a more subdued shell pink. And Diane, feeling adventurous, went for a coral red. "I'll probably want to remove it before long," she confessed to Beverly as they waited at the register. "But it's kind of fun."

"This has all been fun," Beverly admitted. "And so out of the norm for me."

And because Adelaide was now on a pink mission, they stopped by the T-shirt shop, where she found a cute shirt that matched her nails and hair extensions. Adelaide could not have been happier as the four of them got in the car to head home.

"Thank you for coming with us," Margaret told Beverly. "I know it meant a lot to Adelaide."

"It meant a lot to me too," Beverly confessed. "Thanks for letting me tag along!"

CHAPTER TWELVE

Y ou look so pretty," Shelley told Adelaide when she came over to help with the kids on Friday morning.

"Thank you." Adelaide grinned as she touched her pink hair extensions.

"I might have to try something like that myself," Shelley told her. "For the holidays."

"We got our nails done too." Adelaide held up her hands to show hot pink nails with little yellow daisies painted in the centers. "A lady named Mimi made the flowers. And I got a new pink shirt that matches." She told Shelley how the hair extensions worked, but Aiden was so persistently tugging on her hand that she had to stop. "I think Aiden wants to play," she told Shelley with a maternal-sounding sigh.

"Yeah," Aiden insisted. "Adelaide is here to play with me. Not you, Mommy."

"Aiden"—Shelley shook her finger in a warning— "remember your manners."

Aiden apologized, then tugged Adelaide toward the family room to see the tent he was attempting to make. Meanwhile, it sounded as if Emma wanted out of her playpen. As much as Shelley appreciated Adelaide's assistance, she wished it was more than just as Aiden's playmate. What Shelley wouldn't give for a full-time nanny. Okay, maybe not full-time. But part-time would be nice. Being able to walk out the door and do as she pleased, knowing that the kids were okay...that would be amazing.

And it wasn't that she felt ungrateful for the time Dan had been spending working with Allan either. That was a blessing on many levels. For starters, it brought in a little income. Besides that, Allan was such a great mentor for Dan. And the two men, despite their age differences, got along wonderfully. But perhaps the best part was that Dan was also learning a new skill—frame making—and doing something he enjoyed. He actually came home happy. That alone was worth a lot.

So, really, Shelley told herself as she tended to Emma while attempting to clean house, she should be extremely thankful. Instead, she simply felt tired. She wouldn't admit it to anyone, but she wondered how long she could keep up the late-night hours baking down at the Cove.

She put Emma in the high chair, pouring some Cheerios onto the tray in the hopes it would amuse her for long enough to clean the kitchen. This morning she and Aiden had made waffles—and this time Dan had stuck around long enough to polish off the last one. But the kitchen was a mess.

"This sorry excuse of a kitchen," she muttered as she scrubbed down the stained porcelain sink. She thought about her mother-in-law's kitchen. Remodeled a few years ago, it had sleek granite countertops and stainless steel appliances, including a commercial-grade gas stove and a double oven. Yet did her mother-in-law ever use it? Hardly ever.

"I spent enough time cooking when the kids were young," Mrs. Bauer had recently said. "This kitchen is my reward for all those years."

Naturally, Mr. Bauer had laughed, saying how their new kitchen was all show and no go. "She's never even used the oven."

Shelley wiped off the top of her nearly useless stove and sighed. Sometimes life seemed so unfair. She was just sweeping the gritty floor when the phone rang.

"Oh, I'm so glad I caught you at home," Maddie said cheerfully. "I know you've been busy with your baking business, but I was just going over the details for Benjamin's birthday party next weekend and I noticed that you hadn't—"

"That's right," Shelley said suddenly. "I totally forgot to RSVP you."

"Yes, I was hoping it was simply an oversight."

"Aiden would love to come," Shelley said quickly.

"Oh, that's a relief. Benjamin would've been so disappointed if Aiden couldn't be there."

"I'm sorry, Maddie. I really meant to call."

"No problem." Now Maddie chatted on about how it was a cowboy theme and there would be ponies to ride, so the kids should dress appropriately.

"Yes, I'll see what I can do." Shelley could see that Emma's patience with the high chair was wearing thin now.

"And the birthday cake is going to be shaped like a bucking bronco," Maddie said. "I ordered this cake kit online and it's really going—"

Her words were interrupted by a loud wail from Emma. Kicking her feet and flailing her arms, she was clearly finished with her Cheerios.

"Sorry, but I have to go." Shelley balanced the phone between her shoulder and ear. "But Aiden will be there next week. I promise."

"Don't forget he needs to dress up like a cowboy," Maddie said as Shelley unbuckled the safety strap on the highchair.

"Right...cowboy." Shelley said good-bye and extracted Emma from the high chair. Sometimes she wondered if Maddie suffered from Supermom Syndrome. A cake shaped like a bucking bronco—*really?*

Shelley had barely finished cleaning house, if one could call it that, because it seemed she barely put one thing away before something else flopped down to replace it, when Dan came home and asked about lunch.

"Here." She handed Emma to him. "You take her, and I'll go fix lunch."

"Sounds like a deal to me," he said cheerfully. Emma let out a chirp of delight as he hoisted her up into the air like an airplane, flying her around and making engine sounds.

Shelley tried to enjoy this bit of "alone" time in the kitchen, but at the same time she felt slightly out of sorts. She knew it was probably more from weariness than anything—after all, she'd gotten all of five hours' sleep last night—but she felt resentful of all the time she spent cooking and cleaning. Wasn't there supposed to be more to life than this?

As she sliced some cheddar for grilled cheese sandwiches, she reminded herself that she *loved* to cook. Usually. As she opened a can of tomato soup, suppressing her guilt for not making it from scratch, she tried not to feel angry. What was wrong with her?

While using the two burners that actually worked, she told herself she should be thankful. At least they were still living in Marble Cove. At least Dan had found some work besides at the dock, where the hours grew fewer by the week. And if Shelley was patient and persistent, it was possible that her baking business would fill the gap too. Life was looking up for the Bauers. Wasn't it?

"This smells great, hon." Dan pecked her on the cheek.

"Will you see if Adelaide is staying for lunch?" she asked him.

"We will." Dan sailed Emma off in search of Adelaide and Aiden, and Shelley had to take in several slow deep breaths to keep herself from feeling angry and put upon. Really, what was wrong with her today?

Shelley kept her feelings inside as she sat down with Dan and Adelaide and the kids. She made cheerful small talk, saw to the needs of her family, keeping up the facade that all was well within her. After all, wasn't that what mothers were supposed to do?

After lunch, Adelaide played with Aiden while Shelley tended to Emma and eventually got her down for an afternoon nap. Naturally, when Shelley announced that it was nap time for Aiden as well, he resisted. But before he could throw a fit, she reminded him about Benjamin Bancroft's birthday party and how only good boys got to go to it. Sure, it was a whole week away, but she could use it as leverage for a while.

Shelley thanked Adelaide for her help, then escorted Aiden to his room, where, still complaining, he took off his shoes and climbed reluctantly into his bed. Shelley wanted to climb in beside him like she used to do sometimes when he insisted he wasn't sleepy. But she still had the kitchen to clean up and things to get lined up so that Dan could watch the kids for her while she headed out to bake at the coffee shop later tonight. Besides all that, she had promised to bake dessert for Diane's friend's dinner party tonight. It was only a pineapple upside-down cake, but just the same, it would take time.

As Shelley worked, she felt like one of Aiden's favorite toys—the electronic hamster that ran and ran on his exercise wheel to nowhere, then through his mazelike cage, then back to the wheel to run some more. Except that the electronic hamster had batteries to keep him going, whereas Shelley felt like she was running on empty.

By the time Dan returned home, dinner was ready and Shelley had everything pretty much set for the rest of the evening, with bottles filled with milk, pajamas laid out, and so on. Shelley, however, was so tired she could hardly put one foot in front of the other.

"Maybe you should take the night off," Dan said to her as she slumped into her chair at the table. "You look whupped."

"I am." She nodded sleepily.

"Then just stay home."

"I can't." She put a spoonful of homemade macaroni and cheese onto Aiden's plate.

"Sure you can," he said. "It's your business, Shell. You get to make the rules."

"Not exactly." She spooned some applesauce into Emma's opened birdlike mouth.

"Why not?" Dan sounded irritated. "What's the point in being your own boss if you can't make the rules?"

"Part of the deal for using the Cove is that I do their baking too," she reminded him in a tired voice. "They depend on me to fill their pastry case. I can't just decide not to show up."

"Oh." He nodded as he forked into his food. "I guess I kinda forgot about that part."

A part of Shelley—the exhausted part—wished she *could* stay home tonight. But another part of her was glad to escape the house that sometimes felt like her prison. She felt guilty for those feelings, but they were still there. As tired as she was, the idea of being free from sticky little hands and never-ending demands was most welcome.

And even though she would be working—without *too* many distractions tonight, she hoped—she knew she would be able to think her own thoughts, to daydream, and to simply enjoy a small, temporary escape from her everyday reality. Was it wrong to feel like she needed to get away from her own children, her dear, sweet little family?

Well, if it was wrong, maybe she didn't want to be right.

Chapter Thirteen

Diane was pleasantly surprised by her e-mail on Friday morning. The publisher had finally made the necessary changes to the contract, and there it was, attached to the e-mail from Jane. In her excitement, Diane immediately called her agent's cell phone. Then, as the phone rang, Diane wondered if this was appropriate. She didn't want to turn into one of those authors who were constantly bugging their agent.

"Frieda Watley," the agent said briskly.

"Sorry to bother you—" She paused, realizing she hadn't identified herself. "It's Diane Spencer. I just received—"

"Oh, Diane, I was just about to call you. I read over the new contract yesterday and all seemed in order, so I asked Jane to send it on to you."

"And she did!" Diane exclaimed happily. "I have it right here on my computer."

"Yes, I know. She copied me on it."

Diane looked more closely to see this. "Oh yes," she said. "I hadn't even noticed."

"So anyway, I think we're good to go on it. That is, unless you see something that needs changing."

"I don't think so." Diane continued skimming over the words. Some of the legalese went over her head, but the important parts—like her name, the titles of the books, the deadlines, the word counts, and, of course, the all-important advance amount, which would help to support her for the next couple of years—were there. "It all seems to be correct," she said slowly. "I just can hardly believe it though."

"Well, believe it," Frieda told her. "And sign it."

"Sign it?" Diane stared at her computer screen.

"Print out three copies. Sign and date them. Then return all three to Jane."

"Oh yes." Diane felt silly. "Of course."

"Then go out and celebrate, Diane. Your career is officially launched."

"Thank you! This is so exciting."

"Sorry I have to run," Frieda said. "But congratulations!"

After Diane hung up, she began printing out the copies of the contract. Holding the actual paper in her hands was even more thrilling than reading it on the screen. She carefully signed and dated each one. After copying them, she stapled them and slipped them into a large envelope addressed to the publisher.

She walked them down to the post office, where she sent them Priority Mail. "It's a *three-book* contract," she told the postal worker.

His brows shot up. "You're a writer?"

She nodded eagerly. "And this is the moment I've been waiting for—to actually sign and return the contract."

He grinned. "Well, now…good for you."

Diane felt like celebrating as she walked through town, but when she glanced into the Shearwater Gallery, she could see that Margaret was showing an elderly couple through the gallery. Not wanting to disturb an encounter with real customers, Diane continued on her way. By this time of day, Shelley would probably have the kids down for naps. And Beverly was probably working. She would have to figure out some sort of celebration with them later. Maybe during the weekend.

In the meantime, all she really wanted to do was write. Amazing how an actual book contract suddenly made the writing process feel more authentic and validated.

Diane was caught off guard when Barbara called that afternoon, saying that she planned to have several guests for dinner tonight. "I just wanted to be sure that the dessert you're bringing will be large enough to serve eight."

Diane wondered who the other six guests would be. But, not wanting to be nosy, she declined to ask. "I'm sure it will be plenty," she assured her, "but I'll check with Shelley just in case."

It wasn't until later, as she drove out on the beach loop road, that she became rather curious. Just who did Barbara know in Marble Cove anyway? Diane didn't know anything about the house where Barbara was staying, but she'd assumed it was simply a vacation cottage since there were many of them out this way. Perhaps somewhat rustic and probably small.

She couldn't have been more surprised when she pulled up to an enormous home. It looked new but obviously had been constructed before the economy went south. Not built in the usual beach house style with shake shingles and painted trim, this house, with its modern lines and numerous multileveled decks and large windows, looked like it belonged more in Southern California than Maine.

She pulled into the circular drive where several other cars were already parked and, gathering up her pineapple upside-down cake, prepared to go inside.

"There you are." Barbara, dramatically dressed in a colorful caftan and wearing long dangly earrings, opened the double doors wide and smiled. "Come in, come in."

Feeling underdressed in her khaki pants and turtleneck sweater, Diane found herself standing in the great room where a number of men and women, all more formally dressed, were sipping drinks and cheerfully visiting around a massive stone fireplace.

"Margot," Barbara called toward the kitchen, "please, come and get this cake from my guest."

A young woman appeared and took the cake. Barbara introduced Diane to a familiar-looking couple named Wallace. "Vance and Lynne," Barbara said. "They own the bed-and-breakfast on Water Street."

"Oh yes." Diane nodded. "My late husband and I stayed there a time or two. Such a lovely place."

"And maybe you already know Evelyn Waters," Barbara continued, "the mayor of Marble Cove."

Diane shook her hand. "I haven't had the pleasure, but your son and I are already old friends." Diane told Barbara about Lee Waters and the Pet Place. "Lee takes good care of Rocky and me."

"Speaking of Rocky." The local veterinarian stepped up to shake Diane's hand, smiling warmly into her eyes. "How is he doing?"

"Dr. Spangler," she said with surprise. "So nice to see you again. Um, Rocky is just fine. He runs as if he'd never been hurt."

"Please, call me Leo," he told her.

"Leo lives next door," Barbara said. She introduced Diane to the others, names Diane recognized as prominent business owners in Marble Cove.

"You've been here less than a week, and it seems you know half the town already." Diane used a teasing voice for Barbara. "How did you do that so quickly?"

"Oh, you know me," Barbara told her. "I'm a bit of a social butterfly."

Diane looked out the large window that overlooked the ocean, where the last rays of sunlight were slowly fading. "What a spectacular view." She spotted the mysterious-looking white tower in the dusky blue light. "You can even see the lighthouse from here."

"Yes." Barbara nodded eagerly. "In fact, that is something I want to talk to everyone about tonight. It's part of my reasoning for inviting you all here like this. That, and a need for a little fun." She turned and grinned at Leo. "Well, except for you. I invited you here simply because you're my neighbor."

Diane felt her brows arch as she wondered if those were romantic sparkles glowing in Barbara's eyes. Why should Diane care if they were?

"Do tell us what's going on, Barbara," Evelyn said. "I'm simply dying to hear what you're planning and why you've gathered us here."

Barbara walked over to the window and pointed toward Orlean Point Light. "I want to purchase the lighthouse."

Diane felt a tightening in her stomach. So she really meant to do this.

"You must be joking." Evelyn chuckled. "Whatever for?"

Barbara turned to the Wallaces now. "For a bed-and-breakfast." She gave them a reassuring smile. "Not to be in competition with yours, of course. Although I would appreciate your professional advice in this matter."

"Turning a lighthouse into an inn?" Lynne Wallace frowned. "It sounds like an impractical undertaking to me. I can't even imagine where you'd begin."

"Oh, don't be too hasty," her husband said to her. "I happen to know of several B and Bs in lighthouses—quite popular too." And suddenly they were all discussing the pros and cons of running a lighthouse as an inn. No one even seemed to question whether or not this crazy idea was even a real possibility.

"Is the lighthouse for sale?" Diane asked quietly when there was a brief lull in the conversation.

"No, I believe it's owned by the state or maybe the port authority," the mayor informed them. "As far as I know, there hasn't been any talk of selling it."

"In my experience, everything's for sale," Barbara added glibly, "if the price is right. And really, if no one is using it, it's just a big white elephant."

Several guests laughed over this. Diane held her tongue.

Margot came out to announce that dinner was ready, and they moved to the dining area.

With her head still slightly spinning over Barbara's crazy-sounding announcement, Diane took her place at the elegantly set table. Then as the lobster bisque soup was served, she questioned her choice of pineapple upside-down cake for dessert. What had she been thinking?

"I have always loved Orlean Point Light," Barbara told her guests as the glazed salmon was served. Then she went on to explain how her family vacationed here during her childhood and how the lighthouse was always a key part of their visits.

"I can relate to that," Diane said. "But I wonder if it would take something away from the lighthouse if it was a bed-and-breakfast. For me, the most interesting thing about the lighthouse was the sense of awe and mystery I got from it as a child. I'm not sure I would've felt that way if guests had been coming and going from it."

"That's a good point," Leo said. "I feel a bit like that myself."

"But think of the business it could bring to Marble Cove," the mayor said. "And in a downturned economy, it could be quite a boon to be a town with a lighthouse B and B."

The conversation was off to the races again. Everyone, it seemed, was convinced that turning Orlean Point Light into an inn might be a very good idea. But to Diane it seemed blasphemous. Okay, *blasphemous* was too strong a word. But it did seem irreverent and improper and just plain wrong. Not that she would say such things. Not here and now. So for the course of the meal, Diane held her tongue.

"I understand you're a writer," Evelyn said to Diane as the table was being cleared. "What do you write?"

The others at the table grew quieter now.

"Diane *used* to write for a newspaper," Barbara answered for her.

"But I retired from that."

"I think she's far too young to be retired," Barbara said teasingly. "Can you believe that we went to college together more than thirty years ago?"

Now the conversation switched over to disbelief. "You must've been a child prodigy," Vance said to Barbara. "Were you six years old in college?"

She laughed and waved her hand. "Go on."

They did go on for a while, and Barbara just seemed to eat it up. Then, when there was another lull in conversation, Leo spoke up. "Diane, I thought I heard you were writing a book. Is that correct?"

"A book?" Barbara looked surprised and skeptical.

"As a matter of fact, I am." Diane smiled at Leo.

"What sort of book?" the mayor asked.

Diane explained about the mystery series and how she had recently changed it from a continuing series to a stand-alone series. "I've learned that publishers can be a fickle bunch."

"So is this a self-published book?" Barbara asked. "You know, so many people are doing that now. I've thought of paying for one myself."

"No..." Diane took in a slow breath, willing herself to be patient with her "old friend." "It's a contracted series with a New York publisher. They pay me—not the other way around. As a matter of fact, I just mailed off the signed contract today."

Leo held up his water glass as if to toast. "Well, here's to having a famous author in our midst."

"Oh, I wouldn't go that far," Diane told him.

"Well, it is exciting," the mayor said. "And it's good for our town too. I hope you'll do some book signings and promotions when the book comes out."

"If anyone is interested, I'd be more than happy to."

"Things are looking up for our sleepy little town," the mayor said. "An author living here in our midst, and perhaps a bed-and-breakfast at Orlean Point Light. This is quite a newsworthy evening, folks."

Diane studied Barbara as she seemed to bask in this light. "I would think that it might be tricky getting permits and approval for the lighthouse to be rezoned as an inn," Diane said carefully. She explained about her young friend who couldn't even get her kitchen approved for a home baking business.

"Oh, that's state law," the mayor explained. "It has more to do with the health department than zoning." Evelyn winked at Barbara. "I suspect that getting the lighthouse zoned for another use shouldn't be too difficult. You just need to talk to the right people."

Several of them chuckled, and Diane suppressed the urge to react. "So does this mean you will become a permanent resident in Marble Cove?" Diane asked Barbara.

Barbara seemed unsure. "Well, I don't know. Of course, I'd have to hire someone to renovate the lighthouse. Who knows how long that might take. Then I'd need someone else to operate the B and B for me. But it might be fun to stick around just to see how it's all done." She frowned slightly. "Although the winters here can be a bit formidable. I might need to be a snowbird and flit off to warmer climes sometimes."

Now the dessert was being served and it took all of Diane's self-control not to apologize over its humble appearance. Even with the whipped cream on top, which Shelley had insisted upon, it looked rather homespun. Still, if anyone complained, and surely no one would be so ill-mannered, Diane would never reveal who had baked it.

To Diane's relief, the response to the pineapple upside-down cake was nothing but positive and glowing. So, feeling a bit motherly toward Shelley, Diane bragged about her talented neighbor and friend. "I'm sure some of you have already tasted Shelley's other delectable goodies at the Cove."

"I have a perfect idea," Barbara announced. "I will ask Shelley to be the chef for my B and B."

The others began to discuss this possibility, and Diane again decided to keep her opinions to herself. The chances of Shelley ever agreeing to something like that seemed unlikely. Besides, it was a long way off. And she hoped it would never happen.

"You know"—Barbara held her coffee cup in midair and smiled happily—"I wondered how my friend Diane managed to downsize her life from living in the bustling city to a small place like Marble Cove. But I think I'm beginning to appreciate it. And I am beginning to feel right at home."

Diane pasted on a polite smile and wished most ungraciously that Barbara had never set foot in this town. More than that, Diane wished she'd never agreed to join Barbara for dinner tonight. Suddenly it seemed that all that Diane loved most about Marble Cove...and the lighthouse... was starting to unravel.

CHAPTER FOURTEEN

Two things were troubling Margaret of late. First, she was not the least bit excited about being involved in the chamber of commerce. It seemed they only wanted to put more demands on her. Upon her first visit, they began suggesting she play the role of a volunteer art consultant to the city. As if she didn't have enough on her plate. Good grief, who did they think she was—Superwoman?

The other troubling thing, although she tried to appear nonchalant about it, was Adelaide's new "love interest." Thanks to Adelaide's constant chatter about how Hank had done this or that, Margaret's own curiosity over the young man was growing daily.

"Why don't you go on down there and have a conversation with him?" Allan suggested to Margaret. He and Dan had just delivered several of his latest creations into the gallery.

"It's as if Adelaide thinks he hung the moon," she said. "And it's starting to worry me more than I care to admit."

"Just go talk to him."

"I wouldn't know what to say." Margaret watched as Allan scooted a contemporary-style buffet into place against the brick wall. It was a lovely piece with an intricate inlaid border of mahogany, cherry, and zebrawood strips.

"How about we invite the young man for dinner?" he suggested.

Margaret gave Allan a horrified look, but instead of giving him a verbal response, she simply ran a dust cloth over the sleek surface of the buffet. What was he thinking?

"Oh, I get it." Allan chortled. "I suppose that might be sending the wrong message."

She shook the dust cloth at Allan. "Do you truly want Adelaide to get married?"

He scratched his head. "Well…only if Adelaide wanted to marry. Then I suppose it would be all right."

"But how would that actually work?" she asked. "In real life, I mean? Have you considered it?"

He shrugged. "Not fully. But Adelaide has a right to happiness…wherever she finds it."

"But she *is* happy."

He frowned.

"And we take *care* of her," Margaret reminded him. "She needs us. She would be lost without us."

"But there are ways that a marriage like that, a *special* marriage, can work." He adjusted the buffet to be more evenly spaced against the wall.

"How so?" Margaret didn't like challenging her husband like this, but she did not understand his reasoning. Not at all. Did he honestly expect Adelaide to marry Hank and that they would live happily ever after?

"I've done some research." With hands on his hips, Allan stepped back to study the buffet. "Lots of people like Adelaide find happiness in marriage."

"Yes, I've read up on it myself. But still."

"I'm not saying I want Adelaide to get married, Margaret. I'm just saying we have to let her live her own life...to the degree she can."

Margaret knew that he was probably right. But it was hard to admit this.

He put his hand on her shoulder now, looking deeply into her eyes. "If it's meant to be, it'll be. Right?"

She nodded reluctantly. "I suppose."

"In the meantime, would it hurt to get to know the fellow? Not have him over for dinner. But maybe I'll pick Adelaide up at the center today. And while I'm there I can just mosey in and say a quick hello." He chuckled. "And determine if his intentions are honorable."

She gave him a gentle shove on the chest. "Yes, I'll just bet you will."

"I'll simply be friendly," he assured her, "and observant."

"And maybe I'll do the same," she told him. "Not today, since you've got that handled. But later this week, I'll make an effort to get better acquainted with Handsome Hank too."

"Handsome Hank?" He grimaced.

"That's what Penny calls him. Well, not to anyone except me, I suspect."

"So is he quite good-looking?" Suddenly Allan seemed a bit worried.

"He's got nice brown eyes and thick blond curly hair." She shrugged. "He's on the skinny side with a bit of an overbite. Not my cup of tea, but our daughter thinks he's stunning."

"Oh." Allan opened and closed a drawer of the buffet. Like with all his furniture, the mechanics were impeccable.

"It's a beautiful piece," she told him.

He nodded with a distracted expression. "And let's not forget, Adelaide has some competition in regard to Hank."

"You mean Lisa?"

"Yes." He brightened. "It's possible that Lisa and Handsome Hank are already in a relationship. Maybe *they* want to get married."

"Wouldn't that be a relief?" Margaret sighed.

His smile faded. "Unless it broke our little girl's heart."

"Oh my...I think we need to ask God to help in this matter, Allan. I'm afraid we're in over our heads."

He nodded with a wistful expression. They both just stood there with only the quiet strains of Miles Davis playing in the background.

"Not to change the subject." She nodded toward the counter. "But there's a message from one of the giclée printing companies. It seems they're offering a special deal. And I think it's the company we liked."

Allan went over and played back the phone message. "Do you want me to call them back?"

"I don't know." Margaret joined him. "I guess I'm still concerned about quality control." She frowned. "Can you imagine how we'd feel if a lot of giclée prints came out with the wrong colors?" She glanced up at a seascape. "Take that painting, for instance. I had such a hard time making the sunset colors look realistic with that layer of fog out on the ocean. If the giclée printer didn't reproduce the colors exactly as I painted them, it would end up looking all wrong."

"Surely they have worked out a way to manage the color, or else people would never buy giclées." He paused. "I don't really see a downside here, Margaret."

"Go ahead and call the company if you want, just to get the information. I'll trust you to make this decision. I have enough to think about right now. What with the chamber trying to get me to jump through their hoops and my daughter threatening to elope with Handsome Hank."

Allan's brows shot up.

"Just kidding. But, really, Allan, I'll trust you to figure things out in regard to the giclée printers."

Allan looked relieved. "Thanks. I'll spend some more time looking into it. And Dan is making good progress with the frames. As well as helping me with the woodworking end of things. That boy's a fast learner. And it's nice having company."

"So maybe it's just a matter of timing."

"Like life."

After Allan left, Margaret went to the back room to continue working on her current painting. Despite how quiet the gallery had been lately, she still felt distracted, as if she wasn't accomplishing as much as she had hoped. She could blame it on the chamber of commerce, but she knew that most of her uneasiness was due to Adelaide's recent romantic interest. She couldn't imagine what she'd do if Adelaide decided to get married.

Yet at the same time, she knew that Allan was right. Adelaide needed to live her own life. With her parents' help, of course. But if Margaret tried to smother her daughter, it would surely backfire. It felt like a balancing act. When to step in…when to step back… Prayer might be her most efficient tool.

Hearing the back room phone ringing, she was tempted to ignore it and let the machine answer, but then she heard the voice on the other end saying it was Charlotte Vincent. With paintbrush still in hand, Margaret went over to better hear what the chairwoman of the chamber of commerce was saying.

"I'm calling to ask you a favor, Margaret. We have a very special project that I think you'll be interested—"

"Hello, this is Margaret." She set her paintbrush aside and listened.

"Oh, Margaret, I'm so glad I caught you."

"What can I do for you?" Margaret braced herself. She hoped this wasn't about coordinating all of the city's future art and cultural events, because Margaret was just not up to it.

"Well, you've heard about the Cannery, haven't you?"

"Yes. It sounds like a wonderful way to preserve an old building as well as bring in some new business."

"Precisely. But there's a huge blank wall on the inside and we were discussing the possibility of painting a large mural. You know, something that represents Marble Cove. Naturally, your name came up right away. Do you think you would possibly have time to help with something like that?"

While flattered to be asked, and relieved it was something smaller than organizing the entire town, Margaret wasn't too sure. "How big is the mural to be?"

"The wall is about sixteen feet high and thirty feet long."

"Oh my!"

"But we could get some high school art students to help with it. As long as you directed the project. You could have them do most of the work."

"Oh, well, that sounds more doable."

"So you'll agree?"

Margaret looked longingly at her current project. "Well... perhaps I should examine the wall first. Just to be sure it's a wall that will lend itself to a mural."

"Yes, that's an excellent idea. How about if you meet me there this afternoon? Around two?"

"Sure."

"Thanks, Margaret."

After she hung up, she wondered if this was wise. But just because you were invited to do something didn't mean you had to say yes. Margaret could easily thank them for the honor, then pass.

But when she got to the old building, where workers were in full gear, and when she saw the wall, and when Charlotte gushed on and on about how wonderful it was going to be and how Margaret was the perfect person to do this mural, it was just impossible to say no.

"I do like the idea of high school students helping me," she told Charlotte as they stood by the main entrance looking back toward the wall. "I can imagine a seascape with a lot of layers of blues and greens, and that would take some time to paint."

"Yes, and we want the mural done in time for the Christmas shopping season. That's when the Cannery is scheduled to open. The same weekend as the Christmas parade."

Margaret blinked. "That's only five weeks away."

"But it's doable, right?" Charlotte looked concerned.

"Sure, it's doable. But for that reason, I think I should keep the painting simple. Just to ensure that it really is completed in time."

"Yes, that sounds wise." Charlotte opened the door. "Oh, I'm so glad you agreed to this. The chamber will be thrilled to hear you're onboard."

"And I'll put together some preliminary sketches," Margaret said as they exited. "I assume the chamber will need to approve them?"

"Yes." Charlotte nodded. "For sure."

"Well, this should be fun." Margaret glanced back at the building, hoping she hadn't just bitten off more than she could chew.

"Thank you so much!" Charlotte vigorously shook Margaret's hand. "And, naturally, we'll have the newspaper do a piece on it. Maybe even get it into some of the other larger papers. After all, you're becoming a big name in these parts."

Margaret chuckled. "Well, I don't know…"

Still, as the two women parted ways, Margaret couldn't help but feel good. It really did feel as if her career had experienced a big jump start this past year. It was all so much more than she'd ever dreamed of. Sometimes she felt like maybe she should pinch herself just to make sure it was real.

CHAPTER FIFTEEN

The one thing Shelley could always count on her mother-in-law for was to do something unexpected. Whether it was a drop-in visit, a critique of Shelley's housekeeping, an impromptu invitation to a family event that had been planned for weeks, or giving unsolicited parenting tips, Frances Bauer had a knack for pulling the rug out from under Shelley.

For that reason, Shelley had long since told herself that when it came to her mother-in-law, just like she learned in her Lamaze birthing class, she should expect the unexpected. Even so, she still got taken by surprise.

"Hello in the house," called a painfully familiar voice. "Aiden, Emma, Shelley? Grandma's here!"

Shelley looked around the family room with a sense of desperation. Aiden, still wearing pajamas (ones that were too small) and part of his breakfast on his face, was sprawled in front of the TV where his favorite Spider-Man cartoon was playing a bit too loudly. Shelley, wearing her usual grubby warm-ups, was also on the floor, surrounded by Emma's toys and the diaper bag (with all its contents splayed out from her search for a diaper, which she had not found) and Emma, still smelling stinky (for lack of said diaper), was wearing only a faded pink onesie that was stained from a formula spill.

"We're in here," Shelley said weakly. Whatever happened to knocking?

"Oh my!" Frances looked around the room in dismay. "Is someone sick?"

Shelley forced herself to her feet. "No. No one's sick. Uh, how are you?"

"I'm just fine." Frances looked puzzled. "But you're sure no one's ill." She sniffed. "What's that smell?"

"It's Emma's diaper." Shelley took in her mother-in-law's burgundy pantsuit and pale pink shirt and suspected she was on her way to someplace special. At least more special than here. With luck, this would be a short visit. "If you'll excuse me, I'll run and get a fresh one."

"Of course."

Shelley tried not to fume as she hurried to Emma's room, gathering up some diaper-changing supplies and a fresh coverall. Frances' sense of timing never ceased to amaze. Just create a big mess and wallow in it a little, and the next thing you know, voilà, Frances shows up.

As Shelley returned to the family room, she could hear Frances questioning Aiden's viewing habits. "Your mother actually lets you watch *that*?"

"Yeah. It's Spider-Man, Meemaw. He's a good guy. He saves everyone."

"You look all dressed up," Shelley said as she knelt down to rearrange her daughter's appearance. "Are you on your way someplace?"

"Just church. Our women's ministries group has a planning meeting for the harvest party."

"Oh, that sounds interesting." Shelley focused her attention on Emma, deftly removing the offensive diaper and going through the regular cleaning routine as swiftly as possible.

"Oh dear!"

"What?" Shelley glanced over her shoulder to see an anxious expression on Frances' face.

"Is that how you do it?"

"Do what?"

"Change poor Emma's diapers?"

"Yeah." Shelley turned her focus back to her daughter as she put the clean diaper in place and adhered the sticky tapes.

"Oh my. Well, you young people do things in your own way. But back in my day, I would've worried about diaper rash."

You're welcome to change her yourself, she wanted to say. "Well, Emma's in good shape." Shelley pulled off the dirty onesie and began maneuvering the wiggling child into the coverall.

"Do you know that I never used disposable diapers at all? Not on any of my kids."

"Yes, uh, you've mentioned that." Shelley made a face at Emma, which made Emma laugh.

"And now with all this concern over the environment and being green, I hear that cloth diapers are coming back into vogue." Frances laughed as if this amused her.

Now Shelley stood back up with Emma in her arms. "Surely you didn't stop by here to discuss cloth diapers." She offered Frances a stiff smile.

"No, no, of course not." Frances glanced at her watch. "I just had a few minutes to kill, and I thought I'd pay my grandkids a visit." She looked over at Aiden, who was still glued to the TV.

Shelley considered turning it off, but she knew that would only cause a conflict with Aiden, and she'd already bribed him with Spider-Man in order to get a few minutes of peace. "Here." Shelley held Emma out to Frances. "Maybe you'd like to bond with your granddaughter while I go put these things away and clean up a bit."

"Oh?" Frances blinked as if she was unsure about her burgundy suit and the women's planning meeting. But then she took Emma, albeit gingerly, in her arms.

"I'll be back in a couple of minutes." Shelley felt like a bandit as she grabbed up the diaper bag things and made off to the bathroom, where she locked herself in and counted to ten. Then she cleaned up a bit, brushed her teeth and hair, and, finally feeling a bit more human, emerged.

She found Frances and Emma strolling through the kitchen, looking at the breakfast dishes still on the table and last night's dishes still piled in the sink. Even the pot of spaghetti, with leftovers that were now rendered useless, was still on the stove.

"Kind of messy in here," Shelley said lightly.

"I'll say."

Shelley explained that she'd had a late night at the Cove. "I had several special orders and it was past midnight when I got home." She took the pot of spaghetti, dumping it into the sink, before she remembered the defunct disposal.

"It's important to organize yourself when you work outside of the home," Frances told her.

Like Shelley didn't know that. "Organization is not my strong suit." Shelley began to load dishes into the dishwasher. At least that still worked…somewhat efficiently.

"Does your baking business really help the family budget that much?"

Shelley set a plate into the rack with a loud clank that sounded as if it could result in a chip.

"I mean, you have to look at the big picture," Frances continued. "Maybe it would be better if you stayed home for now. You know, while the children are younger."

Shelley turned and stared at her. "You were the one who told me, not so long ago, that it was my job to help Dan out, and that I needed to contribute financially to the household. Remember?"

"I'm not sure you understood me correctly, Shelley. Yes, you need to contribute. But perhaps not outside of the home." She glanced around the messy kitchen as if this made her point.

"It doesn't always look like this," Shelley told her. "The kids and I were just having a laid back morning. I was tired and—"

"I didn't come here to argue with you, Shelley." Frances frowned. "I suppose it's up to you how you spend your time."

Shelley knew exactly what that meant.

"I mostly came by to ask you a favor."

"A favor?" Now this was a new twist. First criticize, and then ask for help. Interesting strategy.

"Yes." Frances handed Emma back to her and smoothed out the front of her jacket. "It's Ralph's birthday, you know, in early November. And I'll be so busy with the harvest party that the church has on Halloween, which I hope you and Dan will attend with the children. Anyway, the gist of it is that I don't think I'll have time to bake Ralph a cake this year."

"You want me to bake the cake?" Shelley was surprised. Was it possible that Frances finally respected her for her baking skills?

"Yes, if it's not too much trouble. It's Ralph's seventy-fifth birthday, and I want it to be special. I'm hosting it at the church's reception room and inviting about fifty people. Can you make a cake that large?"

"Of course. I'd be glad to."

"And naturally, I'll expect you and Dan and the children to attend." She glanced at Shelley's frowzy warm-ups. "And please dress up, because I plan to have a professional photographer there. I want to get some nice family photos to use on our Christmas card this year. Do you think you can manage that, dear?"

"Yes, of course." Shelley felt frustration rising.

"I'll let you know the color scheme later."

"You mean for the cake?"

Frances waved her hand. "Well, that too."

Shelley gave her a questioning look.

"I'm referring to how you and Dan and children should dress for the party. The photographer suggested that everyone in the family wear similar colors to make the photo look coordinated. I'll let you know what you should wear."

"Oh." Shelley licked her finger and wiped a splotch of dried baby food off Emma's cheek.

"Anyway, I better get going. Don't want to be late." Frances gave the kitchen one more disdainful look, then turned away with a loud sigh. "Have a nice day!"

Shelley tried not to picture the Wicked Witch of the West as her mother-in-law scurried out of the house. But it was all she could do not to let out a frustrated scream as the front door closed.

"I'll get you, my little pretty," Shelley cackled to Emma. "And your little dog too!"

Emma giggled.

Thinking of little dogs, Shelley suddenly remembered that Prize hadn't been let out this morning. She hoped it wasn't too late. Oh, the daily glamour of a mother's life!

Chapter Sixteen

As much as Beverly wanted to keep Jeff Mackenzie out of her life, she knew it was not going to happen until she met with him. And now that he had their home phone number and the chance of her father answering the phone, possibly questioning how Jeff knew his daughter...well, it was all too disturbing. For that reason, she agreed to meet Jeff on Thursday night.

"Great. How about Captain Calhoun's Crab and Lobster House?" he said cheerfully. "Around six?"

"No," she said firmly. "Not for dinner."

"Oh...okay. Dessert then?"

"Coffee."

"At the Cove?"

"No." Beverly wasn't sure if the Cove was even open at night, especially during this time of year, but even so she didn't want to chance being seen by Shelley there. "Captain Calhoun's is fine. We can get coffee there. But I can't make it until after eight. If that's too late for you, I'm sorry." She wasn't really sorry. In fact, she hoped he might not be able to make it.

"Eight is fine."

"It might be more like eight thirty," she told him. "I want to be sure my father has gone to bed. He, uh, has some health issues." She knew this was partly true, but partly an excuse as well. "I live with him so I can help with his care."

"Eight thirty is fine too. In fact, I'll just plan to arrive at the restaurant an hour or so earlier. I'll order some dinner and just wait for you. You come whenever you like. I won't be going anywhere."

"Right..." She wanted to ask him *why*. Why was he digging in his heels like this? Why didn't he understand that she didn't want to see him? Why couldn't he grasp that she simply wanted to pretend they'd never met? Hadn't she made that perfectly clear that night at the lighthouse?

"See you tonight then," he said lightly.

She reluctantly confirmed this and hung up. What was he really up to? He'd claimed he'd been at the lighthouse in order to do some research. But research about what? She knew it was paranoia on her part, but the only thing she could imagine him being in Marble Cove to research was her. But how did he know she'd moved back here? And how did he know about her interest in the lighthouse? None of it made sense.

For that reason alone, she was a tiny bit interested in meeting with him. Curiosity was a compelling force. Of course, she needed to bear in mind what it did to the cat.

"Everything okay?"

She jumped to hear Father's voice behind her. She had assumed he was still outside raking leaves. She'd been so glad to see his energy and interest in doing a little yard work returning to him.

"Yes." She nodded eagerly. "I'm fine. Did you get the leaves all raked?"

"Mostly." He looked concerned. "You don't seem fine, Beverly. You have that look. The same look your mother got sometimes, as if you're quite worried about something." He gently touched her cheek. "Is something disturbing you?"

She forced a smile. "No, Father. Really, I'm fine."

"But you'd tell me if something was troubling you?"

"Yes, of course." She turned away and pretended to busy herself with rinsing a coffee cup in the sink. "It's such a nice day today... I think I might take a little walk on the beach. Do you want to come?"

"I'd rather get the rest of those leaves raked up before the weather changes. The forecast is for rain this weekend."

She reached for her jacket, hanging by the back door. "I guess that's just one more reason for me to take a walk today." She turned and smiled. "Don't overdo it with the raking, okay?"

"No worries there. I plan to put my feet up for a bit. Then I'll go back and finish this afternoon."

Promising to be back in time to fix lunch, Beverly made her exit. But instead of walking like she'd told him, she decided to make this a jog. Maybe the exercise would help clear her head.

But with each step she ran, the same questions pounded in her head. *Why is he here? What does he want? Why is he here? What does he want?*

Finally, not far from the lighthouse, she quit jogging and simply walked. Still breathing hard, and with her gaze fixed on Orlean Point Light, she asked herself the question that was most mystifying to her: *Why had Jeff been at the lighthouse that night?*

She experienced the same rush of shock as she recalled her feelings at seeing his face when the lighthouse door had opened. It was as if she'd seen an actual ghost. Short of seeing her deceased husband's face in front of her, nothing could've been more unsettling or disturbing.

What had he really been doing there? Even if Jeff had been telling her the truth—that he was doing some kind of research that was unrelated to her—what kind of research did one do at night? Astronomy? And why this particular lighthouse? And why had he flashed that light out? And why had he acted so mysteriously? At the very least, it seemed to suggest he was up to no good. But mostly, it didn't make sense. And Beverly liked things to make sense.

But how was she going to make sense of seeing him again tonight? And how was she going to maintain a cool, calm demeanor? And what if someone she knew saw them together? How would she explain it? It seemed that all Beverly had was questions. More and more questions.

As she reached the lighthouse, she came up with an answer. Just like that, she realized how she would get through tonight's unwelcome meeting with Jeff: she would have a list of her own questions for him. And certainly, she had plenty. That way, if his line of conversation grew too uncomfortable, which was likely, she would be ready to bombard him with questions of her own. She would demand to know why he was here and what he was doing at the lighthouse. If he refused to answer her, she would just cut their appointment short.

She leaned against the lighthouse. As was often the case on a sunny day, its hard surface, after absorbing the morning sunlight, felt warm to her back. So comforting. She leaned her head back, looking up at the bright blue sky overhead. These autumn days were meant to be relished and enjoyed. She peered out over the ocean, seeing a bank of fog rolling in. The weather system could completely change before nightfall. Kind of like life.

Beverly longed to talk to someone about all these unsettling things—these interruptions to what would otherwise be a satisfying life here in Marble Cove. But who could she open up to? Despite his assurance that she could confide in him, her father would be greatly disturbed to hear about Jeff Mackenzie and how he was connected to Beverly. For all Beverly knew it could even be hazardous to his health. No, she couldn't tell Father.

She had considered opening up to Diane before. In fact, she had very nearly spilled the beans and told Diane everything not so long ago. She wasn't even sure why she trusted Diane so much. Perhaps it was her age, or maybe it was her general sense of stability, or maybe that she'd suffered some losses of her own. But from the first time she'd met Diane, when her new neighbor had been concerned for Beverly's father's health, Beverly had sensed something safe and comforting about Diane.

Beverly patted the lighthouse. Not unlike her old friend Orlean Point Light. But despite that sense of a kindred connection, what would Diane think if she knew the whole truth about Beverly? What if that ruined everything? And just when Beverly had begun to feel a real sense of friendship with Shelley and Margaret as well. What if Jeff's presence in this town unraveled all of it?

Beverly couldn't bear to imagine what that would feel like. Especially after making her break from Augusta. What would she do if the sweet little life she'd been building in Marble Cove came tumbling down? Where would she go? Who would she turn to?

"God, help me!" She closed her eyes and prayed quietly. "Help me to find my way. Send Your light to show me what to do, where to go." With her eyes still tightly shut, she imagined God as not so different from a lighthouse—a functioning lighthouse. She imagined Him shining a long, bright beam before her, showing her which way to go, guiding her to safety. She imagined God illuminating her life... bringing her a sense of understanding...hope and peace.

And when she opened her eyes, she felt it too. A sense of peace and calm...and safety. God would protect her.

Now if only she could hold on to this when the storms began to rage. Because she had a feeling there was a storm moving steadily toward her.

★　　★　　★

All day long, Beverly tried to maintain that sense of calm that had filled her by the lighthouse. She focused on it while fixing lunch, making Father's favorite clam chowder. She reminded herself of it throughout her workday. She tried to hold on to that peace while helping her father get ready for bed. Not that he needed her help so much anymore. Perhaps it was more for her than him that she turned down his bed and set the glass of water and his reading glasses on his bedside table.

But as the minutes ticked stubbornly by, the calm feeling seemed to steadily fade. It seemed to be nearly gone as she went to her room to freshen up. And, seeing her reflection in the mirror as she gave her hair a quick brush, her sense of peace disintegrated. She stared at her image and shuddered. That woman in the mirror was nothing but a phony. And perhaps it wouldn't be long until everyone, even her father, found out.

She changed her shirt. Not to impress Jeff, but because she'd splattered it with bacon grease when she'd sautéed the onions for the clam chowder. She really didn't care what she looked like for this meeting—or even that she still smelled vaguely of onions and clams. In fact, as she pulled a black turtleneck over her head, she realized that she wanted to look plain tonight. She wouldn't freshen her lipstick or put on jewelry. She wanted to do nothing to give him the wrong impression.

She checked on Father to see that his light was turned off, and his even breathing suggested he was already sleeping soundly. His exercise of raking leaves had worn him out nicely. He had seemed happily tired as they'd chatted over their chowder tonight. And, in some ways, it was one of the sweeter times they'd shared a meal together. Beverly hoped that didn't mean it was going to be the last one...or that Jeff was going to pull the switch that would detonate her life.

No, she told herself as she put on her trench coat, she was being melodramatic. She slipped her cell phone and list of questions into her coat pocket. As well as some cash. There was no way she would allow Jeff Mackenzie to buy her anything—not even a cup of coffee, which she wouldn't touch anyway. It would simply be a prop to make it seem that there was a reason to meet up with him tonight. To drink coffee.

She slipped out of the house without turning on the porch light. Quietly locking the door behind her, she pulled up her collar against the damp fog that was already rolling in. Hard to believe it had been so sunny and clear today.

She felt conspicuous as she walked down Newport Avenue, but no neighbors popped out to greet her. No one even seemed to look out their windows. By the time she got to Main Street, which looked fairly deserted, she felt like she might be able to pull this mission off unobserved. But then she noticed Shelley's car parked in front of the Cove. Of course Shelley was baking tonight. Still, she reminded herself as she hurried across the street, Shelley would be back in the kitchen. She wouldn't observe Beverly going into Captain Calhoun's.

Taking in a deep breath, Beverly braced herself as she pushed open the heavy wooden door. The warm lights and pungent smell of seafood cooking greeted her as she stepped in. The restaurant portion of the business looked pretty sleepy, but the bar side sounded as if it was hopping. But Beverly knew that Captain Calhoun's lounge had a reputation all its own.

Although she tried not to show it, Beverly spotted Jeff Mackenzie almost instantly. Seated in a corner booth and looking strikingly attractive in a light blue chambray shirt, Jeff smiled brightly and waved. As she approached the table, he stood and greeted her, acting as if they were old friends and that meeting like this was the most natural thing in the world.

Beverly felt the eyes of the pretty waitress watching as Jeff reached out to shake her hand. For that reason, and many others, she barely shook it, awkwardly pulling her hand back too quickly.

"We're only serving the lounge menu now," the waitress told her, smiling at Jeff as she refilled his cup.

"That's okay. I only want coffee. Decaf, if you have it, please. And cream." As Beverly sat down, she wondered if the waitress had been taken in by Jeff's good looks and easy charm. Perhaps she was even feeling disappointed that Beverly had shown up.

"How are you?" he asked lightly.

"I'm doing well, thank you." Beverly loosened the belt of her trench coat but didn't remove it.

The waitress set a cup on the table, filled it with coffee that looked black as ink, and set a stainless steel pitcher of cream beside it. "Anything else?"

"No, thank you." Beverly gave her a stiff smile. Then, slowly inhaling, she willed herself to get and stay calm...steady... unruffled. Slipping her hand into her coat pocket, she felt for her cell phone, the slip of paper, the cash, and her house key. She would conduct this meeting as quickly as possible. Then leave.

"Marble Cove appears to be the kind of town that rolls up its streets at five o'clock," he said casually.

Nodding, she added cream and stirred without looking up. "It gets even quieter here in the wintertime."

"Charming."

She looked directly at him now, challenging him with her eyes to get on with it. However, it seemed that he wanted to play games first, because he simply proceeded to make meaningless conversation. First he inquired about Augusta and her job. Then he moved on to why she'd moved to Marble Cove, her father's health, and a plethora of other minutia.

Beverly played his game, tossing the ball right back at him as she asked similar trivial questions about his life, carefully keeping everything on the uppermost surface level. But for some reason, his answers seemed to slip right over her head, never fully lodging in her consciousness. Whether it was due to the stress or just a general lack of interest, she suddenly realized she didn't even recall where he'd said he was living these days, let alone what he was doing for a living. She knew he'd been quite well off the last time they'd met. Perhaps he was independently wealthy and didn't work at all. What difference did it make?

By the third time the waitress refilled her coffee cup, which despite her earlier resolve she'd managed to consume, partly out of nerves and partly as a distraction, Beverly knew she was in over her head. She also knew that the only way she was going to survive this evening would be to take charge.

"So why are you here?" She'd thrown down the gauntlet.

"At Captain Calhoun's?" He smiled mischievously. He obviously knew what she meant but was still intent on game playing. Perhaps she should simply excuse herself and get out of here.

Beverly glanced over to where the waitress was noisily counting out the till. She'd already informed them that her shift was ending but that they were welcome to remain since the bar would be open for a couple more hours. And Jeff had insisted on paying the bill and giving her a generous tip. It seemed almost as if he did it to irk her. Beverly told herself it didn't matter—just forget about it. She didn't have a watch on, but she knew it had to be late.

"I think you know what I mean," Beverly said tersely. "Why are you here *in Marble Cove*? And why do you keep calling me?"

"Like I said, I'm doing research."

"On the lighthouse?" Her voice was coated with skepticism.

"Yes." He smiled again.

Did he think that flashy Colgate smile was his golden key? Maybe it had worked for him with others, but Beverly was not going to be taken in. Not this time!

Fighting back rage and frustration, Beverly reached into her pocket. She pulled out her rumpled list of questions and she held them out of sight in her lap. Time to pepper him. If he wasn't going to disclose why he had invited her here, she would at least try to extract some information regarding the lighthouse.

However, her questions seemed less pertinent than they had earlier. And when she asked them, they didn't seem to come out quite right. She reminded herself of a bumbling schoolgirl. However, Jeff was more forthcoming in his answers about the lighthouse than she'd expected. And she was surprised to discover that he'd actually done some real research on the history of Orlean Point Light. He even shared some tidbits of information with her. Some things she already knew. Some she did not.

And, although she couldn't hide her mutual interest in the lighthouse, she tried to hold her cards close to her chest. She had no intention of letting him in on the things that she and her friends had recently uncovered. The bottom line was she did not trust him.

"The only thing I don't understand about your 'research,'" she said finally, "is the real reason you're doing it."

"The reason...?" His mouth twisted to one side like he was thinking. "Well, I just happen to find this lighthouse very interesting."

"Interesting? In what way?" She watched him closely now, trying to determine his motives.

He tapped the cheap metal spoon like a drumstick against the worn wooden tabletop. "Historically," he finally said. A defiant look crossed his face.

"Historically?" She waited, still studying him.

With a firm mouth, he nodded.

"Is it something you're studying academically, then? Or is this a professional interest?"

His brow creased and he set the spoon down. "Neither."

Now she was perplexed. What other explanation could there be? "So would you say it's just a personal interest in the lighthouse?"

He barely nodded. She could tell he was holding something back now. But why? What could he possibly know about the lighthouse that should be so important as to be kept secret? It made no sense. And, naturally, that made her even more suspicious. Really, why was she here with him? What was the point?

"It's late," she said suddenly. "I need to go home. I shouldn't have left my father alone this long." She stood and started to leave, but he stood and moved right with her, opening the door, walking her outside, dogging her heels as she crossed the street.

And now he started to talk quickly, as if he realized this was his last chance, and he wanted to convince her that he was legit and only wanted to befriend her and that she could trust him. His words rushed over her, getting lost in the foggy night air. She just wanted to get away from him.

"Please," he begged her, "I didn't mean for it to go like this tonight. But when I saw you, I was taken aback. And then I could see it in your eyes. You were already judging me, and that made me mad. And, well, I just acted like a jerk. I'm sorry. Please, can we try again?"

"Try what?"

"To talk. Like two rational adults. Just talk, Anna."

She glared at him.

"I mean 'Beverly.'" He leaned his head back and exhaled sharply. "Sorry."

"Why should we talk?" She felt so tired now, like getting the words out took more energy than she had left. "What difference would it make? What's done is done. Let's just let it go and move on."

"I know there's a reason we met again," he insisted. "Couldn't you sense it? That night at the lighthouse?"

She looked into his eyes and wished she could see what was underneath all this. But all she saw was his handsome veneer, looking even more mysterious in the misty lamplight. "I have to go." She turned and hurried away.

A part of her wondered if she was just being melodramatic with her hasty exit. It wasn't as if he was dangerous. More likely, she was simply being practical. She'd always been a self-preservationist at heart. Even more so after Will had died.

Still, as she walked down Newport Avenue, she felt a sense of dismay. She wished she could replay more of their conversation, but it felt so fragmented and confused. There had been a few moments when she had wanted to trust him. But she'd kept her guard up.

For a while, she had actually started to believe that Jeff Mackenzie's only purpose for being in Marble Cove was to research the lighthouse and that it was purely a coincidence that they'd bumped into each other that night. She'd been almost convinced of this.

Almost.

CHAPTER SEVENTEEN

As a teen, Shelley had dreamed of a glitzy, lime-lit show-biz career. It had all started out when she got the lead role in their high school musical as a sophomore. Bolstered by this achievement, she'd gained the confidence to try out for the Junior Miss pageant. When the big night came, she'd blown the talent competition by forgetting the words to "Somewhere Over the Rainbow," a song she'd known by heart since childhood. There went her chances for a life of fame and fortune.

Of course, when she had fallen in love with Dan, those shallow ideas of running off to Hollywood had evaporated faster than an August morning fog. And, really, being a wife and a mom had been her biggest dream. But sometimes she wondered about what might've been. What if she had met Dan later in life...after she'd had a chance to chase some other dreams first?

These were the kinds of things she ruminated on as she measured and mixed, baking her goodies late into the night in the Cove's kitchen. Fortunately, she had the place to herself tonight. For that reason she'd brought some of her own CDs to play. The jazz music piped throughout the coffee shop was okay sometimes, but she was really a country music fan at heart. And with no one to hear her, she belted out some songs right along with Shania Twain and Taylor Swift. Occasionally she would hold the wooden spoon like a mike and strut and dance as she checked on the oven or rinsed a bowl.

It was hard to admit, especially since these late nights wore her out, but baking in the coffeehouse kitchen, especially when she was here by herself, was becoming her favorite time of day. It was very fulfilling to bake undistracted, checking on her muffins, cookies, pies and cakes before they were overdone. Seeing these goodies lined up, browned and pretty, cooling on racks, smelling the spicy-sweet aromas, was its own reward.

Even the cleanup time was a treat. She loved being able to set everything back to order, leaving the stainless steel countertops gleaming. The whole process was surprisingly satisfying. And, she reminded herself as she turned off the lights, it was helping her family buy groceries and make house payments.

Balancing a basket of goodies to take home with her, she dug in her jacket pocket for the front door key, then paused to look outside. She was surprised to see a couple across the street. It was past midnight on a Thursday, so it was unusual to see anyone out. She paused, unsure she wanted to disturb them. They looked romantic standing there in the fog, illuminated by the streetlight, almost like a scene from *Casablanca*. The woman was even wearing a trench coat.

Well, it was fine for them to enjoy this romantic interlude, but Shelley was sleepy, and her bed was calling. She started to open the big glass door, but the woman turned slightly, and Shelley blinked in surprise and wondered if her eyes were betraying her. Because, as strange as it seemed, that woman looked just like Beverly. In fact, Shelley knew that it was indeed Beverly!

Even more shocking was that the man with Beverly was the same handsome stranger they'd met in the lighthouse several weeks ago. That Jeff Mackenzie. But Beverly had gone to such great lengths to play down this guy, acting as if their odd meeting was simply a fluke. And yet here she was looking at him in a way that suggested something more than just a casual acquaintance.

They didn't kiss or touch or anything that could be misconstrued as romance, but something in their demeanor and posture suggested intimacy. Or else it was just Shelley's overactive imagination running away with her again. Probably fueled by singing along to those corny country love songs tonight. She should probably go back to listening to jazz.

She quietly stepped out and silently locked the door. But by the time she turned around, the couple had parted. Beverly was headed on foot toward Newport Avenue, and Jeff was going in the opposite direction.

Shelley frowned at her car parked in front of the coffeehouse. Why hadn't she just walked tonight? Then she could have jogged and caught up with Beverly. Shelley would've acted perfectly natural as she questioned Beverly on their way home. By the time they got there, she would've known everything.

But Dan had insisted she drive to work tonight. For whatever reason, and despite her reminder that gas was not cheap these days, he always seemed overly worried about her safety. And now it was too late to do anything about it. She couldn't even call out and offer Beverly a ride because she was well out of sight. Oh well, knowing Beverly, she probably would've been evasive anyway. Beverly could be a very private person.

Shelley got into her car and started the engine. Suddenly she felt weary to the bone. Like she could lean her head into the steering wheel and fall fast asleep and not wake up until morning. Perhaps the police would find her snoozing here.

Be strong, she told herself as she drove down the quiet street, *and don't let on that you're so tired.* It was weird...even though she enjoyed her time at the Cove, she had no idea how she would keep up this pace. Baking was just one part of the business. There was also the online orders and learning to use things like PayPal, plus marketing and bookkeeping and shopping...and on top of all that she still needed to be a mom and wife? What if she failed or fell apart? She couldn't help anyone if she had a nervous breakdown or had to be hospitalized for exhaustion.

As troubling as her fears were, she also knew they would remain her secret. If Dan had any idea how exhausted she was he'd probably put his foot down—hard. But right now they needed this extra income. For the sake of her family, she had to make it work. Besides, this was Shelley's first real business—and she was determined to make it succeed.

As she tiptoed into the house and locked the door behind her, she was dismayed to see that, besides leaving all the lights on, Dan hadn't picked up a single thing. The house looked even messier than when she'd left. She knew she shouldn't be irritated, especially since it was obvious from the toys spread out all over the place that he and the kids had enjoyed a good time together.

Stuffed animals were lined up on the furnishings like a zoo. And Aiden's train set was set up, along with what looked like hundreds of Legos and blocks that had been used to create buildings alongside the tracks.

She picked up a pacifier and an empty baby bottle and carried them to the kitchen, where the dirty dinner dishes were still on the table. She glanced at the stove. He'd put the leftovers away this time. That was something. She rinsed the pacifier and dropped the bottle in the sink, and for a brief instant she even considered cleaning up the messy kitchen. It would be so pleasant to wake up to some order in the morning. But her feet ached, and it felt like someone had shackled lead weights around her ankles. Chaos Central would have to wait.

As she brushed her teeth, she wondered if she would ever spot the light at the end of this tunnel. Would life ever slow down or become fun? Would she and Dan ever be able to catch up financially?

She dropped her toothbrush into the cracked ceramic lighthouse toothbrush holder and thought about Beverly and Jeff. How romantic they'd looked tonight. A quiet little longing rustled inside of her—the hint of romance, adventure, and perhaps something else. Maybe it was that pure sense of freedom. What would it feel like to be that free? To be out at night without feeling exhausted or guilty, enjoying a sweet interlude with the one she loved? She sighed and just shook her head. What was wrong with her?

Dan made a sleepy groan as she climbed into bed. Feeling guilty for her discontented musings, she reached over and stroked his head. Really, she was happy. She loved Dan. She loved her kids. She was simply tired. Very, very tired.

★   ★   ★

By morning, Shelley had almost completely forgotten last night's discontentment. By morning, she was thankful to be in her own home, despite the mess, doing her usual thing with her kids.

Shortly before noon, Shelley enticed Aiden out for a walk. With Emma in the stroller and Prize leashed up, the four of them set out to walk the neighborhood. Shelley's secret mission was to run into Beverly and subtly inquire about last night's liaison. Unfortunately, Beverly was nowhere to be seen. Even Mr. Wheeland seemed to be lying low. Finally, knowing that the kids were hungry for lunch and that nap time was nigh, Shelley herded them all back toward home.

"Shelley!" It was Diane. She crossed the street from her house and joined them. "I was just looking for you. Your upside-down cake was a hit. Thank you again for making it."

With Prize at his heels, Aiden ran up and hugged Diane's legs and began jabbering at her about ideas he had for his Halloween costume.

Shelley tugged Prize's leash a little closer to her, then bent down to put Emma's pacifier back in. She was already beyond fussy, and, with the stroller stopped, she could be close to pulling a full-blown fit. "Glad it worked for you," she said to Diane. "What's up?"

"I'm having a little dinner party tomorrow night."

Shelley perked up. "A dinner party?"

"Yes, just some of the neighbors and, uh, a friend of mine from college."

"Oh?" Shelley gave Diane a sly grin. "A *guy* friend?"

Diane laughed. "No. A woman friend. Anyway, I was hoping you and Dan could join us." Diane glanced down at the kids. "And the children too if you like, although it's not until seven thirty."

"That's a little late for them." Shelley jiggled the stroller.

"I mentioned this to Margaret, and she suggested that if the kids were in bed, or nearly, perhaps Adelaide could sit with them."

Shelley hesitated. "I don't know about that." It wasn't that she didn't trust Adelaide—she absolutely did. It was simply that she didn't know. Although Adelaide was a perfect mother's helper, Shelley had never left her alone with the kids. Had never intended to.

"Yes, I wasn't sure if you'd be comfortable with that or not. Although I did mention to Margaret that I'll bet your baby monitor might reach to my house." Diane smiled knowingly. "And you can actually see your house from my front window. Perhaps if Emma was already asleep. And if Aiden was nearly ready for bed, or had a good DVD to watch…"

"Let me think about it," Shelley told her. "And let me ask Dan." She brightened. "I'd love to come, Diane. Let me get back to you."

"Great!"

Shelley felt hopeful as she rounded up her little group and herded them back to her house. Going to a grown-up party on Saturday night could be fun. Also, she remembered, Aiden had Benjamin's birthday party on Saturday, so the chances of his being worn out that night were good. Plus, if he had one of his favorite movies to watch, and if Emma was asleep…maybe it would work.

But she did still need to run it all by Dan first. If he had reservations about Adelaide being on her own here, Shelley would acquiesce, although she knew they couldn't afford a real sitter. Adelaide always refused pay, although Shelley sometimes exchanged baking lessons with her.

But perhaps Dan's mother wouldn't mind sitting with her grandchildren. Although she'd never sat with them before—not here in the house. Sometimes Dan and Shelley dropped them off there, but that was always complicated, and often Dan's mom would complain that Shelley had forgotten something or else they stayed out too late. As a result, they left them there less and less. But maybe Frances would be feeling generous.

Shelley laughed wryly as she sliced an apple to go with the kids' lunch. That was highly unlikely. Even if Frances did agree, there would be a price to pay. For starters, Shelley would receive an unwanted critique of her housekeeping and parenting skills. Even if Shelley scoured her house from top to bottom and if the kids were perfect, which never happened, Dan's mom would find some reason to complain. No, it would be better to just spend the evening at home. That was...unless Adelaide was really up to this.

By the time Dan got home, after a full day of working down in the shipping yard, he was tired and, judging by his expression, on the verge of grouchy. But when she greeted him with an icy soda and a warm smile, he seemed to lighten up. She'd fixed meat loaf and mashed potatoes— his favorites—and she already had the kids fed and in their pajamas, and she had even taken a few minutes to spruce herself up. So far, so good.

"Hey, are you just trying to show me up?" he asked as he kicked off his boots and sank into his favorite chair. He gave her a sheepish smile. "Sorry about the mess last night. Aiden and I were building a railroad town."

"That's okay," she said. "That's nice you guys had fun."

He looked slightly suspicious as he sipped his soda. "So what's up? It's not our anniversary, is it?"

She playfully punched his shoulder. "No. If it was our anniversary you'd be in trouble."

"Right." He studied her closely. "So, seriously, Shell, what's up?"

So she told him about Diane's dinner party and the idea for Adelaide to sit with the kids. At first he frowned. But then she explained about how she'd have them ready for bed and how they'd use the baby monitor and everything. He agreed to think about it.

Shelley got Emma down for bed and Aiden occupied with a movie so that she and Dan could sit together, just the two of them. This was part of her plan.

"Wow." He looked around the tidy kitchen and then to the candles glowing on the table. "I feel like I'm in someone else's house."

"I decided we need a little grown-up time," she told him. "Also, this is an experiment. I figured if this went smoothly tonight, it might go smoothly again tomorrow night." Then she told him about Aiden's big day tomorrow and how she would try to wear Emma out.

Finally, as she was serving dessert—hefty pieces of French apple pie à la mode—Dan gave in. "I'm convinced, Shell. Let's give Adelaide a try tomorrow night. We'll just have to make sure we're all set like we are tonight."

Shelley leaned down and kissed him on the cheek. "You have no idea how much hope this gives me." But more than just hopeful, Shelley felt confident. Maybe she was getting a handle on this thing called motherhood. Maybe life was going to get better.

CHAPTER EIGHTEEN

After a quick run to the grocery store, Diane had just pulled into her driveway when she saw someone hurrying down the sidewalk toward her. It was already dark out and well past the dinner hour, but it looked like Beverly coming toward her. She was dressed in jeans and a sweatshirt, and she was waving as if something was amiss. Diane hurried to get out of her car. "What's wrong?" she asked as she went to meet Beverly.

"Oh, Diane." Beverly looked as if she'd been crying.

"Is it your father?" Suddenly Diane imagined Mr. Wheeland unconscious…perhaps even dead. "What happened?"

"No, no. Father is fine. It's me." Beverly pulled a tissue out of her pocket and blew her nose. "I know it's late. But do you have time to talk?"

"Sure." Diane reached in the car for her purse and her bag of groceries. "Come inside."

Diane led Beverly into the house, greeted Rocky, then sent him out into the backyard. "Sit down, Beverly." Diane pointed to the living room. "Can I get you something? Tea? Water?"

"Water. *Please*." Beverly slumped onto the sofa like a rag doll. "I feel like I'm falling apart."

Diane went into the kitchen, getting them both a glass of water as well as a box of tissues, and saying a silent prayer for Beverly, she returned and handed her the water, setting the tissue box nearby. "Everyone falls apart sometimes," Diane calmly told her. "Feel free." Diane sat down across from her and waited.

"I probably look like a crazy woman." Beverly took a long sip of water. "I was actually trying to talk to my father about it just now. But I could tell he was feeling stressed, and I realized I couldn't say too much. You see, it was always my mother that I talked to about...about these sorts of things. But by the time I could talk about this, she was already gone."

"I'm good at keeping confidences, Beverly." Diane had known for months that something was bothering Beverly. Even more so in the last few weeks. She had always hoped that Beverly would come to her.

"I sensed that." Beverly reached for a tissue.

"And as far as falling apart, well, I've found that sometimes it's in the falling apart that we're put back together again." Diane gave her a wistful smile.

"I don't know." Beverly sniffed. "Sometimes I feel like if I let myself go...if I really give in to it...that everything will just spin apart."

"Maybe it will." Diane took a sip from her own water glass. "For a bit anyway. But then maybe it will fall into place."

"Do you really think so?" Beverly looked hopeful.

Diane shrugged. "It's hard to say. But consider the alternative. I mean, if you keep holding it all inside of you... where will that get you?"

Beverly pressed her lips together, sadly shaking her head. "I'm afraid if I keep holding it in...I'll probably just go to pieces anyway. It seems that's—that's what's happening." She started to cry again.

"Just take your time," Diane spoke in a soothing tone. "Take a couple of slow, deep breaths. There's no hurry."

Beverly did as told, and eventually she began to calm down. "Do you remember when you asked about my husband...about Will?"

"I vaguely remember." Diane tried to think back. "It was months ago. Back when we first met."

"Yes." Beverly blew her nose. "You said something back then, and I suppose you hit a nerve. As usual, I tried to brush you off."

Diane gave a meek smile. "Well, you know me. I'm a bit on the nosy side. It's the reporter in me. Inquiring minds, you know?"

"Well, you were absolutely right. You nailed it, Diane. I do *not* like talking about him. I never have."

"But sometimes it helps to talk about things...things that make us uncomfortable. I know it helped me a lot to talk about Eric and his death. It was part of the grieving process for me."

Beverly's eyes grew dark. "Maybe for some people. But I'm not sure if it can help me."

"But you seem so unhappy."

"I am unhappy. If I could have my way, I would never talk to anyone about Will...or how he died. I wanted to believe that the past is the past. Buried and gone. Just like Will. I wanted to be done with it."

"But you're not done, are you?" Diane studied her, trying to figure out what was really going on. This seemed to be something more than just grief.

"No...not done." Beverly twisted a tissue between her fingers. "I don't even know where to begin."

"How about the beginning?"

Beverly slowly nodded. "Well, the truth is that our marriage was never what I'd call a good one, Diane. Not like yours and Eric's. Oh, I tried to convince myself it was good, at least early on. I honestly felt I was lucky to get him. Will Parker was this successful architect, respected in the city, charming, distinguished, older and, I had supposed, wiser. I know my mother had questions about him, but she kept her concerns to herself. At first, anyway."

"As a mother, I can understand that."

"You see, it was Will's third marriage, and he had two nearly grown children. They're young adults now. And I suppose I should've seen it as a red flag when Will had me sign a prenuptial agreement. But at the time I felt blindsided."

"A prenuptial agreement...?" Diane tried to imagine how she would've felt if Eric had suggested such a thing.

"Yes. It was his first wife's suggestion. I thought it was a little odd that she would interfere, but, like I said, I felt blindsided and slightly humiliated. Anyway, I didn't question it. After all, I was in my early thirties at the time, in a good career. I was strong and independent. But early on in the marriage…I knew we had problems." She paused to take a sip of water.

Diane waited.

"This is hard to say. I've never told anyone. But I'm fairly certain Will wasn't faithful to me during our marriage." She shook her head. "Then…something happened yesterday. It was like a blast from the past, and it shook me up. It triggered so many memories that I couldn't even sleep last night. So all day long, I thought I would tell my father everything. I knew he'd be shocked, but it seemed the best thing."

Diane nodded.

"So after dinner, we settled down in the den, and I was about to just spill the whole ugly story. But seeing him, happily sitting there by the fire—and you know, he's feeling so much better now, and his memory is improving. And suddenly I realized I would be heaping so much stress on him. What if it was more than he could handle?"

"That could be a concern." Diane knew that despite Mr. Wheeland's progress, he was still relatively frail.

"My parents' marriage was so happy and normal. And I know how Father wanted the same for me. It would be so hard on him to know the truth. I think it's actually easier for him to see me as a widow than as someone who'd been miserable in her marriage."

"I can understand that."

Beverly began to cry again. "Despite all that I just told you and what I want to say, I really did love Will, Diane. I truly did."

"Of course you did."

"And I never, never wished any harm to come to him." She looked at Diane with sad eyes. "Do you think it's possible for a person to be a jinx?"

"A jinx?"

"You know, like bad karma or just plain unlucky. Sometimes I feel like I'm cursed, like everyone I love or try to become close to ends up suffering. Even now, I feel guilty for pouring my problems out on you. What if I'm bringing bad luck into your life?"

"Oh, don't worry about that, Beverly. I'm not the least bit concerned."

"Maybe you should be." She choked back a sob. "I had a boyfriend in high school...he broke his neck in a skiing accident. Then I had another boyfriend, about ten years later, who got MS. And then, after Will, my mother died. And even with my father...and his diabetes and then those ministrokes... I think I brought my bad luck onto my father."

"That's ridiculous, Beverly. You've been nothing but good for him. And your father loves you dearly. Honestly, I can't imagine how you could bring him anything but joy."

Beverly pulled out another tissue, wiping her fresh tears. "But isn't it strange? The way everyone around me seems to suffer? I know I'm not imagining these things."

"Suffering is everywhere," Diane said. "But so is happiness. We have to take the bad with the good, the rain with the sunshine. Sometimes it seems unbalanced, but I do believe that eventually the positive overcomes the negative. It's been true in my life."

"But there's more to my story, Diane." Beverly's voice grew quiet. "You see, Will was on medication. A very serious medication. For seizures. Somehow it became my job to remind him to take his pills. Maybe I was codependent, or he was in denial. But it was an unhealthy situation."

Diane felt somewhat lost but tried not to show it.

"Whatever it was, our relationship seemed to be slowly unraveling. Or disintegrating. Will took me for granted. He acted like an irresponsible adolescent and treated me like I was his paid caregiver. I began to resent that role. Sometimes it felt like he needed a nursemaid more than a wife."

"Unfortunately, a lot of marriages fall into that pattern. Some women are natural caregivers. Some men take advantage. I even think some women unconsciously seek out men who will need them more as mother than wife."

"I suppose. And I honestly think I wouldn't have minded playing the caregiver if I'd felt confident in Will's fidelity. Or if he'd treated me as an equal. Instead, I felt used and unappreciated."

"No one could blame you for that, Beverly."

Beverly pressed her lips together, staring into the darkened fireplace as if she was considering her next words. "So one day Will and I were supposed to go boating with one of his clients. But that morning, Will and I got into a huge fight, and I didn't want to go with him. I don't even remember what the fight was about, but Will made a big fuss. He laid a guilt trip on me, insisting that I come." She sadly shook her head. "I honestly think he only wanted to bring me along as eye-candy, if you know what I mean."

"That had to be hard." Diane had no idea where this story was going, but she could tell it was serious—life-and-death serious. She sipped her water, waiting for Beverly to continue.

"It *was* hard. But I gave in and went with him. And it turned out that..." She swallowed. "It turned out that Will's client was a great guy." She looked directly at Diane now. "Jeff Mackenzie was much closer to my age than my husband. He was extremely attractive. He was wealthy and had a big, beautiful boat. I'm ashamed to say it, but the two of us really hit it off."

Diane felt a slight shock run through her. "Jeff Mackenzie? The stranger at the lighthouse?"

Beverly nodded.

"You said you two had met before."

"We had barely met, Diane. We only knew each other for a few hours. A few horrible hours that I wish had never happened."

"Oh." Diane tried not to register her surprise. All the while, almost against her will, her fertile imagination was supplying storylines for what happened.

"Looking back," Beverly said, "I realize I probably acted like a little fool. I'm sure I simply ate up the attention Jeff gave me. Partly because I wasn't used to it…" She sighed. "And partly to get back at Will."

The room got very quiet. Diane waited for Beverly to continue. Years of writing for the newspaper had taught Diane when it was time to probe deeper and when it was time to remain silent and simply let someone tell her story.

"It was a gorgeous day. Blue sky and sunshine. Will decided to go swimming, and he asked me to go with him. But I was still feeling out of sorts, and I told him I didn't want to swim. So Will went in by himself. I stayed onboard the boat with Jeff, just enjoying his company and totally ignoring my husband. Acting like a spoiled brat." Beverly began to cry again. "The next thing I knew—" Her voice choked. "We saw Will facedown in the water. He was lifeless."

"Oh dear!" Diane just shook her head. "I'm so sorry, Beverly. How horrible!"

"We tried to resuscitate him… We called 911…but it was too late. He never regained consciousness."

"That must have been awful."

Beverly nodded and blew her nose. "What I never told anyone, not Jeff, not the paramedics, no one…was that Will was an *excellent* swimmer. He never should've drowned like that."

"Why then? What happened?"

"He hadn't taken his seizure medicine that morning. In the heat of our argument at home, I had completely forgotten to remind him."

"Oh…" Diane set down her water glass as the implication sunk in. "And you feel guilty for that."

"Of course I do. Whether it was right for him to make me do that or not, it's a job I had been doing. And I forgot! Wouldn't you feel guilty?"

Diane shrugged. "I don't know... I mean, I wasn't in your shoes. And I can't begin to imagine how you must've felt that day, to be treated like that by your husband, to feel objectified, to be so unsettled in your marriage. It must've been extremely stressful. And stress makes us do strange things. It can impair your memory or your reasoning skills. And I can see you're stressed about it even now."

"I am."

Diane was thinking hard, trying to come up with the right things to say, but everything about Beverly's experience was so foreign to her, so totally different from Diane's own personal loss, that she didn't know how to encourage or advise this young woman.

"So now I feel like a hypocrite," Beverly continued. "Whenever people hear that I'm a widow, they show me sympathy—sympathy I don't deserve. And that makes me—"

"Wait a minute." Diane held up a hand. "That's where you're wrong, Beverly. You *do* deserve their sympathy. Probably more than people realize. Because, although the loss of my husband was excruciating—and trust me, it was very painful—I do have the comfort of knowing that he loved me, *truly loved me*, and I know that I loved him. I still do. And although our marriage wasn't perfect—but whose is?— it was very, very good. And that is a huge comfort to me."

"He must've been a wonderful man."

"He was." Diane nodded. "But you see, Beverly, my point is that *you* didn't get left with that kind of comfort, did you?"

She shook her head.

"And that makes me feel very sad." Diane reached for a tissue for herself. "You have my deepest sympathy, Beverly. I am so sorry that Will wasn't the kind of man that allowed you to mourn your loss in the way that I do for Eric. Does that make sense to you?"

Beverly's eyes lit up ever so slightly. "It does make sense."

"It sounds to me like Will tortured you a bit in life. But it's up to you as to whether he continues torturing you in death. You've punished yourself enough, Beverly. I think it's time you let go of your guilt. You need to stop beating yourself up for something you had no control over."

"Do you really believe that?" Beverly looked astonished. "You don't think that I should be blamed for my husband's death?"

"Of course not. He was a grown man, Beverly. He forgot to take his medicine. He chose to go swimming. What happened just happened. It was not your fault."

Beverly started to cry even harder, and Diane wondered if nothing she'd just said had soaked in. She went over and sat on the couch, slipping an arm around Beverly's shoulders. "Really, sweetie, if your mother were here, I know she would agree with me." Diane pushed a damp strand of dark hair away from Beverly's face. "This is exactly what I would tell my own daughter if she just told me what you said. Can't you trust me?"

Beverly looked at her with misty eyes. "I do trust you, Diane. I—I'm sorry to keep crying. But I...I think these are tears of relief." Beverly threw her arms around Diane. "I feel like a huge burden has been lifted."

They sat there together for a moment, and Diane rubbed her back. She could feel Beverly's tension seeping away with every tear.

"You mentioned something earlier," Diane began, "something that happened yesterday that triggered your memories. I'm just curious what it was."

Beverly got an uneasy look. "Oh yes, I nearly forgot about that part."

"What happened?"

"Jeff Mackenzie."

"Is he back in town?"

She nodded. "Ever since that night at the lighthouse. He'd been calling me to meet with him. I was trying to ignore him, but he got our home phone number and actually spoke to Father."

"Oh dear. Did he upset your dad?"

"Not that I know of. But I was worried he might. So I agreed to meet with him last night."

Diane felt her eyes widen. "How did that go?"

"I don't really know." Beverly looked confused.

"What did you talk about?"

She shrugged now. "I think I was in partial shock, Diane. I sort of blanked out the first part of our conversation. But, really, it was mostly small talk. Then we talked about the lighthouse."

"The lighthouse?"

"Yes. I wanted to know why Jeff was here in Marble Cove. He said he'd come to research the lighthouse."

"And it's just a coincidence that you were here?"

"He claims that." She frowned. "But I'm not so sure. Maybe it was just my imagination, but I got the feeling there was something more going on."

"Such as?"

"Well, what if he was here to blackmail me?"

The fiction part of Diane's mind had already come up with that idea as well. "How would he blackmail you? Could he?"

Beverly held up her hands. "I don't even know. To be honest, it sounds silly to say that out loud. I suppose it was just my paranoia talking...from all this guilt I've been carrying."

"You need to let that guilt go, Beverly."

She just sighed.

"And maybe Jeff Mackenzie really is here only to research the lighthouse. We had heard that someone had been doing some investigations, and we found him there that night. It's possible that it's simply a coincidence that he bumped into you, Beverly." Diane turned to face Beverly directly. "You have to tell me: why did he call you 'Anna'?"

Beverly gave her a wistful smile. "That's my name, Diane. I used to go by 'Anna.' Back before all this happened. Back before the day Will drowned. After that...I changed my name. I decided to go by my middle name. I've been Beverly ever since. I don't know why I felt such a need to change that too. Maybe it's because so much had changed...I didn't want anyone to know about who I used to be. Or who I felt like I was. It was my secret."

"But doesn't it feel good to tell someone?"

She nodded. "I didn't think it would, but you were right. Thanks for listening."

"And, do you know what's amazing? It's as if the lighthouse brought Jeff to you, Beverly. Did you think of that? If it's really true that he's here to research Orlean Point Light, and we have no real reason to doubt that, then it drew him here—where you live now. It's why we all ran out there that night, to find out who he was and why he was interested in the lighthouse. Remember?"

"That's true."

"As strange as it sounds, it's as if the lighthouse is helping you to heal this old wound, Beverly. This is a part of your life that you need to make peace with, and it's as if the lighthouse is giving you the chance."

Beverly looked just as stunned by this realization as Diane felt. Was it possible that the lighthouse not only played a role in saving the life of a drowning swimmer caught in the riptide and a wounded dog caught in the tidal pools, but a woman who'd been trapped in the past as well? What kind of lighthouse was it?

CHAPTER NINETEEN

After hearing of Barbara's disturbing goal to transform Orlean Point Light into a bed-and-breakfast, Diane decided that some kind of intervention was necessary. And so, on the morning before her dinner party, she gathered her friends for a quick meeting over coffee and blueberry scones, compliments of Shelley, to give them a heads-up about Barbara's activities during the past few days.

"At first I thought she couldn't be serious," Diane told them. "To honestly think she could purchase the lighthouse! Not to mention turn it into a bed-and-breakfast. But she's a very determined person. Already she has the mayor and several other influential citizens listening to her."

"You've got to be kidding!" Shelley was outraged. "She can't come in here and just buy our lighthouse. I don't care how rich she is. She can't have our lighthouse. Not without a fight."

"I don't want to fight," Diane admitted. "I mostly just hoped that we could talk some sense into her."

"Or tar and feather her and run her out on a rail," Shelley declared. Then she giggled. "Sorry. Just kidding. But that's our lighthouse, girls. We have to protect it."

Even their normally calm Margaret seemed fit to be tied as well. "If Barbara thinks this town will sit idly by while she comes in and tries to take over our lighthouse, she will have to think again."

"That's right," Beverly said. "We Mainers don't like outsiders pushing us around."

★   ★   ★   ★

Shelley felt like she was almost keeping up today. For starters, she had Benjamin's birthday party with which to lure Aiden into his best behavior. He'd already eaten all his breakfast, gotten dressed, straightened his room, and taken Prize out to the backyard to play during her coffee get-together with her friends. At this rate, she'd be sitting pretty by the time she dropped Aiden off at the birthday party.

Her plan after that was to come home and put Emma down for a nap. She would use the nap time to take a long, spalike shower, do her hair, and get everything ready for Adelaide's arrival later on this evening. She'd pick Aiden up at three, and, if the good weather held out, she'd take the kids to walk and play on the beach—something guaranteed to thoroughly wear them out. By the time Adelaide arrived at seven, Emma would be in bed, and Aiden would be tired and in his jammies and ready to watch his favorite DVD.

She and Dan would stick around for a while to ensure the plan was going well. And then, with baby monitor in hand, they would slip out and across the street where they would enjoy a night out with adults! It seemed almost too good to be true.

So when her mother-in-law showed up at their door at noon, just as Shelley was giving the kids lunch, she was still in fairly good spirits. "Hello, Frances," she opened the door wide. "We're just having lunch. Care to join us?"

"Oh no, dear. I don't have time for that. I just stopped by to ask you another favor."

"Oh?" Shelley led her back to the kitchen.

"Yes, I'm just so swamped with the church harvest party." She let out a weary sigh as she sat down on one of the kitchen chairs. "I wish I'd never agreed to help. But there's no backing out of it now. Anyway, since you're baking Ralph's birthday cake, I wondered if you could coordinate a few other things too."

"Other things?" Shelley spooned some soup into Emma's mouth.

Frances waved her hand. "Not too many other things. But since you're baking the cake, I thought you could pick out the plates and napkins and some decorations and whatnot. Naturally, I'll give you a budget. But if you could just make sure that it all comes together nicely, you know, make it look like something Ralph would like..." She laughed. "Whatever that might be. Well, I'd greatly appreciate it."

"Oh." Shelley didn't know what to say. Did Frances really expect her to do all this? Did she actually trust Shelley with so much? "I'm surprised you didn't ask Vera to help." Shelley knew that Frances usually relied on her oldest daughter for things like this.

"Well, Vera is so busy with her new job."

"Right..." Shelley put some more apple slices on Aiden's plate.

"But if this is expecting too much from you..." Frances reached for her purse. "I suppose I could just—"

"No, no," Shelley said quickly. "I can do this. It's no problem."

Frances smiled and opened her purse, removing a piece of paper. "I already made you out a check in the hopes you'd do this. I think it should cover the expenses." She handed it to her.

Shelley looked at the check and tried not to show her disappointment. It seemed a little skimpy. "Did you say you planned on having fifty guests?"

"That's right." Frances stood, closing her purse with a loud snap. "I think that should be plenty as long as you can stay on a budget." She smiled. "I remember when I threw a golden anniversary party for Ralph's grandparents. There were more than a hundred guests, and I spent about a third of that. So you should be fine."

Shelley wanted to ask how long ago that had been. In the Dark Ages? Instead she promised to do her best, and she saw Frances to the door.

"Is it time for the birthday party?" Aiden asked eagerly.

Shelley glanced at the clock, then told him he needed to wash his face and change his shirt. "And then we still have to wrap Benjamin's present."

Of course, this resulted in a conversation about why Aiden couldn't just keep the birthday present for himself. She explained that it wasn't his birthday. Finally, feeling tired and harried but still happily anticipating the quiet afternoon ahead, she loaded the kids into the car and drove over to the Bancrofts'. Maybe she'd get lucky and Dan would come home early from working with Allan and offer to pick Aiden up for her.

"Here you go." Shelley smiled at Maddie as she handed over her son. "I'll see you in—"

"Wait." Maddie put her hand on Shelley's arm. "You can't go yet."

"Huh?"

Maddie took Shelley aside as another mom came to the door. "Howdy, partners," Maddie said cheerfully to them. The little boy had on a cowboy hat and western shirt and chaps and boots and even six-shooters in his holsters.

Maddie whispered in Shelley's ear, "Aiden was supposed to dress like a cowboy, remember?"

Shelley put her hand over her mouth. "I totally forgot."

"Mom," Aiden began in a whiny voice.

"Well, maybe I can help," Maddie said quickly. "Bring Aiden to the boys' room and—"

"But Emma's in the car."

"Then bring her in. You meet me in their room, and we'll see what we can put together. Now hurry."

Feeling like an incompetent mother, Shelley ran back to get Emma. By now Aiden knew exactly what was up and was on the verge of tears. But before long, they were in the boys' room and Maddie was digging through their walk-in closet. "Here." She thrust several things at Shelley. "These should work. But I need to go." She smiled. "Meet us in the backyard and I'll—"

"But I have—"

"You've got to see this, Shelley." Maddie winked at her. "I mean it. See you in a few, okay?"

Shelley just nodded as she slipped the western vest over Aiden's shirt and tied the red bandanna around his neck. With the black cowboy hat in place, he looked almost like the real deal. She owed Maddie now. Big time.

And so, with Emma in her arms, Shelley followed Aiden out to the backyard where the birthday party was in full swing. To her surprise, a number of the other moms and a few dads were sticking around.

"Come and see." Maddie took Shelley by the arm. "I know you'll appreciate this." She led Shelley over to the food table and showed her the enormous cake. It was more than two feet tall and looked exactly like a bucking bronco. Even the saddle was perfect.

"You made this?" Shelley asked with wide eyes.

"Uh-huh." Maddie nodded proudly. "Didn't it turn out great?"

"It's absolutely gorgeous." Shelley stared at the amazing cake. The horse was chocolate brown with a black mane flowing in the breeze. Even the bridle had shining candies that looked like silver. "You could be a professional."

Maddie waved her hand. "Oh, I'll leave that to you. But it certainly was fun. I highly recommend those cake kits.

Now come on over here and meet Harrison's mom. She's been asking about the mom who bakes for the Cove, and I promised to introduce you. You go sit down, and I'll get you a strawberry lemonade."

"But I didn't plan to stay—"

"Just stick around a little while," Maddie pleaded.

"Just a few minutes," Shelley said reluctantly. Soon Maddie had introduced her to the moms at a table, and Shelley sat down with her drink. Of course, that was when she noticed that she was still wearing her grubby house-cleaning sweats.

"I didn't really plan on staying," she explained to the moms, who all seemed to be dressed impeccably. She centered Emma on her lap, trying to use her to hide the stain on the front of her sweatshirt. "I have a million things to do at home. I just wanted to drop Aiden and make a fast break."

"Just relax and enjoy," Harrison's mom told her. "And tell me how you make those incredible blueberry scones."

"Or that chocolate zucchini bread," another one said. "It's amazing. In fact, I'd like to buy a whole loaf of it for a luncheon I'm having next week."

Shelley started to relax a bit now. Okay, maybe she did look like a frazzled mom, but at least these women seemed to respect her for her baking abilities. That was something.

"I don't know how Maddie does it all," one of them said. "Four kids. And her house is perfect. And she throws parties like this."

"She makes me sick," another one said with a teasing smile.

"One day my husband compared me to her," Harrison's mom said, "and I nearly decked him."

"I call it MBS," someone said.

"What's that?" Shelley asked.

"Maddie Bancroft Syndrome."

Everyone laughed.

"Well, I actually admire Maddie," Shelley told them. "I know I'll never have it together like she does. But I think it's great she can do all this." She waved her hand. "And she's really generous too."

Now the conversation shifted, and instead of bashing their hostess, the others actually said some nice things. Shelley suspected that these young moms, like her, suffered some twinges of jealousy from time to time. But what good did it do to be mean?

Soon they were talking about Halloween and what their kids were going to dress up as. And suddenly Shelley felt guilty. She didn't want to admit that she didn't have anything ready for her kids yet. She'd figured Aiden would be content to wear a set of superhero pajamas, and she'd put Emma in her bunny sleeper and call it good. No chance that she'd ever develop a case of MBS.

Emma was starting to fuss now, and Shelley was feeling even more out of place than when she'd arrived. "I should probably get this little girl home for her nap."

"Not so fast." Maddie joined them. "It's time to light the candles and cut the cake."

Feeling trapped again. Shelley sat back down and waited as the birthday song was sung and candles blown out, watching as the amazing bronco birthday cake was cut open and served. Jiggling Emma on her knee, no longer concerned about the spot on her sweatshirt, she forked into the cake and took a bite.

It was barely in her mouth when she realized something— it tasted horrible. A combination of sawdust and chocolate-flavored cardboard. It was all she could do not to spit it out. She glanced around the table at the other women. Their expressions conveyed the same thing.

"Well, I hate to eat and run." She stood. "But I need to get Emma out of here before she gets really fussy."

Harrison's mom gave Shelley a wry smile. "You didn't finish your cake."

Shelley grinned back. "I had enough."

"Me too." Another mom slid her cake plate into the center of the table.

"Too bad *Shelley* didn't bake the cake," someone said.

Shelley just chuckled as she bid the moms good-bye. Seeing Maddie still happily and obliviously serving the bronco cake, Shelley mouthed "Thank you!" and made a quick exit.

Yes, it really was too bad Shelley hadn't helped with that cake. Maybe that's what the adage meant—you can't have your cake and eat it too. She wasn't sure. But as she drove Emma home, she couldn't wait to get the taste of sawdust out of her mouth.

Chapter Twenty

As Diane put the final preparations on her dinner, she still felt a bit nervous about how the evening would go, but she knew her friends would be there for her. They would have her back. She took in a long, deep breath as she set a stack of her best dishes on the dining table, praying that all would go well tonight.

Given the size of her small cottage, and because there would be nine diners here this evening, she'd decided to serve the meal buffet style. But now she was second-guessing herself. She hoped no one would mind about having to fill their own plates, gather their own utensils, and eventually find a comfortable corner in which to sit and eat.

As she set a large bowl of tossed salad on the counter, she remembered how she and Eric had served buffet dinners... back in the day. Sometimes they would accommodate a crowd of up to fifty, and people would clump here and there. Some would sit on the stairs, some would eat standing, but they always seemed to have a good time. So she hoped they'd be fine tonight too.

Originally she'd thought they would have only eight for dinner—and she could've accommodated that number at the dining table. However, Barbara had misunderstood the invitation and had invited her neighbor Leo Spangler to come with her.

"That's fine," Diane had assured her. "The more the merrier." And it wasn't that she didn't like Leo. She most certainly did. Not only was he a fine veterinarian, he was a fine person too. Not to mention handsome. It was just that one more guest changed the dynamics. Going from eight to nine felt awkward to her. And, as silly as it seemed, she felt that she would be the odd one out now. Margaret and Allan were coming together. As were Beverly and her father. Also Shelley and Dan. And then Barbara and Leo. It was times like this that she really missed Eric. Still, there wasn't time to dwell on that tonight.

Besides, perhaps casual would be better. She didn't want to admit, not even to herself, that her hidden agenda for having this dinner party was not merely social.

"Okay, Rocky, time for you to go out and enjoy some fresh air." She held up the enticing bone that she'd gotten for him. "This place will be too crowded for you tonight." He wagged his tail happily as she led him to the back door and handed over his reward. "Be good."

Back in the house, she removed the lasagnas from the oven, setting them aside to set. She was just filling the water pitcher with ice and lemon slices when she heard someone at the door.

"Come in," she told Margaret and Allan, taking their coats.

"We came a few minutes early." Margaret nodded across the street. "We walked with Adelaide. She's getting settled in at the Bauers'. And I thought maybe I could help you."

Hearing a timer in the kitchen going off, Diane handed her back their coats. "Perhaps you could be the coat person. I planned on stashing them in my office."

"Would you like me to put another log on your fire?" Allan offered.

"Yes. Thank you!" Diane headed back to turn off the timer and to check on the vegetable dish. Soon Allan and Margaret had joined her, and they visited congenially as she put the finishing touches on dinner.

"I told Margaret she had to wait until Barbara finished her meal before bringing up the subject of the lighthouse," Allan said as he munched on a celery stick.

"And I told Allan that I would have no control over whether or not Barbara introduced the subject herself," Margaret retorted.

Diane laughed. "Well, I don't want to create any fireworks tonight. But I think an open, honest discussion is perfectly acceptable."

It wasn't long before the others arrived, and suddenly Diane's dinner party was in full swing. To her relief, Barbara melded fairly easily into the group as they loaded their plates and found places to sit in the small living room. As they commenced to eat and visit, the topic of the lighthouse didn't come up.

It wasn't until some of the guests returned for seconds that Barbara told Shelley about her bed-and-breakfast idea. "And I would seriously consider hiring you to cook for me," she said.

Shelley blinked in surprise. "Well, thank you. That's very kind." She turned, smiling nervously at Dan.

"How soon would you plan to begin this venture?" Dan asked Barbara.

"I'm currently in the process of trying to determine the best way to go about it. Fortunately your kind mayor is helping me a lot. And I have a real estate attorney working with me as well. But, naturally, there are still some obstacles to overcome."

"I would imagine there would be some land-use concerns," Margaret said as she rejoined them. "Not to mention red tape regarding the wetland issues."

"Wetland issues?"

Margaret sat down, setting her plate on her knees. "You didn't know that there are wetland preserves south of the lighthouse?"

"The mayor didn't mention anything about wetlands." Barbara adjusted her pretty beaded jacket, sitting straighter on the sofa. "I'm sure if she thought it was going to be a problem she'd have told me."

"Perhaps she's more focused on the commerce a new bed-and-breakfast would bring," Beverly said a bit tersely. "It's not really a mayoral responsibility to be concerned with environmental issues, especially those outside of the city limits."

Suddenly, they were in an animated and somewhat heated discussion over whose responsibility it was to protect the environment. Diane tried to remain neutral, but it wasn't easy. Eventually, she simply excused herself to the kitchen to see about dessert.

"I'll help," Shelley offered eagerly.

"And I'll slip across the street to check on Adelaide and the kids." Dan stood, moving toward the door.

The debate continued. What had started out as a nice little dinner party was suddenly threatening to turn into something rather ugly. Diane wondered if she'd been mistaken to attempt to do something like this. Perhaps mixing food and politics was a big mistake.

"It's getting a little hot in there," Shelley said quietly as they both stood in the kitchen.

Diane smiled nervously. "Good thing we're all mature adults, right?"

Shelley chuckled.

"These pies look fantastic," Diane told Shelley as she cut into the lemon meringue. "I don't know how you find time to do everything you do, Shelley."

"Well, I already had the crusts made," Shelley said. "Adding the other ingredients was fairly easy."

Diane studied Shelley. "But you do look tired. You're sure you're not burning your candle at both ends?"

Shelley seemed to force a laugh. Then she told Diane about going to a kids' birthday party where the cake had tasted like sawdust.

Diane laughed. "Sounds like you've had a busy day."

They set the servings of pie on the table for guests to help themselves, and Diane checked on the coffee. She could hear the conversation continuing. Beverly seemed the most informed of the group. Margaret was the most opinionated. Leo turned out to be more concerned with protecting the environment than encouraging development. Dan, who had found the kids to be doing fine with Adelaide, had his own views on conservation and how it sometimes went too far. And Allan was attempting to be a peacemaker.

"Dessert is served," Diane announced. "And I have coffee and tea in the kitchen. Everyone feel free to help yourselves."

The debate over the lighthouse continued during dessert, and it seemed that if the controversial topic was put to the vote in this house, Barbara would definitely go down. By the time they were having second cups of coffee, Diane was feeling a bit guilty. She could see that Barbara was not enjoying herself.

"Maybe we should talk about something else." Diane put a hand on Barbara's shoulder. "As you can see, the fate of the lighthouse is a touchy subject among the locals."

"It never occurred to me." Barbara looked over the group. "I thought everyone would love the idea."

"I think the idea of another bed-and-breakfast in Marble Cove is great," Margaret said. "Just not in the lighthouse."

"The lighthouse is more than just a structure," Shelley told Barbara. "It's more like a friend to some people."

"And there's a mystery attached to it," Diane said.

"A mystery?" Barbara's eyes lit up.

"Some of us think it's a mystery," Beverly said quickly. "There are others who don't."

"What sort of mystery?" Barbara asked curiously.

Diane and her friends exchanged glances. Now Diane wished she hadn't mentioned it. What if the idea of a mysterious lighthouse encouraged Barbara to dig in her heels even deeper?

"Well, it's not like it's a secret," Beverly said. "If you asked around, you'd be sure to hear about it."

"About what?" Barbara persisted.

Beverly looked at Diane as if uncertain, but then she continued. "Strange lights have been seen coming from the lighthouse," she said cautiously.

"But it's decommissioned, isn't it?" Barbara asked with a puzzled expression.

"Yes," Margaret told her. "But these aren't ordinary lights."

"Do you think it's haunted?" Barbara directed this to Beverly.

Beverly shrugged with a perfect poker face that almost made Diane laugh. It was sweet how she was coming to the lighthouse's defense. It was obvious that Beverly was changing in a number of ways.

"Some of the local kids, mostly teens, like to pretend that it's haunted," Shelley said eagerly. "Especially this time of year. Sometimes there's vandalism there on Halloween."

"Vandalism?" Diane was shocked. "To our beloved lighthouse? I didn't know that."

"It's true," Dan said. "One Halloween, just a couple years ago, the lighthouse got covered with graffiti."

"And there was glass all over the place," Shelley said. "From broken alcohol bottles."

"Oh no!" Diane shook her head. "That's just wrong."

"Yes, it looked terrible," Margaret told her.

"A group of us took it upon ourselves to clean it up and get it repainted," Allan said. "But it took almost until Christmas before we raised enough money to purchase paint to repaint the lighthouse."

"And then we had to wait until spring," Margaret said. "Until the freezing temperatures let up."

"In the meantime it was a real eyesore." Shelley shook her head. "I remember taking Aiden in the stroller down the boardwalk, and I'd see the defaced lighthouse and just break into tears. It was like seeing an old friend who'd been brutally beaten."

"You'd think that the police would keep an eye on the lighthouse," Diane said. "Especially on Halloween. I wonder if we should say something to Fred."

"That's not a bad idea," Beverly said.

"It sounds like you people really do love your lighthouse." Barbara looked around the group with a curious expression.

"We do love it," Allan told her. "It's not only historically significant. It's a symbol of hope too." He glanced at his wife. "Some locals have their own special stories to tell... related to the lighthouse. I personally think it would be very sad to see it turned into a commercial venture."

"And you mentioned an interest in hiring me," Shelley said, "but I could never agree to bake anything that would be served at a bed-and-breakfast in the lighthouse. That would just feel wrong to me."

Barbara looked shocked. "You're all really this opposed to the idea?"

"There are other pieces of real estate that would make nice inns," Beverly suggested. "In fact, I just heard about an old stone mansion up on the bluff that will be going up for sale soon. The Hemphill House."

Suddenly the conversation switched over to how that property would be the perfect location for a bed-and-breakfast. And by the time the dinner party began to wind down, Diane felt hopeful that Barbara was seriously rethinking her lighthouse bed-and-breakfast plan.

"You know," Diane said as she was helping people with their coats, "we should consider forming a Friends of the Lighthouse club. We could do fund-raisers and whatnot to generate interest and help for the lighthouse."

"That's a great idea," Margaret said.

And so, what had threatened to turn into the worst dinner party ever, turned out to be rather nice in the end. Thanks to good friends.

CHAPTER TWENTY-ONE

Margaret decided to use the community center's Hallow-een party as an excuse to do some friendly spying. Of course, she would be very discreet about the whole thing. No one would suspect her of espionage. She even made brownies with pumpkin-orange frosting and candy corn sprinkles to sweeten her presence. Her mission: to determine the motives of Handsome Hank.

Adelaide's attraction to Hank seemed to be on the increase. Hardly a day went by now when they didn't hear Hank's name. And whenever Adelaide spoke of her friend, her brown eyes grew a little dreamy—and Margaret grew a little more nervous.

Friday, while in the waiting room at the dentist's office, Adelaide had told Margaret she wanted to get married.

Margaret had closed her *Reader's Digest.* "Married?"

Adelaide had nodded.

"Who would you marry?" Margaret had tried to keep her voice calm.

Adelaide got a thoughtful look. "Hank."

"Hank?" Margaret set the magazine down.

"In a wedding."

"A wedding?" Margaret knew she was parroting her daughter, but she didn't know what else to say.

Adelaide held up the very dated magazine in her hands, pointing to a photo of a beaming celebrity couple with megawatt smiles. "Like that."

"Oh." Margaret nodded, trying to take this in.

"I want a pretty dress like that." Adelaide smiled dreamily again.

"That *is* a pretty dress."

So on Friday night Allan and Margaret had agreed that, as responsible parents, it was time to get more involved. Or at least to make a determination on how serious this relationship had gotten.

Feeling a bit uneasy about her spying mission, Margaret walked into the community center with Adelaide. Trying to act casual, she watched as her daughter went over to join her friends at a table that was covered with newspapers and pumpkins. The party was to begin with a pumpkin-carving contest, and Adelaide was anxious to get started.

"It's so nice that you could join us today," Penny told Margaret as she eyed the brownies. "And those look yummy."

"Yes, please." Margaret glanced nervously toward the activity table.

"Want me to take them to the kitchen for you?"

Margaret nodded and gave her a grateful smile. Penny probably suspected why she was here, but Margaret was relieved she didn't say anything. Margaret walked over to watch as the pumpkin carving continued. Mostly she wanted to see how Hank and Adelaide interacted.

But nothing out of the ordinary seemed to be happening between them. No flirting, no coyness, and they barely exchanged words as they worked on their pumpkins. They didn't even sit together. And, as they worked to hollow out their pumpkins, they never even seemed to make eye contact. A few bantering words were tossed out here and there. But, really, nothing to suggest a budding romance was going on.

Hank reached up to push a curly strand of blond hair away from his eyes, smudging some pumpkin goop across his forehead as he intently worked on cutting a triangle-shaped nose in his jack-o-lantern. Dressed in a yellow oxford shirt and neat brown corduroy pants, he was attractive in a scrawny, boyish sort of way. But he seemed like nothing more than a sweet young man—far more interested in carving his pumpkin than he was in Adelaide. Perhaps Margaret's worries were for nothing.

Margaret went over to get a cup of coffee, watching the group of enthusiastic pumpkin carvers from a distance.

"We have some fun prizes for the contest," Penny said as she joined her. "We have so many categories that everyone will win at least once."

Margaret laughed. "Maybe that explains their enthusiasm."

"But they don't know that everyone is getting a prize."

"Oh…" Margaret frowned.

"Are you worried about something?"

So much for her secret mission. Margaret went ahead and sheepishly explained Adelaide's comments about wanting to get married to Hank.

"Really?" Penny looked shocked.

"Do you think this is something I should take seriously?"

Penny rubbed her chin, looking over to the pumpkin area with a bewildered expression. "Well, I haven't seen anything between them that, you know, I would consider romantic behavior. Oh, sure, they're good friends. But they've never held hands or kissed or anything."

Margaret felt a wave of relief.

"Unless they've done it secretly. I suppose that could happen." Penny told her about a couple from a few years ago and how they'd had a clandestine romance.

Margaret's relief evaporated.

"So, can you tell me what the context of the conversation was, I mean when Adelaide said she wanted to marry Hank?"

"We were in the waiting room at the dentist's office."

"Oh, well, then...maybe it's not such a big deal."

"What do you mean?"

"It's just that I remember being in grade school and how I loved to dress up like a bride, and my friends and I would play wedding. We'd use my mom's nighties and scarves and jewelry, and we'd pick bouquets." She laughed. "We must've looked ridiculous, but we sure had fun."

The light went on in Margaret's head. "So maybe that's what Adelaide meant? She liked the idea of a wedding? Dressing up like a bride? Carrying flowers?"

"Maybe so." Penny nodded. "What girl wouldn't?"

"I sure hope you're right."

"In fact, that gives me an idea: we should have a formal dance here sometime. A chance for all the girls to dress up, wear corsages, and get their hair done."

"Oh, Adelaide would love that."

"Maybe we could have a prom in the springtime."

"I'd help out," Margaret said. The idea of helping with a prom was much preferable to planning a wedding.

"And that would give everyone plenty of time to find their dresses and everything."

Margaret patted Penny on the back. "That's a lovely idea. No wonder you're such an asset to the community center."

"Looks like they're starting to finish up their carving." She turned to Margaret. "Say, would you like to help judge? Being that you're an artist and all?"

"Absolutely." Margaret nodded eagerly.

By the time Margaret left the center, it was as if a load had been lifted from her shoulders. She'd seen nothing to suggest that Adelaide and Hank were about to embark on some crazy romantic ride. Penny would tell her if she thought it was going the wrong direction. And now she and Adelaide could start planning for a spring prom. What fun!

Feeling greatly encouraged, she found Allan in the gallery and quickly relieved his fears that his only daughter was going to elope with Handsome Hank.

"That's wonderful, Margaret." But now his smile faded.

"Yes...then what's wrong?"

"Bernadette Lassiter stopped by here to see you."

Margaret let out a groan. Bernadette was another artist who lived in town. And last week the chamber of commerce had surprised Margaret by deciding that both Bernadette and Margaret should work on the mural together. It wasn't that Margaret wanted the project all to herself, but she'd already invested a fair amount of time preparing her preliminary sketches. Plus, she knew that involving another artist would complicate things. Not only that, but when Margaret had arranged with Bernadette to meet at the Cannery, Bernadette was a no-show. And that had irked Margaret.

"Do you think you should give Charlotte Vincent a call?" Allan asked with concern. "I know how stressful this has been for you."

"I can do better than that," Margaret told him. "If you don't mind watching the shop a while longer, I will pay the good chairwoman a visit."

He grinned. "Good luck!"

Allan knew as well as Margaret did that Charlotte was a determined woman who was used to getting her way. Just one reason she made a good chairwoman for the chamber. But Margaret didn't have time for this. She needed to make some boundaries when it came to her art and her time and her life. Thinking perhaps this was a good day for missions, Margaret marched down to the chamber building and found Charlotte in her office.

"Good morning," Charlotte said cheerfully.

Margaret cut straight to the chase. "I already tried to convey my concerns about involving another artist on the mural project," she told her. "And now I'm here to say I'm afraid this is all a big mistake."

Charlotte looked surprised. "Why is that?"

"For starters, Bernadette didn't even meet me when we scheduled it. Beyond that, we have very different styles, and I—"

"But Bernadette told me she called you."

"She left me a message—but that was just this morning. Before I return her call, I wanted to speak to you."

"Isn't there some way you can work this out with Bernadette?" She smiled hopefully. "You're just the right person to take Bernadette under your wing, Margaret. Wiser and more experienced and so successful. And if you work it right, you could have Bernadette do most of the work for you. You simply direct the project and put her in charge of the students. She can stick around to make sure they don't mess anything up. You know how crazy teens can get if they're unsupervised. I'd think that having Bernadette on the project should free up more of your time."

"But Bernadette is an artist," Margaret protested. "It seems unlikely she'd want to work as a supervisor for a bunch of high school kids."

"She just wants to be involved," Charlotte assured her. "It's a community project, Margaret. What's the harm of letting more helpful hands from the community participate?"

"But Bernadette's art is so different from mine," Margaret pointed out again. "What if she wants to be involved in the creative portion of the work?"

"Oh, Margaret, I have no doubts you can work the little bumps out with her. Bernadette is a reasonable woman."

"I don't know... Perhaps it would be better if I just bowed out now. Let Bernadette take—"

"No, no!" Charlotte said. "We can't have that. Please don't desert us on this project. We need you, Margaret. The community knows and respects you. We all love your art. We want you to take the lead."

"Then why are you bringing on Bernadette?"

The phone rang, and Margaret gathered from Charlotte's conversation that it was a call from the mayor. As she waited out the call, Margaret surmised the Bernadette thing was probably political. Maybe someone who knew somebody wanted Bernadette involved in this.

"I wish I could do something to make you feel better," Charlotte said after the call. "But whatever you do, please don't abandon us, Margaret. We need you."

In the end, Margaret agreed to stay on. As she walked back to the gallery, she wondered if she should have her head examined.

"Did Bernadette tell you why she didn't show up to work with me on the mural last week?" Margaret asked Allan as she set her purse down on the counter with a thud.

He shook his head, but she could tell by the firm line of his lips there was more to the story.

"Allan?"

"Well, Margaret, she did say that she'd just been down at the Cannery, and that she'd looked at the sketches you'd started…and…well…" His voice trailed off.

"Those were the sketches Bernadette was supposed to help me with," Margaret added crisply. She wanted to ask why Allan hadn't mentioned this earlier, before she'd paid Charlotte that visit. Still, she reminded herself, this wasn't Allan's problem. And she was the one who'd stormed out of here. "So what else did Bernadette say?"

"Well…she said that she thought they looked, uh"—he cleared his throat—"amateurish."

"Amateurish?" Margaret blinked.

"I know, I know." He ran his hand over his balding head.

"She thought it was amateurish?"

"That wasn't all."

"Oh, good grief." Margaret peeled of her jacket and tossed it onto her purse. "Do tell."

"Now don't shoot the messenger, Margaret. I could just as soon not tell—"

"No, no… I'm sorry, Allan. Just get it out quickly, please."

"Bernadette wants to start all over. She said the seascape looks childish and—"

"She said it looks *childish*?" Margaret could hear the volume in her voice increase. She glanced around the gallery, looking for anyone who might've overheard.

"No one is here," he assured her.

"She thinks the sketch looks childish?" Margaret repeated. She was pacing now. "Childish?"

"And juvenile," he muttered.

Margaret turned to look at him. "Have you ever seen her work?"

He chuckled.

"Her *modern* art looks like something a two-year-old painted. And it's not that I don't like modern art. I do. I just happen to like good modern art. Bernadette's is not good."

"I don't care for her work much either," Allan said.

"Which is why I don't want her work in here." Margaret put her hand over her mouth.

"Do you think that's it?" Allan asked. "Is she trying to get back at you for refusing to show her work here?"

"But I explained to her that the Shearwater is about nature and Maine and seascapes and birds...and that her work wouldn't show well here. I tried to keep it professional."

"I don't know." Allan was getting his jacket now. "But I told her you'd be here this afternoon, so don't be surprised if she pays you a visit."

Margaret groaned. "Great. And I had wanted to get some painting done today. Now I'll be on pins and needles waiting for her to swoop in and call me childish and juvenile, which, by the way, are the same thing."

He chuckled. "Well, I'm sure you can handle it, dear."

"Oh yes, I'm sure I can."

Margaret watched as he left. Lucky man. He got to go home and work undisturbed. He even had an assistant in Dan. Meanwhile, she got to mind the gallery and put up with the likes of Bernadette Lassiter! Of course, he'd interrupted his work to watch the gallery—and dealt with

Bernadette—so she could go off on her crusades. Maybe they were both lucky.

She went to the back room and started to get out her materials. Maybe she'd just tell Bernadette to do the mural on her own. Go ahead and paint some wild, crazy splashes of paint on that wall. Maybe the shopkeepers at the Cannery wanted the wall to look like a bad day at the carnival. Margaret didn't have time for these kinds of games.

She squirted some cobalt blue onto her palette, then realized it was far too much. Taking a deep breath, she attempted to de-stress. Slowly exhaling, she reminded herself to count her blessings. She had a sweet husband and daughter. She lived in a delightful seaside town. She got to paint for a living. She owned her own gallery. And today's best blessing was that her daughter was *not* getting married. She posed her brush over the canvas and smiled. Really, she had so very much to be thankful for.

CHAPTER TWENTY-TWO

B everly hadn't been surprised when Jeff called her a few days after their meeting at Captain Calhoun's. She had tried to be a bit more congenial this time. Not friendly, exactly, but polite as she concocted clever reasons for not seeing him again. It wasn't that she was being dishonest as she told him she needed to be with her father. It was simply that she was perhaps exaggerating the situation. Because the truth was, Father was fine.

But when Jeff called her on the afternoon of Halloween, her excuse was completely honest. "I'm sorry," she told him. "I promised to stay home and help Father with the trick-or-treaters tonight. He loves to see the children in their costumes, but it wears him out to try to handle it on his own." And, although she didn't mention it, Beverly wanted to make sure Father didn't eat any candy.

"Maybe some other time."

"Yes, maybe so." She had injected more hope into her voice than she really felt. Perhaps it was because she was starting to feel just a little sorry for him.

The first trick-or-treaters came just before dusk, and Beverly stood nearby as Father answered the door. He pretended to be afraid of the three little goblins, but then he complimented them on their costumes and plunked generous amounts of candy in their bags.

It wasn't much later that Shelley and Dan brought Emma and Aiden to the door. Aiden, predictably, was dressed as Spider-Man and Emma as a cute pink bunny. Father engaged with them and dropped candy in Aiden's plastic pumpkin.

"We're heading over to the church harvest party," Shelley told Beverly. "But I promised Aiden we'd do our street first."

"There don't seem to be many kids out," Beverly said, glancing down the mostly deserted street.

"I think parties are taking over," Shelley told her. "Parents probably feel it's safer."

Beverly looked at their half-full candy bowl. "Well, maybe we won't run out of treats then." She waved as the Bauers continued on their way.

Father didn't hold out even as long as the candy did. By seven thirty, she could tell he was bushed. "I doubt there will be many trick-or-treaters this late," she told him. "You can go ahead and turn in if you like. I'll take care of any more that come."

Naturally, he protested. But when the doorbell rang again, he flashed a sheepish grin. "I suppose I am a little worn out." As she picked up the candy bowl, he told her good night. She kissed him on the cheek, then went for the door.

This time, the kids were older and the costumes not quite so cute. But she smiled as she plunked candy into their pillowcases.

"I hope you kids won't be up to any tricks tonight," she called out as they hurried down the walk. They just laughed, but suddenly she remembered about the vandalism to the lighthouse. Surely those kids wouldn't do something like that.

She closed the door and considered turning off the light, but decided to wait until eight. Or until the candy gave out. She checked on Father and was relieved to see that his light was already out, and he was sleeping soundly. Then she went to the kitchen and was just putting the teakettle on when she heard the doorbell again. Fortunately, Father's hearing was poor enough that he probably wouldn't be disturbed, but just the same she hurried to grab up the bowl and make it to the door before the bell rang again.

But it wasn't kids this time. To her surprise, it was Jeff Mackenzie.

"What are you doing here?" she asked.

"Trick or treat?" he said with a cautious smile.

She looked blankly at him as she reached into the bowl, retrieved a single minisized candy bar, and handed it to him. "There."

"I thought maybe I could keep you company," he said gently. "Keep the ghosts away."

She wanted to point out that *he* was a ghost, but something about his smile weakened her resolve to hold him at arm's length. And now she heard the teakettle whistling. "Well, come in then." She shoved the candy bowl toward him, then dashed off to quiet the kettle.

The doorbell rang again. She turned off the gas and headed back to the door in time to see Jeff cheerfully giving some teenagers what was left of the candy. "Have fun!" he called out as he closed the door.

She thanked him, then looked pointedly at the empty bowl. "Now what?"

"Want me to run out for more candy?"

She glanced at her watch. It was past eight now. She peeked out the window and found that the other neighbors' porches were already dark. "No." She turned off the outside light. "I think Newport Avenue is closed for the night."

"Did I hear a teakettle whistling?" he asked hopefully.

She studied him, trying to decide whether to throw him out or to invite him for tea.

"You really should turn off the lights inside the house too," he said as he clicked off the light switch in the entryway. "So that kids don't see them from the street and think you're still giving out candy."

"I suppose that makes sense." She went to the library and turned off that light too. Now she was standing in the hallway, which was dimly lit from the light in the kitchen, trying to decide what to do.

"I don't mean to be a pest," Jeff said quietly. "But a cup of tea does sound good."

"Come on," she said, sounding resigned. "One cup of tea, and then you're out of here."

"That's an invitation I simply can't refuse."

She wondered what she was doing as he followed her to the kitchen. Without even asking him what kind of tea he might prefer, she made a pot of Earl Grey. Then she set it and a couple of everyday mugs on the kitchen table. She wasn't about to get out the good china for him.

"Good thing I take it black," he said as she filled the mug in front of him.

She filled her own mug. Then with her elbows on the table, she sat down across from him, just staring. Why was he here?

He sniffed the tea. "*Mmm*, Earl Grey, my favorite."

She rolled her eyes and took a sip. She knew she was acting like a spoiled adolescent, but she just couldn't seem to help herself.

"I'm sorry for barging in on you like this," he said. "But I figured it was the only way I'd be able to finish our conversation."

"I thought our conversation was finished."

"No...in fact, I don't think it has really begun." He pressed his lips together and looked intently at her. "And I'm happy to take that blame for that."

She just shrugged.

"Seeing you that night...when you walked into Captain Calhoun's...well, you kind of took my breath away."

She looked down at her tea, studying the shiny amber surface.

"I know that's not what you want to hear. And it's really not what I came here to say. But it's the truth. And because you took my breath away, well, I just started blabbing about a bunch of really stupid stuff. And I'm sure I sounded like a complete idiot."

"To be honest, I can't remember even half of the conversation that night."

"Well, maybe that's good. Because I never came close to saying what I meant to say."

She looked up at him with curiosity. But she still wasn't ready to let her guard down. "I never said what I meant to say either."

Now he looked hopeful.

"I mean that I had a lot of questions for you."

"Oh." He nodded. "Feel free. And I will attempt to be as honest as possible."

She wasn't quite sure what that meant, but she decided to go for it. "Okay, for starters, I want to know the truth about why you're here in Marble Cove. Is it really to research the lighthouse?"

"Yes."

"But *why*?" she asked. "If what you told me is true, if it's not work-related or academic, why could you possibly have such an interest in this particular lighthouse?"

"I have my reasons."

She narrowed her eyes. "Do your reasons have anything to do with me?"

He gave her a slow smile. "Not exactly."

She wasn't sure whether to be relieved or offended. "So it's a coincidence that you're shadowing me?"

"I'm not shadowing you."

"You keep calling me and—"

"That's not about the lighthouse. That's just because I want to talk to you."

"Yes." She nodded. "And now you have your chance."

"And I appreciate that." He leaned forward. "But at the same time I want to be careful not to overwhelm you, Anna."

"Beverly." How many times did she have to remind him?

"Beverly." He slapped his forehead. "Yes...I know. I'm sorry. It's just so hard not to think of you as Anna... I keep remembering that day."

Panic rushed through her. He wanted to talk about that day. She had known it all along. Why did they need to rehash it? What was the point? She looked at the clock on the stove. It wasn't even nine yet, but she wanted to say it was late... that he should go. Instead she just sat there staring down at her tea.

"I have something to tell you—" He stopped himself. Perhaps he was about to call her Anna again.

She waited, feeling her heart pounding. How much did he know? What difference did it make?

He cleared his throat. "I just want to say I'm sorry... Beverly. I want to say that if I could go back and do things differently, I would. I've felt terrible about this whole thing for years now. At first, I was in some kind of denial. But the truth is I feel that I'm to blame, and I feel I've never taken full responsibility for it. I would appreciate it if you would forgive me."

"Forgive *you*?" She tried to absorb this. "For what?"

"Yes. If I had handled things differently that day, if I hadn't been so selfish…so distracted…well, maybe Will would still be alive today."

She tightly closed her eyes, shaking her head. Was she hearing him correctly? Did he honestly think that he was to blame?

"I know you have good reason to hate me. To be honest, I've spent a fair amount of time hating myself."

She opened her eyes and stared at him. "You think that I think that you—"

"I know you must blame me. And you have every right to. I just want you to consider what I have to say and to give me—"

"I'm not sure I understand." She wrinkled her brow, still trying to take this in. "You honestly think that I blame *you* for Will's death?"

He nodded sadly.

"Oh…" She tightened her fingers around the mug's handle.

"I wrote you letters," he said, "but they were returned unopened."

"Yes…I know."

"You changed your phone number. And your name."

She pursed her lips. Was it possible that she had completely misjudged him? Was he really only hounding her to express his regrets, to apologize to her? This wasn't anything like what she'd expected.

She decided to open up, just a little. She hoped it wasn't a mistake. "I had a lot to deal with back then," she said calmly, almost as if giving a report. "I lost both my mother and my husband in a very short amount of time. I was going through a lot…a lot of grief. It was the hardest time in my life. I suppose you were the last one I wanted to connect with just then. Surely you can understand that."

His dark eyes were somber. "I understand that you would want to ignore me, to keep me completely out of your life. It's only natural. Just like it's natural for you to have blamed me for Will's death." He looked down at his hands on the table.

Despite her resolve to not let him get to her, she felt pulled in. Even worse, she felt sorry for him. "I don't see why you should feel guilty."

"If you and Will hadn't been with me that day…things could've turned out so differently."

"I don't know."

"Beverly, your husband would still be alive."

"I honestly don't know if that's true. But if anyone was to blame…" She felt that familiar lump growing in her throat. "It was me."

"See?" he said suddenly. "That's exactly what has worried me. That you were blaming yourself."

"But what else would I do?" She blinked to keep back the tears. "If I'd been paying more attention to Will, I'd have noticed he was in trouble. I could've even rescued him." She decided to leave out the part about Will and his medicine.

"But can't you see? That's what I should've done. It was my boat. I was the host. I should've been taking better care of things. Instead, I was distracted. I was...flirting with you. Didn't you notice? I was...playing silly games with you. And when Will got in trouble, I never even noticed." He looked at her with sincere eyes. "Can you ever forgive me?"

"Yes," she said quietly, holding back the tears. "I do forgive you."

They sat there just looking at each other, not knowing what to say. But the sound of tapping on the back door made them both turn.

"Who can that possibly be?" Beverly's heart raced. Trick-or-treaters would come to the front door.

"Want me to get it?" He was already there, cracking open the door.

"Beverly?" a woman's voice said quietly. "It's just me. Diane."

"Oh, it's Diane!" Beverly hurried over as he opened the door wider. "My goodness, you nearly frightened me to death." She pulled her into the kitchen. "What are you doing out?"

Diane looked at Jeff with wide eyes. "Trick or treat?"

Beverly laughed. "We're fresh out of candy. Do you remember Jeff Mackenzie?"

Diane nodded, peering at Beverly with curious eyes. "I'm sorry to interrupt. But I got to thinking about the lighthouse and the Halloween pranksters, and I was worried—what if they paint it with graffiti again?" She held up her flashlight and cell phone. "I was going to go on patrol, and I saw your kitchen light on and thought maybe—"

"Sure," Beverly said eagerly. "I'm happy to go."

"Mind if I come too?" Jeff asked.

"I'd love to have a man along," Diane told him.

Before long, Beverly rounded up two more flashlights, they got on their coats, and the three of them headed for the lighthouse. Beverly told Jeff that Diane knew the whole story about Will's death that day. Then, with Jeff's permission, she told Diane about how Jeff had come over to apologize. As they walked, they talked openly about the whole thing. In a surprising way, it felt therapeutic.

By the time they reached the lighthouse, all was quiet and normal. But they decided to stick around a while, just in case. They all sat down, leaning their backs against the lighthouse and watching as the moon played peekaboo with the clouds.

Then, to Beverly and Diane's delight, Jeff began to regale them with some old stories about the lighthouse's past. It seemed that he'd dug up a number of quirky tales recently. Stories of near shipwrecks and other adventures where the lighthouse had played an important role in preserving life. Some tales sounded believable. Some, like the one where people on a stranded boat claimed to be helped by angels, did not.

So, it seemed he was on the level in that regard too. Jeff really had come to Marble Cove to research the history of the lighthouse. The only thing Beverly couldn't quite figure out was... *why?*

CHAPTER TWENTY-THREE

Shelley was trying to maintain a good attitude about Mr. Bauer's seventy-fifth birthday party. Even if she didn't get along that well with Dan's mother, she had always loved and admired Dan's dad. Ralph, unlike his wife, was easygoing and friendly. Even though Dan and his dad weren't particularly close, Ralph had always been kind to Shelley, treating her like a daughter. And, having experienced another kind of dad, one that had walked out on her, Shelley appreciated Ralph even more than she let on. So, she decided, putting this party together for him was just one way to show it.

However, when it came to party planning, Shelley felt seriously challenged. For that reason, just a few days before the party, she called on Maddie Bancroft for help.

"I'm so glad you asked me," Maddie said as the two of them sipped coffee at Maddie's granite-topped breakfast bar. The kids were playing nearby, and Shelley was trying not to have kitchen envy as she eyed Maddie's sleek appliances.

"I'm just at a total loss," Shelley admitted. "And you did such a great job with Benjamin's party—"

"You mean except for the cake." Maddie grimly shook her head. "I never should've trusted the cake mix in the cake kit. I didn't even know until the party was over and I noticed all the uneaten pieces!"

"It probably had to be like that to hold its shape, but there are ways around that." Shelley gave her a sympathetic smile. "Anyway, I figured you might have some ideas for Ralph's birthday."

Maddie picked up another one of the oatmeal cookies that Shelley had brought. "So when is the big event?"

"Saturday."

"Saturday?" Maddie's eyes widened. "As in *this* Saturday?"

"Uh-huh." Shelley took a sip of coffee.

"And you haven't done anything?"

Shelley shrugged. "I have four days to—"

Maddie looked aghast. "Oh, Shelley!"

"I figured I'd just buy some paper plates and balloons. But I just can't decide what colors and—"

"Did you decide on a theme?"

"A theme?" Shelley grimaced. "I can't even decide on what color napkins to buy."

Maddie got out a yellow tablet of paper and a pencil. "First we need to start making a list. How many guests?"

Just like that, Shelley was answering questions, and Maddie was writing things down, telling Shelley where to get what and insisting she get to it right away. "But now we need to think of a theme, Shelley." She bit the end of the pencil with a thoughtful look. "What does your father-in-law like to do?"

Shelley shrugged. "Mostly he just works really hard."

"Any hobbies?"

"Woodworking. I considered making the cake in the shape of a power tool, but Dan nixed that idea."

"I agree with Dan." Maddie tapped the pencil tip on the tablet. "What do you think he likes? You know how some guys like football or poker or boating... What does Ralph like?"

Shelley thought hard, and then she remembered. Just like her, Ralph was very fond of Orlean Point Light. In fact, he was the one who often found her funny little lighthouse images for her ever-growing collection. "Lighthouses," she said suddenly. "Ralph likes lighthouses."

Maddie nodded. "That could work."

"Hey, I'll make a lighthouse birthday cake."

"That could be fun." Maddie wrote down some more things. "We'll go with nautical colors. You know: red, white, and blue. You can rent tablecloths at—"

"I forgot to mention the budget." Now Shelley told her about her mother-in-law's check.

"You're kidding." Maddie scowled. "What a tightwad."

That image secretly delighted Shelley. "Anyway, I guess I need to pinch pennies."

"Well, I saw some cute napkins with lighthouses on them at the dollar store. And I could lend you a few things from my summer party supplies. They're in nautical colors. And we could make some decorations ourselves." Now Maddie was back to her list-making. And then she started gathering up all sorts of stuff from her pantry and closets, piling it all into several grocery bags.

By the time Shelley loaded her kids, plus the bulging bags that Maddie had foisted upon her, into the car, she felt like maybe she'd be able to pull off this party after all. If it turned out as perfectly as Maddie claimed it would, she would owe her Martha Stewart friend big time. Again. If it didn't...well, no one would be terribly surprised.

For the next few days, it seemed that Shelley's every spare minute—not that there were many of them—was spent getting things ready for Ralph's birthday party.

"Are you sure you know what you're doing?" Dan asked one evening when she talked him into helping her cut out construction paper shapes. Maddie had promised they could be transformed into attractive and decorative flags, but, truthfully, Shelley couldn't quite see it.

"Of course," she said. "Keep cutting."

"Well, Vera called me today." He frowned up from where he was sitting cross-legged on the floor. "She's worried that you might be in over your head."

Shelley glared down at him. "And what did you tell her?"

He shrugged, then looked back down at the block of blue paper in his hand.

"You didn't even defend me?"

"I told her that the cake would be good."

She punched him in the shoulder. "Thanks for that vote of confidence."

He looked up at her with a worried expression. "I'm just concerned that you're doing too much, Shell."

"I'm fine."

"But you're either working at the Cove or on this party or with the kids. It's like you're running yourself ragged."

"Really, I'm okay." She forced a smile.

"I don't know." He set the paper aside. "I'm thinking it's too much. All these evenings at the Cove are taking their toll...on both of us."

She closed her eyes and took a deep breath. No point in getting angry. What good would it do? They'd been over this so many times already. "You know that I need to keep baking to keep my business going."

"I know." He nodded as he picked up another piece of paper. "But maybe our timing's wrong, Shell. Maybe this was too much, too soon. The kids and I need you home with us at night."

She stood now, going over to the kitchen table where she pretended to busy herself with the to-do list that Maddie had made for her.

"All I'm saying is, think about it, Shelley. I really respect that you're contributing to our income, but Allan and I were talking today. He thinks that if all goes well they might be able to ramp up the giclée framing operation in the spring, in time for tourist season. If that happens, I'll be busier than ever. You won't need your baking business."

She turned and stared at him. "What if I want it?"

He held his hands up helplessly. "What if it tears us apart?"

She bit her lip. He knew she didn't want that. Why did he always go there? It was like he was baiting her. Well, she wasn't falling for it. Not tonight.

★   ★   ★

By Saturday morning, Shelley knew she really was in over her head. Despite Dan watching the kids and promising to have them dressed in the party clothes she'd laid out for them—colored according to her mother-in-law's decree—she felt seriously worried as she drove Dan's pickup to the church. How was she ever going to pull this off? The back of the pickup was full of boxes of a bunch of things that in no way resembled a party. The only thing that had turned out the way she'd expected was the cake sitting next to her. Secured in a cardboard box, she'd even safely buckled it, in case she had to make a sudden stop.

She reached the church parking lot with no catastrophes, and she proceeded to unload the truck, feeling like a pack mule as she carried everything down to the church basement. Not for the first time, she wondered why no one else in Dan's family had offered to help her. Even Vera's call had been only to inquire if Shelley could pull it off, not to volunteer to help.

Shelley stood in the lackluster room and stared at the boxes of stuff. She didn't even know where to begin, and now she could hear the phone in her purse ringing. She hoped it wasn't Dan calling to say he was having a problem with the kids. "Hello?" she barked into the phone.

"Hey, Shelley. It's Maddie. How's it going?"

Shelley let out a groan. "Don't ask."

"What's wrong?"

Shelley looked at the big clock on the back wall. "Nothing. I just have a little more than an hour to put this whole thing together, and it looks absolutely hopeless. I haven't even started to unpack."

"You're kidding! You should be nearly set up by now. How can you possibly get it ready in time?"

Shelley felt on the verge of tears. "I don't know."

"I'll be there in a few minutes!" The line went dead.

As Shelley started to unpack a box, she wondered if she'd heard Maddie right. Was she really coming to help, or had Shelley just experienced a wishful daydream? But in under ten minutes, Maddie was there, working right alongside Shelley, blowing up balloons, stringing together flags, and basically showing her how to take what had previously looked like chaos and transform it into surprisingly wonderful party decorations.

"This cake is awesome," Maddie said as Shelley set the huge lighthouse-shaped cake in the center of the table.

"Check this out," Shelley said as she slipped the miniature flashlight into the hole she'd made in the top of the lighthouse, turning it on.

"The lighthouse actually works!" Maddie clapped her hands. "Genius!"

Shelley threw her arms around Maddie. "I never could've done this without you. I don't know how I'll ever thank you."

"By promising to make my next birthday cake?" Maddie chuckled.

"I'll make you lots of birthday cakes."

Maddie pointed to Shelley's jeans and T-shirt. "Why don't you go change while I do some finishing tweaks on this? And then I'll have to clear out of here. I promised to take the kids to the roller rink today."

Shelley glanced at the clock. Only fifteen minutes until party time. "Good idea. And if I don't see you before you go, *thanks*!" She hugged Maddie again, then grabbed up her party clothes and hurried to the restroom.

By the time Shelley emerged from her quick change, Maddie was gone and some of the guests were just starting to arrive.

"Oh, there you are," Frances said to her. "Ralph is coming later with some of the others. I thought I should see if you need any help."

"I can't wait to see this," Vera said.

Shelley led them down to the basement, opening the door and hoping that it still looked just as good as she'd left it. But instead, it looked better!

Maddie must've adjusted the lights because it was no longer so glaring. And she'd turned on the strings of white lights that she'd taped under tables and ledges, insisting they'd add to the atmosphere—and she'd been absolutely right. Not only that, but there was music playing. It sounded like an oldies collection—probably something right from Ralph's generation.

"Oh my!" Frances looked truly shocked.

"You did this?" Vera asked with wide eyes.

Shelley nodded. "With a little help from a friend."

The others came in, and suddenly everyone was oohing and awing. Dan and the kids arrived, and even Dan was truly astonished.

But the best part of the day was when Ralph arrived. He was so touched that he actually got tears in his eyes. He didn't know that Shelley had put it all together, so she was able to hear him going on about how it was all perfect and how it reminded him of his navy days. How great the lighthouse cake looked. And tasted even better since red velvet was his favorite. Dan had clued her in on this little detail.

As the party was winding down, Ralph stood up to make a little speech. He looked self-conscious as he told everyone how much he appreciated them and how glad he was that they'd made it here to celebrate with him. "And I don't know how many of you worked on this shindig, but I just have to say that it's been the best birthday party I've ever had. Thank you!"

Frances stood next to him, smiling graciously at everyone and, Shelley thought, almost acting as if she were taking the credit for everything. Shelley nudged Dan with her elbow, exchanging glances. Not that she expected him to do anything besides commiserate with her.

"And, Dad," Dan called out, "you might've guessed that Shelley made the cake."

Ralph grinned at Shelley. "Well, I thought maybe she did." He smacked his lips. "I already sneaked some of the leftovers onto a plate to take home with me. That just might be the best red velvet cake I ever tasted." He winked at his wife. "I can say that without any fear since Frances never made red velvet cake. Right, honey?"

She gave a placating smile. "The cake was very good, Shelley."

"But that's not all," Dan said proudly. "Shelley put this whole party together too. All the decorations and everything. She did it all." He slipped his arm around her and gave her a squeeze.

Suddenly Shelley felt a mixture of pride and embarrassment. It was sweet, but she hadn't really meant for him to do that.

Ralph looked slightly surprised. "Well, good for you, Shelley. I'm most obliged."

She gave him a nervous smile and nodded.

"That gives me an idea," Vera said, turning to Frances. "We haven't decided who's hosting Thanksgiving this year, have we, Mom?"

"No, we haven't." Frances pointed at Shelley. "And since our little Shelley has come such a long way in the art of entertaining, I think it's high time to let her and Dan host Thanksgiving."

"Oh, I don't know," Dan said quickly. "Our house is pretty small, and there's—"

"Your house is plenty big," Vera assured him. "Remember the year I did it in our little two-bedroom bungalow? It was fun."

And just like that it was settled. In under three weeks, Dan and Shelley would be hosting the Bauer family Thanksgiving.

Shelley looked up and noticed that one of the party balloons was almost deflated. She knew exactly how it felt.

CHAPTER TWENTY-FOUR

On Sunday afternoon, Diane enticed her friends to take a beach walk with her. "It's been a while since the four of us got together," she said as they started out.

"That's my fault," Shelley said. "I was so busy with all that birthday party preparation that I missed our coffee date last week. But the party turned out so great that Dan was happy to watch the kids for me today." She let out a tired sigh. "Of course, they're probably sound asleep by now."

"Maybe you should've stayed and napped with them," Margaret said.

"No, I'm glad to be out doing something." Shelley slapped the side of her hips. "Besides, I need the exercise."

Beverly laughed. "I think you must get plenty of exercise chasing your little ones around. I can't even imagine what that would be like."

Diane told them about how she and Beverly and Jeff Mackenzie had ventured out to the lighthouse on Halloween night. "Just to make sure no vandals were out making mischief."

"Was there any damage?" Shelley asked with concern.

"No," Diane said.

"I can't believe you didn't invite me to join you," Margaret said.

"I would've called," Diane told her. "But it was rather last-minute and late at night. I was actually going to go by myself, but I saw the kitchen light on at the Wheelands' and decided to ask Beverly along."

"But how did Jeff Mackenzie end up going?" Shelley asked curiously. "Or was he already at the lighthouse like last time?"

"No," Beverly told her. "He was, uh, just visiting me."

"Oh?" Shelley's brows shot up. "Something we should know about?"

Beverly gave her smirk. "No. Jeff and I are only friends."

"Anyway, Jeff was telling us these great stories about the lighthouse," Diane explained. "He's really done some good research on it."

"Why?" Shelley asked. "What's up with him and the lighthouse anyway?"

"That's a good question," Beverly said. "I'm not really sure."

"Do you think he's writing a book?" Margaret asked.

"He didn't mention it," Diane told her.

"So first we have your friend Barbara getting all interested in the lighthouse," Shelley began, "thinking she can change it into a bed-and-breakfast. And now it's this Jeff guy snooping around. Why can't everybody just leave our lighthouse alone?"

They laughed.

"It's not like we own the lighthouse," Diane said.

"I know." Shelley zipped up her jacket against the wind that was picking up. "But sometimes it feels like we do."

Margaret smiled mysteriously. "Maybe the lighthouse owns us…"

"How so?" Shelley asked.

"Well, remember it helped to save my life. At least that's what it felt like to me," Margaret said.

"And it brought me Rocky," Diane said.

"It brought me back to Marble Cove," Beverly said. "And connected me to my new friends."

"And it connected me to my father-in-law," Shelley said triumphantly. She told them all about the lighthouse cake she'd made for the party. "You guys should've seen it. I even had a flashlight for the beam."

"Did you get photos?"

"Of course!"

They chatted and visited as they walked toward Orlean Point Light.

Diane couldn't help but wonder about Margaret's words. She didn't really think the lighthouse owned them. But it did seem to have some sort of hold on all of them. Something intangible, but real just the same. "Has anyone seen the light recently?" Diane asked as they got closer to the tall white structure.

"Not since the night we found Jeff there," Margaret said. "How about on Halloween?"

"No." Diane shook her head. "Nothing."

"Did Jeff ever explain why he was flashing a light that night?" Margaret asked.

"Come to think of it, I forgot to ask him," Beverly admitted. "But I will."

"I'd sure like to know what he's looking for," Diane said. "And why."

"Well, I'll work on that," Beverly said.

"That must be some fun work," Shelley teased. "Don't you think he looks like George Clooney?"

Beverly laughed.

"Or a young Cary Grant?" Margaret suggested.

"So tell us, Margaret." Beverly was obviously changing the subject. "How's the mural coming?"

Margaret let out a growling sound. "It's not a happy subject."

"What's going on?" Diane asked.

"It's that Bernadette Lassiter." Margaret shook a fist. "She's turning the whole thing into a circus."

"A circus?" Shelley frowned. "You mean the mural is going to be of a circus?"

"Not exactly." Margaret scowled. "Although if she has her way it might resemble a clown act."

"I thought you were in charge," Beverly said.

"I thought so too. But it seems Ms. Lassiter has other ideas. I'm really trying to get out of it, but Charlotte Vincent keeps begging me to stick it out. And now the business owners are getting worried that the mural is going to be a mess. And, really, it is just one great big mess. Why did I ever agree to get involved in city politics?"

"A mural shouldn't be city politics," Diane said as they stopped to gather around the foot of the lighthouse.

"Well, it is," Margaret snapped. "And I just don't have the time or the patience for it. I had the first sketch nearly done when Ms. Lassiter stuck her oar in. Now we're on what must be the umpteenth set of sketches, and no one can agree on anything." She planted one foot on the short foundation wall of the lighthouse and just shook her head. "I want to wash my hands of the whole thing."

"What was the original mural idea?" Shelley asked.

"Just a seascape. I wanted to keep it simple so that the students wouldn't feel overwhelmed."

"That sounds nice."

"Well, not nice enough for Bernadette. She wanted more color, more life!" Margaret threw up her hands. "So then I suggested an underwater scene. I figured sea animals can be pretty colorful. And that would be fun for the students to paint."

"My kids would love that," Shelley told her.

"Too bad." Margaret rolled her eyes. "I had just started sketching it when Bernadette changed her mind again."

Diane patted Margaret on the shoulder. "Sounds like you've had a rough week."

"You can say that again."

"So have you agreed on anything?" Beverly asked.

"Just that we disagree on everything." Margaret pounded her fist against the lighthouse. "How could something so simple turn into something so totally frustrating?"

"Hey," Shelley said suddenly, "why don't you paint the lighthouse?"

Margaret looked like she was going to dismiss that idea, then she turned to stare up at the lighthouse as if considering it. "You know...that's not a bad idea. But I'd need something more than just the lighthouse."

"How about a ship?" Diane suggested. "Like one of the old ones. Maybe it's a raging storm and—"

"And the beam of the lighthouse is working!" Margaret finished for her.

"Wouldn't that be something?" Beverly looked up at the tower. "I'd love to see this lighthouse really working."

"Maybe you will," Margaret said. "At least in my mural."

"Do you think Bernadette will agree?" Diane asked.

"I'll make it my ultimatum. We do the lighthouse, or I walk."

*   ★   ★

It was less than two weeks before Thanksgiving when Diane learned that neither of her children would be joining her this year. She hadn't expected Justin to make it back, not with getting ready for officer training. But she had hoped that Jessica would be able to come. Now that seemed out of the question.

"I'm so sorry, Mom," Jessica said. "But I really like Martin, and I want to meet his family."

Diane sat down in her office, gazing out the window at the morning fog. "When you say *really like* him, what do you mean, honey? Is it serious?"

"I don't know, Mom." Jessica sounded slightly irritated.

"Sorry," Diane told her. "I don't want to be too nosy, but I'm curious. I'd like to meet this mysterious Martin too."

"He's not that mysterious, Mom. I've known him for a couple of years."

"But this is the first I've ever heard of him. And suddenly you're running off to Ohio to meet his parents. That sounds either serious or mysterious. I'm not sure."

Jessica laughed. "Don't make it into more than it is, Mom. I just happen to think he's…nice. I mean, I've known him for a while, but lately we've gotten to know each other a lot better. And he's even nicer than I thought. So I'm trying to be open. You know? And, naturally, I'm curious about his family."

"Naturally." Diane tried to sound supportive, but she really wanted to tell Jessica to just bring Martin here.

"If I was serious, you'd be the first to know, Mom." She giggled. "Or almost the first. I'd have to tell Martin before you."

"Well, I hope you have a good time with Martin's family." Diane tried to insert more cheer into her tone. "And if it gets more serious, you better give me a call. But now, I'm putting dibs on Christmas. Maybe you can bring Martin here to meet me."

"We'll see."

Diane tried not to stew on this after she hung up. After all, she had raised her children to be independent. What more could a mother want? Well, besides having both of her kids by her side for every single holiday! However, she knew from her own experience, especially after she and Eric had married, that it was impossible to make your parents happy all of the time. But she hoped Jessica was right about this Martin fellow and he really was nice. And maybe Diane would get to meet him at Christmas.

She turned her attention back to her computer and her writing. She'd been making great progress lately. Having written for the newspaper for years, Diane knew how to write fast. And she'd recently applied her speedy techniques to her novel. Write it fast, then go over it more slowly later. So far, it seemed to be working. She felt like she was in a groove, and it felt good.

She was just winding down a chapter when the phone rang. To her surprise, it was Gerald Kimball from the newspaper. "Sorry to both-ah you, Diane," he said in his usual thick Mainer accent, "but I'm a-doin' a piece about local authors, and I thought maybe you'd have the time to chat with me some."

"I'd be happy to chat with you, Gerald, but I'm not even a published author yet."

"That's true enough, but I heard you've got a three-book contract with a big publisher as well as a New York agent, and I suppose that's enough news for most folks around here."

"Well, if you think so."

"When would you have time to talk, do you think?"

"Anytime, Gerald." She leaned back in her chair.

"Anytime? *Hmm*. How about now?"

She chuckled. "Now is as good as ever."

"Can you meet me at the Cove in, say, about half an hour, do you think?"

"I'll be there with bells on."

"Well, now the bells might not be necessary. Although it'd add a little extra interest to my piece." He laughed.

Diane saved her work, freshened up a bit, and walked over to the Cove. She still couldn't get over the pleasure of living so close to town that she rarely needed to use her car.

Gerald was already there, so she ordered a latte from Brenna and went to join him.

"Thank you for accommodating me like this," he said as he sat back down. "I'm sure an old newspaper woman like you understands about deadlines and all."

"I certainly do." She tried not to grimace at his use of the word *old*. She knew it was just how Mainers talked.

Gerald opened his little black notebook and began to ask her questions. When had she first begun writing? When did she decide to switch from newspaper writing to novels? What were her novels about?

"I'm afraid my answers aren't terribly interesting," she said.

"Nah, that's pretty much what I expected." He smiled. "In fact, I can relate to your answers."

"Yes, I figured you could. Especially when it came to newspaper writing."

He closed his notebook and leaned forward conspiratorially. "You see, I'm writing a novel too."

She felt her brows lifting. "Really?"

"Uh-huh. Oh, I don't have a big fancy New York agent like you do. Not yet anyway. But my novel is good. I can tell you that for sure." He looked hopefully at her. "Any chance you'd have time to read it? I thought perhaps you'd want to endorse it and maybe you'd introduce me to some of your publishing friends."

She felt a moment of dread in the pit of her stomach. How could she possibly endorse anyone at this point in her career?

"What kind of novel are you writing, Gerald?"

"It's a sci-fi story. It's set in a faraway planet, where the Galaxians are being attacked by the—"

Diane held up her hands and smiled. "Sounds fascinating, Gerald. But I don't know that I'm qualified to comment on sci-fi. I could lend you my agent reference books if that would help you find an agent that specializes in that genre. That's how I found my agent."

"Thanks, Diane! That would be great. I knew you'd be a great resource."

Then he promised to call her if he came up with any more questions for his article.

As she walked home, Diane wondered whether today's interview was about her as an author or about her as someone who might be able to help his own career. It wasn't that she didn't want to help others. It was simply that she barely knew what she was doing herself. It would be like the blind leading the blind.

Still, as she went into her house, she felt like someone had let the air out of her balloon. Although it was likely just a bunch of hot air that needed letting out. But, feeling less like a famous novelist and more like an "old newspaper woman," as Gerald had so bluntly put it, she went back to her office and turned on her computer.

She reminded herself, as she pulled out her chair, that first and foremost, being a writer was simply a matter of sitting down and writing.

CHAPTER TWENTY-FIVE

Margaret, who normally slept peacefully, tossed and turned like a ship in rough waters. All night long she was plagued with worrisome thoughts and bad dreams—not about Adelaide eloping because her crush on Hank seemed to be dying a natural death—but about Bernadette Lassiter and that confounded mural at the Cannery.

Finally, she couldn't take the torture anymore. She quietly slipped out of bed, pulled on some clothes, left Allan a note, and sneaked out of the house. Although it was still dark out, she hurried to town and went straight into the gallery. If she couldn't sleep, at least she could paint. She turned on the lights and found her way into the back room to begin to get things set up.

Painting always helped to clear her head. She'd be accomplishing two things—she would preserve her sanity and perhaps finish this seascape. It felt so good to get lost in her painting. It was almost as if she had stepped away from her problems by entering a whole different world. She lost track of time.

She was just putting the finishing touches on a cloud when she heard the front doorbell tinkling. Oh dear, had she forgotten to lock it? Or maybe it was Allan coming by to check on her. She looked at her watch and was surprised to see that it was already past ten in the morning. Could it possibly be a customer?

"I'm back here," she called as she set down her brush. "Coming." She hurried out, peeling off the flannel shirt she'd been wearing as a smock.

"Bernadette." Margaret took in a deep breath when she saw her visitor. "I'm surprised to see you here. I lost track of time in the back and forgot to put up the Open sign."

Bernadette waved her hand around the gallery. "The lights are on, but nobody's home?" She laughed as if her attempt at humor was amusing.

Margaret made a tolerant smile. "Is there something I can help you with?"

Bernadette was walking around the gallery now. Dressed in her usual Bohemian style, with a long colorful skirt and lots of beaded jewelry, and with her long curly hair piled dramatically onto her head, she actually looked right at home in here. In fact, if Margaret liked her better, she would even consider her an interesting subject to paint. As it was, Margaret wished the young woman would leave.

"We really are a mismatch, aren't we?" Bernadette turned to face Margaret now.

Margaret held up her hands. "I'm afraid we are. The question is, what are we going to do about it?"

"Try to get along better?" Bernadette smiled slyly. "Learn to play well with others?"

Margaret sighed. "The head of the Society for Beautification paid me a visit yesterday."

"Whatever for?"

"They're worried that the mural is never going to be finished on time, which is a legitimate concern." Margaret tried not to remember how horrible the wall had looked when she'd left it yesterday. With Margaret's realistic sketch of Orlean Point Light on one side and the rough sketch of a silly-looking pirate ship on the other, it was no wonder that people were uneasy. "And they're also worried that if it gets finished it will need to be painted over."

"Yes," Bernadette sighed. "I've heard the rumblings."

Everything in Margaret wanted to give up now. She would love to tell Bernadette to take the project and do as she liked with it. Except that the business owners had been pleading with her to rescue this mission.

"I thought you knew that we wanted to open up for business the last weekend of November," Lucy Andrews had told her just yesterday. "We wanted to make a big splash." She'd frowned up at the mural. "But not like that. Surely you're not going to allow that comic book ship to remain, are you?"

"I don't know what to do about it," Margaret had told her. "Bernadette and I have two completely different styles."

Poor Lucy had just shaken her head, mumbling under her breath as she'd returned to the boutique she was working so hard to get ready.

Margaret studied Bernadette now. "Do you have any ideas? Suggestions for how we can make the mural work out and make everyone happy? You know that the high school students are scheduled to begin working on it starting tomorrow. Do you really think we're ready for that?"

Bernadette folded her arms across her front with a stubborn expression. The same expression Margaret had seen too many times before.

"I'd honestly like to quit the project," Margaret told her. "And then you could paint whatever you like and sort it all out yourself."

Bernadette looked slightly surprised, but said nothing.

"Except that I gave them my word." Margaret sighed. "I really thought that you liked the idea of the lighthouse and the ship at sea. I thought we could make it work."

"I did like the idea." She held up her hands. "It's just that I envisioned it differently."

"Because you and I have completely different styles," Margaret said for what felt like the hundredth time. "And I really don't feel our styles are compatible." She took in a deep breath. "And for that reason, I think it would be best for everyone if I stepped down."

Bernadette's dark brows arched. "You'd really do that?"

"I believe I just did." Margaret felt as if a weight had been lifted. She walked over and stuck out her hand. "And I truly wish you the best, Bernadette."

Bernadette shook her hand with a dumbfounded look.

"You are in charge, and I will be very curious to see how it all turns out. Maybe you will even make the deadline now."

She smiled a genuine smile. "Now, if you'll excuse me, I need to go wash my brushes."

"Just like that?" Bernadette still looked perplexed. "You're going to give up and walk out on me just like that?"

Margaret felt herself tensing up again. "What else can I do? For the sake of the business owners and the chamber and the high school students and even the Society for Beautification, I feel I have to step down. Otherwise we'll continue in this stalemate, and nothing will get done."

Bernadette's brows drew together as she stepped closer, glaring at Margaret. "Are you doing this on purpose? Just to make me look bad?"

"No, of course not." Margaret firmly shook her head. "I don't want anyone to look bad. I just want to see the project finished—and in a way that doesn't look ridiculous. I honestly don't know how else to do it. But I'm open to suggestions. So far the only thing I hear from you is that you don't like my ideas. And we can't keep going back to the drawing board."

Bernadette started strolling around the gallery again, slightly bent forward as if she were thinking deeply. Then suddenly she stopped, whirled around, and faced Margaret. "Fine," she snapped. "We'll do it your way."

Margaret blinked. "But I... Are you sure?"

Bernadette put her hands on her hips now. "You are just like my mother, Margaret."

"What?"

"My mother has always made me feel like I'm not good enough. Whether it's my art or my clothes or the men in my life, my mother is always looking down her nose at me. Just like you do."

Margaret walked over to look more closely at her. "I do not look down my nose at you," she said quietly.

"Yes, you do."

Margaret pressed her lips together, trying to determine if this were true. "I know we're different sort of artists," she said gently, "but I honestly don't think I look down on you."

"But you refused to hang my work in here." Bernadette waved her arm.

"Because it doesn't fit in here. I already explained that to you."

Bernadette took on a pout now.

"You know, Bernadette," Margaret spoke slowly, "when I was younger, when I first started painting, I was still learning. And if that younger me walked in here today, and if she wanted to hang those paintings in my gallery, I'd have to say no to her too. It's nothing personal. It's just that I'm going for a certain look in here." Margaret looked closer at Bernadette's beaded necklace. "And just for the record, I love the way you dress."

Bernadette brightened. "You do?"

"Absolutely. In fact, I was thinking I'd love to paint you. Not that I'm terribly good at portraits. But you are so dramatic looking. And your clothes and your jewelry, well, it's just so wonderful and colorful."

"Are you serious?"

"Yes." Margaret pointed to her necklace. "Where do you find these pieces? They truly are works of art in and of themselves."

"You think so?" Bernadette fingered the beads and smiled. "I make them myself."

Margaret was surprised. "Really? You make them?"

She nodded.

"Do you sell them anywhere?"

Bernadette shook her head. "No. Sometimes I give pieces to friends."

"I want to sell *those* in my gallery," Margaret told her.

"Seriously?"

"Oh yes. Can't you just imagine an attractive wooden display case filled with a beautiful selection of your pieces?" Margaret pointed to one of Allan's custom cabinets. "I'd have Allan make something special."

"Really? You'd honestly carry my jewelry in here?"

"Absolutely. Do you think you'd be interested?"

Bernadette nodded. "I think so."

"Great." Margaret smiled. "At least we agree on something."

"And since we agree upon that, I have a suggestion for the mural now." Bernadette's mouth twisted to one side. "How about if you take the lead, Margaret? You go ahead and do the preliminary sketches in your very realistic style. Then I'll follow behind you, working with the high school students to fill it in with color, according to your specifications. Would that make you happy?"

"It would make me happy to simply get the mural done," Margaret said. "I actually had nightmares about it last night." Maybe, just maybe, she wouldn't have to spend Thanksgiving Day worrying about the mural not being finished.

"That's too bad." Bernadette patted her on the back. "And just so you know, I actually love the lighthouse idea. I think it'll be stunning when we're finished."

"Here's to finishing."

CHAPTER TWENTY-SIX

The day before Thanksgiving, Shelley thought she must've been certifiable to have allowed Frances and Vera to corner her into hosting it this year.

"Well, it's too late now," Dan told her as he put his dish in the sink.

"But it's nuts." She tipped her head toward their stove and scrubbed scorched oatmeal from the saucepan. "I only have two burners that work."

"Yeah, but you know everyone brings food anyway. All you really have to cook is the turkey and dressing, and that's in the oven. And then the potatoes and gravy. And also the—"

"Stop!" She held up the scrub brush. "I know exactly what I have to prepare, Dan, and I don't need you to lecture me on it. I'm just saying that we, out of all your family members, should not be hosting Thanksgiving this year." Now she pointed to the sink. "I mean, look, even the garbage disposal is on the blink!"

"Remember the pilgrims, Shell. They didn't have garbage disposals or any fancy appliances, and they still managed to have a pretty good time."

She held up the stainless steel pan like a weapon now, tempted to really use it.

"Just sayin'." He backed off with a guilty smile.

"Well, here's what I'm saying, *Daniel Bauer*. I expect you to help me big-time with this dinner. That doesn't just meaning watching the kids either. You have to peel potatoes and chop vegetables and—"

"Gotta go, Shell. Remember I'm working down at the docks today." He patted Emma on the head and blew Shelley a kiss. "See ya 'round five."

"Have a good day," she said, her tone less than sincere. Oh, she knew she had a bad attitude. And she hoped she'd get over it by tomorrow. In the meantime, she had a bazillion things to get done. Thank goodness Adelaide was coming to help out today.

Shelley continued to clean the kitchen. With luck, Aiden had taken her warning seriously and was getting dressed in his bedroom. Although it was more likely that he was sitting in the middle of his room, half dressed and playing with his Legos.

"Hey, little girl," she called to Emma, who was starting to bang on her high chair tray impatiently. "I'm coming. Just let me finish wiping down these countertops, okay?" Then to further distract her restless daughter, Shelley began to sing nursery rhyme songs. That usually bought her a couple of minutes.

"There," she said as she threw the dishcloth into the sink. "At least that's done." She went over to extract Emma from the high chair, feeling a little more hopeful about her day.

She'd decided at the beginning of the week that, in order to survive Thanksgiving, along with all the extra baking she'd taken on at the Cove, she would have to stay on top of her household chores. So far she was managing to do so. Was she exhausted? Well, of course! But at least her house wasn't a chaotic mess. Plus, she could look forward to slowing down a bit next week. She couldn't even think about Christmas yet.

She put Emma down on the living room floor, setting some toys around for her to play with. Emma had woken extra early today, and it was getting close to her morning nap time, but Shelley wanted to be sure she was nicely worn out first. Then, while Adelaide was playing with Aiden, Shelley could get more things ready for Thanksgiving.

She still needed to give the bathrooms a thorough scrub. And she needed to put some things in the garage and rearrange the furniture in the living room, since that was where she planned to set up the tables so everyone could sit together. Which meant she needed to wash the big window in there, since the kids' greasy, grimy handprints were entirely unappetizing.

Thanks to Maddie's influence, Shelley had turned into a list-maker. She was surprised at how much time and stress this saved. Was she ever in danger of getting a real case of MBS—Maddie Bancroft Syndrome? Probably not. But at least she might pick up some helpful habits.

Shelley had just put Emma down, and Adelaide and Aiden were playing happily and noisily in the family room, when she heard someone step onto the front porch. She hoped it wasn't anyone who wanted to stay and visit. She hurried to open it before whoever it was rang the doorbell and woke Emma. To her surprise, it was Dan's father.

"Ralph, hi! Please, come in."

"Frances asked me to drop the dishes by."

"Dishes?"

"Yeah, they're in the car. I wasn't sure you were home. I'll run and get them."

She followed him out, then helped to carry one of the large plastic crates into the house. "Are these Frances' Thanksgiving dishes?" Shelley asked nervously. She remembered Frances' beloved set of china. Decorated with turkeys and cornucopias, it made an appearance once a year. Sure, these dishes were kind of pretty and festive, but there was so much of it, and with Shelley's undependable dishwasher, it would all probably need to be washed by hand afterward. That could take days.

"Yeah. She thought you'd want them."

Shelley grimaced. "I was...uh...actually thinking of using paper plates this year."

One of his brows lifted. "Well, now."

"I mean, they'd be the good kind, the ones that are heavy duty and big and everything. I already bought them. They were on sale this week."

He just nodded.

"Frances won't like that, will she?"

"Probably not." Ralph gave her a crooked smile. "But Frances isn't hosting this dinner, Shelley. You are."

She felt a smidgeon of hope. "You think it would be okay?"

He grinned and patted her on the back. "I think it would be better than okay. The point of Thanksgiving is to get together. Shouldn't matter what kind of dishes you use, right?"

She nodded eagerly. "Yeah, that's what I think."

"How about if I take these dishes back home?"

Shelley's optimism faded. "But Frances will see them and wonder why I'm not using them."

He nodded, rubbing his chin. "Want me to stick them in a closet or something?"

Shelley giggled. "How about the garage?"

"Fine by me." He chuckled.

They carried them out to the garage and set them in a corner. Shelley felt a tiny bit guilty, but more than that, she felt relieved. "And maybe I'll change my mind," she told Ralph as they went back inside. "And use them after all. I mean, they are kind of pretty."

"It's up to you." He sniffed the air. "Got any coffee?"

"Sure. Would you like some?"

Soon they were sitting at her kitchen table with coffee and a plate of Shelley's pastries.

"Oh, Shelley," he said as he smacked his lips, "this is about the best cinnamon roll I've ever tasted."

She grinned. "Thanks. I made those at the Cove last night." She explained how she made some of her baked goods for them and some for her Internet customers, and how she brought an assortment home with her each night. "It's a wonder I'm not packing on the pounds."

"How is that working for you?" he asked. "Baking at the coffee shop at night? Seems like a lonely kind of job."

She forced a smile. "It's okay, I guess. And it's kind of *my* time, you know?"

"You don't miss being at home with your family in the evenings?"

She felt her chin begin to tremble. "Well, yeah, sure. It's been kind of stressful. Like I'm torn between two worlds." Tears slipped out. Embarrassed, she got up to get a paper napkin. "I know Dan doesn't much like it either." She blew her nose with her back to him. "But it's what we have to do...for now. And my business is really growing. I'm getting more and more orders each week."

"That's good." His voice sounded doubtful.

"It is good. But I don't want my family or my marriage to suffer because of my business," she confessed. "More than anything, I want to be a good wife and mom. I know I've got a lot to learn about that, and I know that Frances thinks I'm hopeless. And I'll admit I've been lazy in the past, or maybe I was just plain tired, but I'm really trying, and I think I'm getting better."

She couldn't believe how much she was telling him, but it was like the cork had popped off and it all just came pouring out. "It hasn't been easy for Dan and me. You know how the job situation is...and that can be stressful...so I think it's important I contribute financially. And I'm seeing that I really can lighten Dan's load. But it's still hard. It's hard on all of us."

"Sometimes it's the hard things that make us strong," he said quietly. "It's like the glue that holds us together."

"So I don't want to give up on my business. Not yet." She went to get one of the glossy brochures that Beverly had helped her to make, handing it to him. "See, everyone is finally starting to take me seriously. I can't just quit while I'm barely getting started."

"I understand that, Shelley. But can't you figure out a way to do your baking at home?"

"I wish I could." Now she explained about state laws and kitchens that didn't comply and how the department of health could shut them down and fine them. "It's possible to have a home kitchen meet those standards, but not for us. Not now. Believe me, I'd love to have a commercial-grade oven and all that." She let out a resigned laugh. "Right now, I'd be thrilled just to have four stove burners that worked at the same time, or even a garbage disposal."

"Your stove's not working?" He went over to look at it, fiddling with knobs. "That's the problem with these smooth-top ranges. You can't just pull out an element and replace it like you could with the old-fashioned stoves."

"I know. But it came with the house. Most of the time it's not a big deal."

He went over to look at the disposal.

"Dan already checked it," she told him. "He said it's just plain worn out."

Ralph nodded, rubbing his chin. "Maybe this wasn't such a good idea—asking you kids to host Thanksgiving this year."

"It's too late to back out now." She forced a smile. "Besides, I'm actually sort of looking forward to it. I've got it all planned out. I'll do most of the baking at the Cove tonight. Then it's just getting the turkey into the oven tomorrow. At least that works." She laughed. "And, like Dan reminded me just this morning, the pilgrims made do without any of this, so we can too. Thanksgiving will be fine."

He grinned. "You're a trouper, Shelley."

"But sometimes I march to a different drummer... different than Frances' drummer anyway." Shelley sighed. "I hope she doesn't mind if I don't use those dishes."

"Can I tell you something?" His expression was hard to read. "Off record?"

"Of course."

"My wife, God love her—and I do too—can be a little persnickety sometimes, if you know what I mean. And it wouldn't hurt her to eat a meal or two off paper plates. So you just forget all about those fancy dishes, Shelley. Do Thanksgiving your way, and let the chips fall where they may."

She nodded. "I will."

"Thanks for the coffee and the treats." He turned to leave.

"Wait," Shelley called as she hurried to get a small paper sack, slipping the last two cinnamon rolls into it. "Take these with you, Ralph."

He chuckled. "Don't mind if I do."

After Ralph left, Shelley felt strangely empowered, as if he'd given her permission to break the rules. Or perhaps to simply make her own rules. Thanksgiving might be a little different this year, but the food would be tasty, and she hoped everyone would have a good time.

★   ★   ★

Shelley wasn't feeling quite so empowered as she came home after a long night of baking at the Cove. But at least she'd gotten all those pies and cakes and rolls finished.

She braced herself as she came into the house. Despite her urging Dan to keep things tidy, she was used to coming home to all sorts of messes. And, although she was tired, she was prepared to stay up late and clean. However, the house looked just as good as, or maybe better than, she'd left it.

"Hello," Dan called from the kitchen.

"You're still up?" She set her basket of goodies on the table and looked around. "And the kitchen is clean." She smiled at him. "Thanks."

"Just finishing." He turned off the faucet and came over to peek in the basket. "Is that for Thanksgiving dinner?"

"No, it's for breakfast, or whatever. Help yourself. You deserve a treat after cleaning up like you did."

He took out a chocolate muffin and began to peel off the paper.

She got him a glass of milk and started herself a cup of tea. "Your dad came by today." She told him about the Thanksgiving dishes. "Do you think it'll hurt your mom's feelings too much if I don't use them?"

He shrugged. "It's your call, Shell. But I vote for paper plates. And I sure don't want to be on KP with all those fancy-schmancy dishes."

"Then it's settled." She sat down at the table with her tea. "It was really nice visiting with your dad today. I think retirement agrees with him. It's like he's opening up a lot more."

"Retirement..." Dan sighed. "Sounds good."

She chuckled. "You're too young to be thinking that."

"Well, sometimes it feels like we're just running and running and never really catching up."

"Your dad said the hard parts of life are like the glue that will hold us together."

Dan took a slow sip of milk, then nodded. "Hope he's right."

She reached across the table, putting her hand on his. "We're going to get through this," she said quietly. "I can just feel it inside of me. This struggle to get by is just temporary, Dan. We'll get past it someday."

"In the meantime, at least we're eating like kings." He popped the last bite of chocolate muffin into his mouth and a slow smile spread over his face. "You're a good woman, Shelley Bauer."

CHAPTER TWENTY-SEVEN

Shelley didn't have to ask twice for Dan to go to the church to pick up folding tables and extra chairs. She knew it was partly because the alternative would be for him to stay with the kids and peel potatoes. Still, she was relieved not to have to leave the house. And, with such a long to-do list, every minute counted.

"Mom," Aiden said with a whine, "I'm hungry."

"You just had breakfast," she reminded him as she chopped celery.

"But I'm hungry."

"Here," she handed him a celery stick. "Munch on that."

He made a face, holding the celery at arm's length.

"How about if I put peanut butter in it?"

"Yeah!" He nodded eagerly. "Ants on a log!"

Shelley sighed as she set down her knife and went to look for raisins and peanut butter. Why was it that when time was limited and she needed to get things done, the kids seemed needier than ever? She finally got Aiden happily settled with ants on a log, but now Emma was fussing, and it was still too early for her morning nap.

Shelley set a teething toy and some Cheerios on the high chair tray. She hoped she could buy enough time to finish chopping up the ingredients for dressing. But now she knew Dan was right: she never should've tried to make homemade dressing. It took too much time and didn't taste that much better than store-bought.

She looked at the clock and wondered why he wasn't back yet.

"Mom!" Aiden screeched.

She turned in time to see him pointing at Prize, who was in the midst of leaving a "surprise" by the back door.

"Oh, Prize!" Shelley dropped her knife and grabbed some paper towels as she hurried over to shoo the dog outside. "You should've let her out," she said to Aiden as she cleaned up the mess. "Prize is your dog. You're supposed to take care of her."

"I *did* let her out," Aiden said in a wounded tone.

Shelley knew she was on the verge of losing it. And she'd been determined to stay even-keeled today. That had been her prayer during her morning quiet time. After disposing of the mess and washing her hands, she closed her eyes and took in a slow, deep breath. She would remain composed. She would not yell at her kids. She would not yell at her husband. Even if everything did not get done just like she wanted, she would not throw a fit. She would not! Still, *where was Dan?*

She was just reaching for the phone when Dan came in. "Hey, Shell," he said cheerfully.

"What took you so long?"

His smile faded. "I ran into Mr. Bannister at the church. He was gathering up folding chairs too. He said Mrs. Bannister wants you to do the baked goods for her Christmas tea."

"Oh." She nodded. "That's great."

"Want me to start setting up the tables and chairs?"

"Thanks!"

As she busied herself she thought of how the guys would be glued to football once they got here. Meanwhile the women would be in the kitchen. Some things never changed. Not that Shelley minded particularly. It wasn't like she wanted to watch football. And she was perfectly comfortable in a kitchen. It was simply that her kitchen was pretty lackluster compared to everyone else's in Dan's family.

Still, she was determined to make the best of it. Maybe they didn't have the latest, greatest kitchen appliances, but at least she could cook.

While Emma was napping and Aiden was playing outside with Dan and the dog, Shelley did her best to pretty up the folding tables. They were lined up in the center of the living room, with enough room to accommodate eighteen grown-up guests. Plus there was a smaller kiddie table tucked in a nearby corner. It would be cozy, but at least they'd be seated together. Last year, when Vera had hosted, their Thanksgiving dinner had been served buffet style, and the men had ended up eating in front of the big-screen TV while the football game blared.

Thanks to Maddie, Shelley had found fall-colored paper tablecloths and napkins at the dollar store. And then Shelley had cut chrysanthemums and other fall blooms from her own yard, which she'd arranged in small, hollowed-out pumpkins for cheap centerpieces. Each one had a rust-colored taper candle in the center. For place cards, she and Aiden had made little turkeys from a pattern Maddie had given her.

She stood back to survey her work, deciding that the overall effect was actually rather festive. She hoped no one would complain about Frances' missing dishes. Certainly no one would be complaining when it came time to clean up!

When the guests began to arrive, Shelley felt surprisingly relaxed. She knew this dinner wasn't picture-perfect. But she realized she didn't really care. Most of all, she just wanted everyone, including Frances, to have a really good time.

She greeted everyone warmly, taking their coats and offering appetizers, which she'd set up on the kitchen table. Comments were made—some sweet, some a bit less than sweet—about the tables set up in the living room.

"This is certainly quaint," Vera said lightly. "And cozy."

"It's the best we could do," Shelley told her. "I just hope everyone doesn't mind squeezing in together."

"What is this?" Frances picked up one of the heavy-duty paper plates and frowned. "I thought Ralph brought you the Thanksgiving dishes, Shelley."

Shelley gave her a rehearsed smile. "Yes, he did. But I was worried that I might break some. My dishwasher isn't as fancy as yours, and sometimes I put a plate in it that's in one piece and it comes out in several. So I decided it was better to be safe than sorry. I didn't think you'd mind."

Frances pursed her lips, then nodded. "Oh, you can't machine wash my china! They have to be hand washed."

"I'm just too afraid we'd break some plates with all that handling," Shelley said.

Frances seemed unsure. "Well, it would be a shame to break any of those pretty dishes. I do so love them."

Shelley did everything she could to make everyone comfortable as they sat down to eat. Of course, there were the usual mishaps. Aiden spilled a whole plate of food on his cousin. Dan's brother Darrell reminded Shelley that he had a nut allergy and couldn't eat the dressing.

But all in all, the sit-down meal went smoothly, and everyone seemed to think the food was delicious. By the time Shelley was setting out the desserts—in her opinion, the pièces de résistance—she was feeling optimistic. Like maybe she hadn't ruined the family's Thanksgiving after all. Even after the guys drifted to the football game and the women were putting away food, the atmosphere remained relaxed and congenial.

"It's kind of nice not having to wash dishes," Dan's youngest sister said as she refilled her coffee mug.

"Maybe we should do paper plates at Christmas too," another sister-in-law suggested.

"But you love my Christmas china," Frances reminded her. "It wouldn't be Christmas without it."

"What's wrong with this thing?" Vera called from where she was standing by the sink.

"Oh dear." Shelley gasped to see that Vera had poured the leftover green bean casserole into the sink, and it was now completely clogged. "The disposal doesn't work."

"Eww." Vera grimaced. "Sorry about that."

Shelley forced a smile. "It's okay. I'll deal with it later. Does anyone want to play board games?" Shelley started to list the games she had, and before long, with seconds of dessert and coffee in hand, the women went to the living room to play Apples to Apples.

Midway through the afternoon, a bunch of them took the kids outside and played some haphazard football. And when guests finally started to leave, it was already getting dusky out.

Dan slipped his arm around Shelley and pulled her close. "You were a great hostess."

"How about if I give you a hand taking these tables and chairs back to the church, Dan?" Ralph offered.

"I'd appreciate that, Dad." They started loading them into Dan's pickup.

"You did a nice job, dear," Frances told Shelley as she slipped on her coat. "Even if you did use paper plates. By the way, Dan put the dishes in my car."

"Oh, good."

Frances gave her an appraising look. "I honestly didn't think you had it in you, Shelley."

"I have to admit I didn't either." Shelley jiggled Emma in her arms. "But it was actually fun."

"Maybe you'd like to offer to host Christmas." Frances peered curiously at her.

Shelley laughed. "Well, it wasn't *that* fun."

"I hope Dan won't mind driving his dad home," Frances told her. "Because I'm tired."

"You go on ahead," Shelley said. "We'll get Ralph home safely."

"Thank you for a very nice day." Frances kissed Emma on the cheek and patted Aiden on the head, then made her exit.

Sighing in tired relief, Shelley closed the door. She was ready to just collapse and relax, but Emma needed a diaper change, and Aiden claimed he was hungry.

She tended to the kids, finally getting them settled in the family room, where she let Aiden put in a Barney DVD. She knew they were both tired, but with hopes of sleeping in tomorrow morning, she wanted to keep them up until their regular bedtime.

"Hey, Shelley," Dan called. "There you are."

She smiled up from where she was stretched out on the floor with the kids and a pile of pillows.

"I hate to disturb you." Dan's expression was hard to decipher. "But I need you to give Dad a ride home."

"Huh?" She sat up.

"It's complicated. But do you mind?"

Of course she minded. "Well…"

"He's outside."

"You left your dad outside?" She stood now, staring at Dan. "Why didn't you just take him home?"

He rubbed his hand through his hair with a strange look. "Dad will explain. Just go ahead and go, okay? It's getting cold out there."

Shelley shook her head. "Fine." She let out an exasperated sigh as she went for her purse and jacket, digging out her car keys as she headed out. Why on earth hadn't Dan just driven Ralph on home instead of dragging him back here? Good grief!

She found Ralph standing by her car with his hands in the pockets of his plaid wool jacket. "I guess I'm giving you a ride." She tried to act like this was perfectly normal as she got into her car and started up the engine.

Ralph buckled his seat belt, then grinned at her. "You probably wonder what's going on."

She glanced curiously at him as she backed out. "Yeah. Kinda."

"Well, I wanted to talk to you, Shelley."

"Oh." Now she felt worried. Was something wrong? Had she offended him somehow? Did it have to do with Frances and not using the dishes? Or was it something more serious? What if someone's health was in trouble?

"You did a really good job today, and the meal was excellent," he told her. "And that was despite not having a fully functional kitchen."

"Don't remind me." She grimaced. "Poor Dan still has to clean out a mess in the kitchen sink. Vera didn't realize our disposal wasn't working."

"So, anyway, I've got an idea, Shelley. And I wanted to run it past you."

"What kind of an idea?"

He cleared his throat. "Well, I've got some investments that need to be turned over or reinvested within the next six months."

"Okay…" She wasn't sure where this was going or how it had anything to do with her, but her curiosity was piqued.

"And I like what you're doing with your baking business. There's no denying you're an excellent cook. So I got to thinking…what if I invested in you?"

Shelley sat up straighter. "In me?"

"Sure. As hard as you've been working to get your business off the ground, and without even having your own kitchen, well, it impressed me. And I got to thinking, what if Dan and I, along with some of my construction buddies, helped you to build a new commercial-grade kitchen?"

"Are you serious?" She turned to look at him as she stopped at the stop sign. With only the lights from the dashboard to illuminate his face, she couldn't read his expression. Was he pulling her leg? She knew Ralph could be a jokester at times.

"You bet. I talked it over with Dan, and he told me that when you did your research, it seemed like the best solution for a commercial kitchen was to build an addition. He and I were talking it over today, and we thought that if we built the addition right off the existing kitchen, it might not be so rough on your family, you know, during the remodel. Then once the new kitchen was done, we'd just gut the old kitchen and turn it into a nice big dining room. It's about the right size for it. So, tell me, what would you think of that?"

Shelley was too stunned to answer.

"Unless you think that I'm interfering. It's always been my rule not to overstep my bounds with my kids. But I do think you have a solid business idea, Shelley. I think you're proving it can work. And, the truth is, I've never really helped you and Dan out much. Maybe it's about time. Anyway, I'd just like to do this. What do you think?"

"I'm totally flabbergasted," she confessed as she turned down their road. "I feel like I must be dreaming. Did you really just offer to build us a kitchen?"

"That's what I'm saying."

"A commercial-grade kitchen for my baking business?" She was trying to wrap her head around this.

"Yep. We can save some money by using our own labor. And you and Dan will still need to help out with the appliances. But I've got some handy friends who owe me. I'm thinking we could get to it during winter when some guys aren't so busy. We ought to have you up and running by springtime."

She pulled up in front of her in-laws' house and got out of the car, ran around to the other side, and opened the passenger door. When Ralph got out, she threw her arms around him and hugged him tight. "I feel like I just won the lottery." She had tears running down her cheeks. "How can I ever thank you?"

He chuckled. "Oh, I'm thinking baked goods will do."

"You got it." She stepped back and looked at him. "Really, I'm just blown away by your generosity. I can hardly believe it." She pulled a tissue out of her pocket and wiped her nose. "No one ever did anything like this for me before. Not ever."

"Then I guess it's time someone did." He patted her on the back. "Now you better get back home to your family, Shelley. You drive safely, you hear?"

"I will." She hugged and thanked him again. And then, with dreams of her new kitchen dancing in her head, she carefully drove home, where Dan already had the kids put to bed.

"I'm in shock," she said as they sat together by the fireplace in the family room. "Total shock."

"Me too," he said.

"You know all about my dad," she said quietly, "how he ran out on us…how he never helped me with anything. It's just so hard to believe your dad would do something like this…for me. I mean, I'm not even his own kid."

"Dad likes you, Shell."

"Well, I like him too. But I'm still pretty stunned that he would do this."

"And he really likes your cinnamon rolls."

"We'll see that he never goes without them." Now she thought of something. "Does your mom know about this? I mean, his generous offer to build our kitchen?"

"I don't know."

"What if she doesn't like this idea?"

Dan laughed. "That's never stopped my dad from doing what he wanted before. I doubt it would now. Besides, she'd eventually come around anyway. She always does."

Shelley leaned her head back and closed her eyes, releasing a long, happy sigh. "We have a whole lot to be thankful for this Thanksgiving, Dan. A whole lot."

CHAPTER TWENTY-EIGHT

Beverly couldn't believe she'd actually invited Jeff Mackenzie to Thanksgiving—or that she was attempting this on her own. Of course, Diane who was also having Thanksgiving dinner with them, had been a huge help in the preparations. But the turkey finishing up in the oven had been Beverly's handiwork. And she'd actually made dressing—even if it was from a mix. Still, her mother would've been proud of her.

At exactly the assigned time, the doorbell rang. Now came the uncomfortable part.

Jeff looked so handsome. That was what she noticed first, despite her determination not to pay attention to such things. He gave her a hug and handed over the pecan pie he'd brought. With a deep breath, Beverly led him in to meet her father and the others.

"Jeff Mackenzie?" Father repeated the name with too much interest as well as a creased brow. Carefully studying Jeff as they shook hands, he seemed almost suspicious. "Have we met before, Jeff?"

"No," Beverly said quickly. "I don't think so."

"But that name is familiar."

"I did live in Augusta for a while," Jeff said.

"Maybe that's it," Father said. "Did we meet—"

"I really doubt it." Beverly wanted to end this. She was still getting used to the fact that her father's memory was improving daily. But surely he couldn't remember anything about Jeff. Why would he?

"I know what it is," Jeff said suddenly.

"What?"

"We spoke on the phone."

Her father nodded eagerly. "Yes, that's it. Jeff Mackenzie. You called here for Beverly." He glanced curiously at her now. "So...Beverly...how do you know Mr. Mackenzie?" he asked.

"Oh, we met back in Augusta," she told him as they headed to the dining room. "Then I bumped into him here in Marble Cove."

"That's right," Jeff added. "At the lighthouse, actually."

"Really?" Father looked far too interested now. "At the lighthouse, you say?"

Diane jumped in. "Mr. Wheeland," she said to Beverly's father, "we have a minute before dinner. Why don't you show me one of the therapeutic exercises you're working on? Did the doctor really prescribe that you write your own memoir? I've never heard of such a thing."

Naturally, Father was eager to show her his work.

Beverly wasn't sure if or when she would tell Father more about Jeff—and more about some of the things she was trying to work her way through. But if he continued to improve, and if it wouldn't be too stressful for him, she might confide in him someday. As for now, Beverly was relieved that they could all be in the same room together...pleasantly. It was more than she'd ever hoped for.

★   ★   ★

Thanksgiving came and went, and the weather at Marble Cove suddenly turned bitter cold, a reminder that winter was around the corner. Beverly wrapped her knitted scarf more warmly around her neck as she hurried toward town on Saturday. The temperature had dropped significantly this past week and the forecast was for snow by early next week.

But today was the grand opening of the Cannery—as well as the unveiling of Margaret's mural. Beverly was well aware that it was Margaret and Bernadette's mural. At least that was how Margaret put it. But everyone who knew Margaret knew that she was the one responsible for the final outcome.

"But Bernadette is making a sincere effort to get along," Margaret had told them last week. "I have to give her credit since she's not used to taking second chair to anyone. At least she's trying."

Beverly had hoped her father would come with her this afternoon, but he was fighting a cold, and they both decided it would be better for him to stay home. She'd left him with a steaming pot of orange spice tea and some of Shelley's lemon drop cookies. As a result, she was a little late. The plan was to meet up with her friends at the Cannery to celebrate the unveiling, and then just pop into the Cove to catch up on the latest.

"Hey, Beverly," Shelley called as she jogged across the street to join her, "looks like we're both running to keep up."

"I hope they won't start on time," Beverly said as they jogged together. "How are you?"

"Great." Shelley grinned. "I thought I was going to have to bring the kids, but then Dan stepped in and told me to just go without them."

"Sweet."

Beverly reached out to open the door, and the two of them made their way into a crowded space where the mayor was in front making a speech. The big mural wall was covered in a patchwork of taped-together tarps. Margaret and Bernadette stood off to one side. Margaret clearly looked uncomfortable. Beverly knew it was because she didn't really enjoy being in the limelight.

"There's Diane," she whispered to Shelley, and they went over to stand with her as the mayor wound down her speech.

"And without further ado, let's unveil the mural and open the shops. I know this is something we've all been waiting for with high expectations."

Beverly knew how much pressure Margaret had been under to get this mural right. Even as recently as yesterday, she had expressed concerns that some of the business owners might be disappointed at the unveiling. "You can please some of the people some of the time," she'd told Beverly as they'd stood in front of the Wheeland house. "But this time…well, I'm not so sure I will please anyone."

"Why not?" Beverly had asked.

"It turns out that everyone wanted something different. During all the various sketching stages, the business owners had gotten attached to different sketches. But then we kept changing it. I'm sure they all felt jerked around."

Beverly didn't have high expectations as she watched the patchwork curtain fall, but what she saw actually took her breath away. And it seemed she was not the only one.

There on the wall, looking almost larger than life, though that wasn't possible, was Orlean Point Light in all its glory and splendor. The sky was dusky blue with clouds rolling in with a misty layer of fog. The ocean was rough and wild looking with whitecaps, and out on the rolling waves was a dark clipper ship with spots of amber light glowing from the portholes. But the most powerful part of the painting was the beam of golden light spilling from the top of the lighthouse. It was as if Orlean Point Light had really come to life.

"It's absolutely beautiful," Shelley whispered.

"Inspired," Diane said quietly.

"Perfect," Beverly declared.

The other comments sounded similar, and Beverly actually wondered if Margaret might've been completely wrong. It seemed that all of the people were pleased.

"Speech," someone called out. "Let's hear from the artists." Others agreed.

Margaret, looking even more uncomfortable, nudged Bernadette to say something. To Beverly's surprise, Bernadette did step forward, and the mayor handed her the microphone.

"Thank you," she said to the crowd. "I would love to say that I'm responsible for this lovely work of art, but that wouldn't be true. Margaret Hoskins is the one who made this mural happen." She turned to Margaret. "And I think she should speak for herself." She tugged her forward as the crowd clapped.

"Thank you very much." Margaret took the mike from Bernadette. "First of all, I would like to thank the art students of Marble Cove High for their hard work in helping us. They put in countless hours, and, without their help, we never would've finished on time. And I need to give Bernadette credit too. It's no secret that we didn't always see eye to eye, but I think our disagreements are what brought us to this particular subject." Margaret turned to look at the lighthouse.

"Orlean Point Light has special significance to me," she said in a serious tone. "I can't even begin to explain how very much it means to me personally. But I feel that it's a symbol of hope and help and stability. Not just for me, but for many of the citizens as well as the visitors to our little seaside town. The lighthouse just seemed the perfect centerpiece for this mural. And I hope that you will all enjoy it, and that it will remind everyone to never give up hope." She smiled at the crowd. "Thank you so much for coming out today and for your support of the Cannery."

Margaret spoke to Allan and Adelaide and then came over to join her friends. "You girls might want to stick around and join the festivities here. That's what Allan and Adelaide are doing. But I want to duck over to the Cove now. I'm a little overwhelmed, and I think I might need some caffeine to settle my nerves."

Naturally, they all agreed to go directly to the Cove with her. Soon they were clustered around a table with their coffees, congratulating Margaret on her success.

"Enough about me," she said. "Tell me what's going on with the rest of you. I've been so busy these past few weeks that I feel like I need to catch up."

"My novel is coming right along," Diane told her. "I feel like I'm in the groove now. I wrote a whole chapter yesterday."

"And the article in the paper was nice," Margaret said.

"Gerald made you sound like you were already famous," Shelley said.

"Well, I hope that doesn't jinx anything." Diane chuckled. "But what about Shelley's big news?"

"What news?" Margaret asked.

Shelley told them about how her father-in-law was going to help her get her commercial kitchen. "Kind of like a silent partner," she said. "Only he's not that quiet."

"That's wonderful news, dear," Margaret said. "What a difference that will make for you."

"I know," Shelley said. "I feel so blessed."

"And what about you?" Margaret said to Beverly. "I was barely catching up with you yesterday, but I never got to ask about Jeff Mackenzie."

Shelley breathed, "Ooh."

"Oh, it was nothing," Beverly said. "He joined us for Thanksgiving, that's all. Along with Diane, Jeff was at loose ends, and so we invited him."

"He showed us some lovely photos he'd recently taken of the lighthouse," Diane told Margaret. "In fact, I'm sure there might be some you'd consider for inspiration for your paintings."

"I'm sure he'd be happy to share them," Beverly said. "He's a wonderful photographer, and he's just a little obsessed with our lighthouse."

Margaret smiled. "Our lighthouse...it belongs to all of us, doesn't it? All who love it..."

They visited for about an hour, and then Diane told them she was going to go to Old First church for the first night of Advent. "They're having a special music program, and I think it's going to be lovely."

"That sounds like a delightful way to start off the Christmas season," Margaret said with enthusiasm. "I'm sure Allan and Adelaide would enjoy it."

"We'd love to come too," Shelley said. "That's where Dan's family goes, and they do have wonderful music."

"And if Father's cold gets better, I'm sure he'd like it as well," Beverly said.

So it was settled: they would see each other the following evening at Old First.

★   ★   ★

The advent service felt inspired. Between the glowing candlelight, the music of a small choral ensemble, and a sermon that warmed the heart, Beverly felt as if she were truly ready to embrace the Christmas season. She and Father greeted friends and neighbors as they headed toward the foyer. They'd ridden with Diane tonight, but she was still chatting with the pastor, Silas Locke.

"I'd like to get some fresh air," Father said as he buttoned his overcoat.

"So would I." Beverly linked arms with him, and together they went outside where the air was crisp and clear.

"No sign of those snow clouds they're predicting," he said, looking up. Overhead, a quarter moon just coming up over the tops of the evergreens and the stars shone brightly.

"Beverly!" called a man's voice.

"Who's that?" Father asked in alarm.

Beverly held more tightly to his arm as she peered out toward the dimly lit parking lot to where a man was waving and jogging toward them. "It looks like Jeff Mackenzie." She held up her hand to wave. "I thought he was coming to the advent service tonight, but he must've gotten the time mixed up."

"But what on earth is he so excited about?"

Jeff was just joining them as Diane stepped out of the church. Jeff grabbed Beverly by the arm. "I was just... at the lighthouse." He paused to catch his breath. "And you're not going to believe this."

"Yes?" Beverly waited anxiously. "What?"

"Something happened—something very, very strange."

Beverly exchanged glances with Diane. "What?"

He held up his camera now. "It's a long story, but I think I got it on film." He shook his head as if he were still trying to figure something out.

"Got what on film?" Beverly asked.

"Well, on the memory card. You're not going to believe this." His dark eyes were wide.

Now Shelley and Dan and the kids joined them, followed by Margaret and her family. "Jeff discovered something unusual at the lighthouse," Beverly explained to them. "He's about to tell us about it."

"I'd rather *show* you," he said urgently. "Does anyone care to come back out to the lighthouse with me? I've got to go back and see it with my own eyes."

"I need to get Father home," Beverly said.

"He can ride with us," Allan offered.

"Do you mind?" Beverly asked her father.

He grinned. "Not at all. But I want to hear all about it when you get home."

Beverly turned to Diane. "Are you in?"

"You bet." Diane nodded.

"All right," Beverly said to Jeff. "Let's get going."

"What about me?" Margaret asked. "Don't I get to come too?"

"You can all come if you want," Jeff said quickly. "But let's get moving, okay?"

"I want to go too," Shelley declared in a dejected tone.

Dan laughed. "You guys and your lighthouse sleuthing." He took Emma from her arms. "How about if I get the kids home and to bed? You run along with them, as long as you fill me in when you get back."

"I'll drive," Diane offered. "We'll all fit in my SUV. And I have a flashlight in the glove box."

As they went to the car, Jeff started pouring out his story. "I'd gone out there to take photos of the sunset. Did you see the sky tonight? It was all rose and orange and lilac. So I thought I'd get some sweet shots of the lighthouse. I had no idea I'd get what I got."

"I heard you have some excellent photos," Margaret said as they reached Diane's car.

"You should see them," Beverly said as she climbed into the back seat. Jeff slid in next to her with Margaret on the other side.

"I'll show you some right now," he said as he turned on his digital camera's viewing screen. "But, trust me, you're not going to believe it."

"What?" Shelley asked from the front seat.

"These photos." Jeff flipped past some sunset scenes.

"Those are gorgeous," Margaret told him.

"I was just snapping shots right and left. But after I left, I discovered something. Something very weird and unexplainable." Jeff's words had an intensity that made the hair on the back of Beverly's neck stand on end.

"I'd taken maybe fifty shots or more," he told them. "And it had gotten dark, so I headed back. But I stopped in town and thought I'd take a peek at the photos, you know, just for fun and to see if any of them had turned out. And what I saw—well, I nearly fell over." Now he stopped at a photo. *"Look."*

Beverly and Margaret both leaned over to see. "What is *that*?" Beverly pointed to what looked like a swirling flash of light.

"Look at this next one, it's even better," he said without answering.

"Was someone flashing a light out there?" Margaret asked.

"No one was out there but me," he said.

Beverly pointed to a cloudy-looking shape by the lighthouse. "What is that, Jeff?"

"Yes," Shelley said with impatience. "Tell us what it is you saw."

"It's not what I saw." He went to the next shot. "It's what showed up in my photos."

"This one!" Margaret pointed to what looked like an apparition and gasped. "It looks like a ghost."

"Or an angel," Beverly said quietly.

"I want to see," Shelley exclaimed.

Soon they were parked by the beach entrance, and all four of the women were gathered in a circle, staring at Jeff Mackenzie's strange lighthouse photos.

"Oh, that's definitely an angel," Shelley declared.

"I agree," Diane said.

"But how is that possible?" Jeff asked them. "I never actually *saw* anything, but it showed up on my camera. How does that happen? And why? I feel like I just stepped into the *Twilight Zone*."

"Or the Angel Zone," Margaret said reverently.

"Do you think those are lighthouse angels?" Beverly asked them.

"I do," Shelley said eagerly. "I really do."

"But why?" Jeff demanded. "And why here?"

"Maybe because we all needed angels," Diane said quietly.

They all looked over at the lighthouse, now lit by the thin, cool blue light of the moon. Silent and still, strong and constant. Even without its light, it remained their beacon of hope. And now angels? What could possibly be next?

Beverly reached for her friends' hands, clasping them warmly in her own, and as if orchestrated, they all formed a circle there on the sand.

"I don't know much about angels," Beverly confessed to them, "but I do know that you dear friends have been like angels in my life. And I know that the lighthouse has brought us together. That's enough for me."

About the Author

Melody Carlson is one of the most prolific novelists of our time. With some two hundred books published and sales topping five million copies, Melody writes primarily for women and teens. She's won numerous honors and awards, including the Rita and Gold Medallion, and some of her books are being considered for TV movies. Melody has two grown sons and makes her home in the Pacific Northwest with her husband. When not writing, Melody likes to travel, bike, camp, garden and walk her yellow Labrador in the great outdoors. Visit Melody at melodycarlson.com.

A Conversation with
Melody Carlson

Q. Which character in Still Waters *is your favorite? Why?*

A. First of all, how do I choose just one? It's like picking your favorite child. But offhand, I'd probably say Diane since we're both writers and I can easily relate to her. Writing alone would give us plenty to talk about over coffee. Also, she has two grown children (as I do) and enjoys walking her dog on the beach, just like I do. I'm sure she'd have lots of questions for me about writing since she's just starting out as a novelist. But I'd also like to hear more about her experiences as a newspaper reporter. Still, I'm not positive she's my favorite since I really enjoy Margaret too. I have a few artist friends, and there are many similarities in how they think and work that compares to writing—and yet it's different. I enjoy hearing artists describe their creative process, so I'd probably have lots of questions for Margaret. Also, I tend to think of her as the wise woman of the group. I think her age and experience set her up for that. However, it's interesting to see how she's portrayed slightly differently when the other authors tell the

Marble Cove stories. But isn't that like life too—seeing people from different perspectives?

Q. Which scene in Still Waters *did you most enjoy writing?*

A. I didn't mention Shelley as a favorite, but she is right up there. And it was fun telling a bit more of her story in this book. And I can relate to her as a frazzled mom just struggling to keep it together. Been there, done that! So I really enjoyed "watching" her plan and pull off her father-in-law's birthday party. It was fun to see Maddie (Shelley's ex-nemesis) helping her. And although I didn't mention this among my diverse careers, I used to plan parties, events and a few weddings, so writing about that felt perfectly natural to me. I also knew that Shelley was going to win over her father-in-law, and I felt she needed this in her life. She and Dan have such struggles, and she so wants to do her baking business. It seemed right that an older family member came alongside them to help. Ralph seemed the perfect guy to do it.

Q. What do you want your readers to take away from your books?

A. I always hope that by writing about characters' personalities, including their strengths and flaws, readers will be reminded of people in their own lives. It's so easy to view people on the surface...to make assumptions...perhaps even to pass judgment. But when you get to know characters through the handy vehicle of story, you're allowed glimpses into the hidden places of their lives. You're allowed to peel back layers and find out why they are the way they are. And I believe that kind of understanding often leads to grace. The more we know about someone (particularly an exasperating someone), the easier it is to show them mercy and kindness. My biggest hope with all of my books is that these stories will encourage readers to look deeper into the lives of those around them and to show them grace and love as a result.

Q. Each of the four women in Miracles of Marble Cove is starting over in her life or career. If you were to start a new career, what would you like to do?

A. I used to dabble in art. I enjoyed pen and ink drawings, watercolors and acrylics, and someday I plan to take it up again. As I mentioned, I really think that art and writing are related, perhaps because I tend to see stories graphically in my head. As a result there's another career that interests me—actually, a facet of what I'm already doing. I'd love to get involved in writing for TV and films. I've written one original screenplay and have had several of my books optioned for TV/movies, but so far none of them have actually panned out. However, I recently adapted one of my own books (a Christmas novella), and it's being considered for a TV movie right now. It was my first adaptation, and I was surprised at how much fun I had doing it. So who knows what's next?

Q. You started writing in your thirties. What career did you pursue prior to being a writer?

A. Although my degree is in early childhood education (and I do love preschoolers), I have so many other interests that it feels like I dabbled in a bit of everything. I'll fill in some of the gaps. Before marrying, I traveled around the world and taught preschool overseas in Papua New Guinea—now that was different! I was a Young Life volunteer when I met my husband. I ran a group day-care center in my home when my boys were in grade school. I also served as their PTA president for several years. I taught wardrobe planning classes and did color-draping. I was briefly involved in politics. Whew! It makes my head spin just to list all of these things. But like I said, I believe these many and varied experiences lend texture and depth to my writing (or I hope they do). My husband is always quick to point out that Louis L'Amour—his second favorite author after me!—had a very diverse background too. So I'm really thankful for my crazy résumé.

Q. Each of the four main characters in Miracles of Marble Cove is strong in her own way. What strong women in your life have influenced you most?

A. I've been blessed with a lot of strong women in my life. I was raised by a single mom who reinvented herself (after my alcoholic father abandoned us) by returning to college to get a teaching degree. She worked hard to support my sister and me, and even managed to build a house in an era when home-building loans were hard to come by for single women. I also had a strong grandmother— my wise woman, as well as a few wonderful aunts I will always be grateful to. And I have a strong friend/sister who has been invaluable as a spiritual influence during adulthood. We raised our children together. She's always been involved in women's ministries and became a pastor a few years ago.

Q. If Diane came to you for writerly guidance, what would you tell her? What is the best single piece of advice you could give her?

A. I think I'd tell her not to take her writing so seriously. I know that probably sounds flippant, but I see her getting so worried about the little details of writing that sometimes I think she forgets to have fun with it. The reason I write as much as I do is because I love doing it. I want Diane to love doing it too. But I think because she worked for newspapers, she's having difficulty just loosening up and going with the flow.

Q. Still Waters *covers the fall holidays. What was your most memorable Thanksgiving?*

A. My most memorable Thanksgiving was giving birth to my second son, the evening before Thanksgiving. That's one way to get out of cooking a turkey!

Baking with Shelley

Mainer Pumpkin Bread

1 (15 ounce) can pumpkin puree
4 eggs
1 cup canola or other light vegetable oil
2/3 cup water
3 cups sugar
3½ cups flour, plus extra for dusting
2 teaspoons baking soda
1½ teaspoons salt
1 teaspoon ground cinnamon
1 teaspoon ground nutmeg
½ teaspoon ground cloves
¼ teaspoon ground ginger
Optional: ¾ cup chopped walnuts or pecans

Preheat oven to 350 degrees. Grease and flour three seven-by-three-inch loaf pans.

In a large bowl, mix pumpkin puree, eggs, oil, water and sugar. In a separate bowl, whisk together the dry ingredients, including spices. Stir the dry ingredients into the pumpkin mixture, just until blended. Fold in nuts, if desired. Pour batter into the prepared pans and bake for about fifty minutes, until an inserted toothpick comes out clean. Makes three loaves.

From the
Guideposts Archives

This story by Chris Merkel of Greeneville, Tennessee,
originally appeared in
the February 1993 issue of *Guideposts*.

When I was little I believed in angels because my mom told me they were real. At bedtime she'd read Bible stories to my brothers and me. She was especially partial to the angel stories, like the one about the angel who promised Paul and his men safety when their ship was about to wreck, or the angel who fed Elijah in the desert. But when I got to be a teenager I doubted angels were actually real. I'd never seen one nor had I ever met anyone who had. Not even Mom. So I figured the stories were more color than fact.

Mom was a true believer, though, and my skepticism didn't deter her one bit. When we went off to school, Mom always appointed an angel to watch over each of us. Even when I was away at college I know for a fact that Mom assigned me a daily angel. It didn't surprise me that after I finished school and moved back home to work with Dad in the family construction business, Mom continued the practice.

Then came a day in January 1991, when I found reason to rethink my doubts. I got ready for work as usual that cold morning. I made sure to put on a lot of clothes, because I'd be working outside digging a ditch and rerouting a city waterline. It would be a hard job. But I like working outdoors. I'm not one to stay cooped up in an office.

As I polished off my breakfast I heard Mom standing over the sink saying her daily prayers: "...and Lord, watch over Chris at his job and charge your angels to keep him safe." I grinned as I put on my coat.

I met up with three of our workers—Terry Carter, Doug Franklin, and Johnny Powers—at the job site along the 11E bypass right outside town. Johnny climbed up into the cab of the Track-Hoe and put the big machine to work excavating the trench we'd be working in. Meanwhile the rest of us unloaded equipment from the truck.

Johnny worked fast. Pretty soon large mounds of red clay dirt were piled up on either side of the narrow, seventeen-foot-long ditch. Terry and I lowered ourselves ten feet to the bottom and began laying the pipe. Doug passed pipe segments down to us while Johnny followed the trench line we'd marked out the day before. Through the soles of my heavy, steel-toed work boots I could feel the vibrations of the Track-Hoe. The job was going smoothly. But as Terry and I struggled with a connection I suddenly felt a large clump of dirt hit my shoulder. Then another. We looked up. In a flash, as Terry started to shout "Cave-in—!" a solid wall of earth came crashing down on us. Before I could react

I was sprawled facedown at the bottom of the ditch with several tons of dirt on top of me.

Everything was black. Frantically spitting dirt from my mouth, I found my face in an air pocket. The crushing pressure made every breath a struggle. At least I had air, but there was no telling how long it would last as the dirt settled. I was being slowly smothered to death.

Terry! Had he survived the cave-in? Fighting for a breath I called his name. No answer. I called again. "Terry!" Even if he had survived, could he hear me? Could he talk?

All the response I got was the sound of my own labored breathing. It was a desperate sound. As I was about to start shouting again I detected a muffled noise somewhere directly above me. Then a voice. It was Terry!

"Terry, are you all right?"

"I think so…hard to breathe."

"We've got to let them know we're alive," I said, coughing and choking on dirt. Every time I spoke a little got in my mouth. "Start shouting."

We shouted like there was no tomorrow. It was an incredible effort. The packed clay earth completely swallowed up our voices. The more I shouted the more panicky I felt. My ears were clogged with mud. Everything sounded so strange. Eventually we had to stop and rest. Despite the chill I was sweating.

"It's no use," Terry rasped.

"Don't talk like that," I snapped. My voice was getting hoarse too. "We can't give up! Terry, think about your wife. Think about your little boy."

I paused. It was getting tougher to breathe. We had to preserve our strength if we were going to get out of this alive. We stayed quiet for a while, then Terry asked, "Chris, do you believe in God?"

"Yeah."

"Me too."

"It's funny," I said, as much to myself as to Terry. "You don't always think about your faith until you get into a bad situation. My mother prays all the time."

"Chris, I believe God hears our prayers no matter what."

Terry started to pray. "Dear Lord, please be with those men trying to rescue us, and guide them. Please be our strength..."

I silently joined in Terry's prayers. I knew they must be digging frantically up above us. They'd probably called in backup by now. I wondered if it would do any good, if this trench would become my grave. Terry's voice began to fade.

Then all was silent. "Terry!" I shouted. "Keep fighting!"

Silence.

"Terry!"

Nothing.

I struggled to move, to claw away at the mud and earth. I was completely trapped. I started screaming again, "I'm here! Here! Help!"

My head was swimming. *I'm only twenty-five. Lord, please...* Suddenly I heard Terry's voice one more time. It was weak and distant. "God, watch over Sheila and little Jarrod...be with them when I'm gone, protect them..."

He was making his final peace, praying for his wife and son. It reminded me of how my mother always prayed for us kids, every morning assigning us an angel. Was she praying for me now?

"Terry? Do you believe in angels?"

But Terry did not answer. I began to slip in and out of consciousness. *Hold on,* I told myself. Hold on! Where was my angel now? "Dear God," I cried, "please send an angel to be with me! Send an angel to the rescue!"

Then, in the dank suffocating darkness, I felt as if I were being lifted up. *You're here!* I thought. I relaxed and everything faded away.

The next thing I knew someone was yelling my name and scraping dirt away from around my face. The tremendous pressure was gone. With a shudder and a gasp I filled my lungs with sweet cold air. I saw people in the ditch with me, Doug and Johnny and others. "Terry," I muttered, "where's Terry?"

"Don't worry, kid," somebody answered. "We got him too. He's fine."

Then they lifted me out and carried me to a waiting ambulance, which rushed me to Laughlin Memorial Hospital for X-rays. I learned that Terry and I had been trapped for over two hours. The doctor who read my X-rays shook his head in disbelief. "I don't know how you two made it. By rights, you should have suffocated. Someone sure must have been looking out for you fellas."

Since that day I've read everything in the Bible about angels. The one passage that keeps coming back to me is from the 91st Psalm: "He shall give His angels charge over thee, to keep thee in all thy ways. They shall bear thee up..."

I've taken a page out of Mom's book too. Every day before I go out on a job, I find myself quietly asking God to assign an angel to each man on the crew, and even to each vehicle and piece of equipment. There's no sense in not using what God has given us to use. Mom taught me that.

True, I've still never actually seen angels. But I've felt their presence and seen their work. And that's good enough for me.

Read on for a sneak peek of the next exciting book in
Miracles of Marble Cove!

A Midnight Clear
by Patti Berg

Margaret turned her head, looking south to the rocky promontory where the lighthouse stood. At the moment, it was partially shrouded in fog. Tall and stalwart and—wait. Was that a glint of light? She was sure she'd seen a quick flash through the windows that stretched all the way around the lantern room at the very top of the tower.

She shook her head, closing her eyes for a moment. It had to be a figment of her imagination. A strange manifestation caused by thinking too much about the lights.

Or...could it be an angel, as Beverly had said? A beacon of light, of hope, that was calling out to her, asking her to come to the lighthouse? Perhaps to help someone in need?

Margaret felt a pair of little arms wrap around her legs, and she looked down to find three-year-old Aiden Bauer's bright blue eyes and freckled face smiling up at her. She lifted the child into her arms and turned to find his mom, Shelley, pushing a stroller toward her. Shelley and Dan Bauer's fifteen-month-old daughter Emma was bundled up in a knitted pink cap, sound asleep beneath a plush, tie-dyed pink and purple blanket.

"What's brought you out and about this afternoon?" Margaret asked the young, pretty blonde who lived across the street from her, as Aiden squirmed out of her arms, too rambunctious to stay put longer than a handful of seconds.

"I had to deliver some of my mini cranberry tarts to Josie at the Quarterdeck Inn. Poor woman's been down with a cold and didn't have the energy to bake anything for her guests' afternoon snack."

"You didn't bake them this morning, did you?"

Shelley sighed and nodded. "Even used my on-the-fritz oven." Shelley sighed, her breath turning to fog in front of her face. "I'll be so happy once my new kitchen's finished so I can do all the baking for my Lighthouse Sweet Shoppe at home. Using the Cove's kitchen after the restaurant closes at night is getting old." She smiled. "But you know what they say. A girl's gotta do what a girl's gotta do."

"Isn't that the truth." Margaret laughed lightly. "I think Josie's been doing far more than a person ought to do too, redecorating the inn mostly by herself."

"I couldn't agree more," Shelley said, "but, oh my, the Quarterdeck is looking absolutely amazing. Oh! Speaking of the Quarterdeck, did you know Jeff Mackenzie is staying there? I don't know about you, but—"

"Mama." Aiden tugged on his mother's coat, interrupting her midsentence, keeping Margaret from finding out what Shelley had against Beverly's photographer friend—or acquaintance, the term Beverly insisted on using for him. "Can we give Miss Margaret her tart?"

Shelley cupped her son's cold and wind-chapped cheek. "Thanks for reminding me, honey."

"I could heat up some leftover coffee," Margaret said, glad to have a little company. She could easily put off going home for another half hour or so. "If you don't mind it a little strong."

"Actually, I wanted to talk with you anyway," Shelley said. "About the photos Jeff Mackenzie showed us last night."

"Oh yes." Margaret nodded slowly. "The…angels."

"I couldn't sleep much last night, thinking about what we saw in those photographs." Shelley's words came out in a flurry.

Margaret held the door open for her friends, locked up again, and led them back to her studio. While Shelley shrugged out of her pale pink, full-length down coat, Margaret quickly heated a mug of very dark coffee, then set it on a small corner table. She pulled a bucket of crayons out of a storage cabinet, along with an inexpensive sketchbook, and sat Aiden down on the floor to draw her and his mommy some pretty pictures. Just when Margaret relaxed in a chair, ready to settle down for a nice chat about *the* photos, Emma began to fuss.

Shelley plucked the blanket off the toddler, pulled her into her lap, and kissed her pretty pink cheeks before settling her down on the floor beside her brother. The little girl was instantly on her tummy, a fat red crayon in hand, helping Aiden with his picture, making squiggly lines all over the paper.

Margaret turned to Shelley. "Now, let's talk about the photos."

Shelley shook her head and rolled her eyes. "They've been bugging me since Jeff showed them to us last night, and I've just gotta ask. Do you think they're real?"

Margaret hadn't even contemplated that question. "They looked real. Or as real as angels or ghosts—or mysterious beacons of light—can possibly look. Have you asked Diane and Beverly what they think?"

"I tried to get ahold of Beverly first thing this morning," Shelley said, "but Mr. Wheeland told me that she and Diane had gone to Augusta to do some Christmas shopping. But I have the feeling they were just as shocked by the photos as I was."

"We were all shocked, Shelley. I don't think any of us expected to see photographs of the lights; as far as I know, no one's ever captured them on film." Margaret pinched off a bit of crust from the cranberry minitart Shelley had given her. "But I've seen the lights. You've seen the lights. Why shouldn't they show up in Jeff's photos?"

"But if Jeff Mackenzie's photos are real, I mean honestly and truly real, the world will soon know—and believe—that some unknown and unseen force is making lights shine from the top of the tower, when we all know there's no bulb, no candle, no source in the dome that can give off light."

Shelley had gotten herself so worked up over the photos that she swallowed a gulp of the coffee, then grimaced at the taste. Margaret had been right that it was strong. Shelley picked reached for a packet of sugar and stirred it in.

"If Jeff releases those photographs, and if people believe what they see," Margaret said, all of a sudden feeling completely uncomfortable, "Marble Cove will be overrun with people hoping to see the lights."

"Can you imagine the ghost hunters who'd show up here?" Shelley gripped her mug even more tightly. "Or producers of some of those paranormal TV shows? I don't want that. But…"

"But what?" Margaret asked. She took another bite of the cranberry tart, hoping the sweetness would help calm her sudden foreboding.

"Well," Shelley said hesitantly, "the first time we met Jeff, he was up in the top of the lighthouse shining a flashlight down on the water. It's like he was trying to pull a fast one, as if he'd heard the stories and was trying to make unsuspecting people think there really are mysterious lights."

"But we've seen them, Shelley," Margaret emphasized. "Even though Fred Little questions our sanity sometimes, we've all seem them."

Shelley nodded. "True. But maybe he's trying to make the naysayers believe there are magical lights for reasons that aren't exactly on the up-and-up."

"You mean trying to profit on their gullibility?"

"Exactly. And now he pops up with photographs of odd lights fluttering around the lighthouse. Maybe, just maybe, he's doctored his photographs, played around with them on his computer to make them look like angels or ghosts are flying around and then put them back in his camera to show us."

"I suppose it's possible," Margaret said. "Creative people can do just about anything with computers these days. But I don't want to believe Beverly's friend is involved in something nefarious."

"I don't want to believe it either. But what do we know about him, other than the fact that he's good-looking? And Beverly won't tell us anything other than she met him years ago."

"She must have her reasons for being so secretive." Margaret swallowed the last bite of her tart. "And let's face it. Beverly's never been big on sharing all the ins and outs of her life."

Shelley pushed out of her chair, crossed to the sink, and dumped out the last of her coffee. "I admit I've got a skeptical streak that's a mile long. My mind was racing, thinking about the photos and whether or not I've really seen the lights. Kept me awake all night—that and our old boiler grumbling and groaning all night long. Try as he might, there was nothing Dan could do to settle it down to putting out heat instead of noise."

Shelley glanced at her watch. "I'd better get these kiddos home." She gave Margaret a quick hug, then bundled up Aiden for the walk home and tucked Emma back into the stroller.

Standing at the door now, Margaret watched as Shelley and the children crossed Main Street's cobblestones. When they were safely on Newport Avenue, Margaret turned to look at the lighthouse. Dark clouds were dipping down, almost touching the domed roof. The wind had picked up and she knew the storm wasn't far away. She should go home, maybe take a nap, or buckle down and work on her Christmas cards.

But she couldn't. Even though she'd seen only one glint of light, she felt sure the lighthouse had called to her nearly an hour ago. She had to go there now.

She just hoped she wasn't too late.

A NOTE FROM THE EDITORS

We hope you enjoyed Miracles of Marble Cove, published by the Books and Inspirational Media Division of Guideposts, a nonprofit organization that touches millions of lives every day through products and services that inspire, encourage, help you grow in your faith, and celebrate God's love.

Thank you for making a difference with your purchase of this book, which helps fund our many outreach programs to military personnel, prisons, hospitals, nursing homes, and educational institutions.

We also create many useful and uplifting online resources. Visit Guideposts.org to read true stories of hope and inspiration, access OurPrayer network, sign up for free newsletters, download free e-books, join our Facebook community, and follow our stimulating blogs.

To learn about other Guideposts publications, including the best-selling devotional *Daily Guideposts*, go to Guideposts .org/Shop, call (800) 932-2145, or write to Guideposts, PO Box 5815, Harlan, Iowa 51593.